BLACK ZONE

FUTURE WARS, BOOK 2

CONNIE SUTTLE

subtledemon.com

Print ISBN-13: 978-1-63478-043-8
eBook ISBN-13: 978-1-63478-042-1

Published by: SubtleDemon Publishing, LLC
PO Box 95696, Oklahoma City, OK 73143

Cover by Renee Barratt @ The Cover Counts.

To Walter, Joe, Larry, Lee, Dianne, Sarah, Mark, Denise and Brett.
Thank you.

ACKNOWLEDGMENTS

As always, this book is the result of collaboration. If it weren't for the support of my editor, my cover artist and my beta readers, it would be less than it is. All mistakes, as usual, are mine and no other's.

About the Author:
Connie Suttle lives in Oklahoma with her husband and a conglomerate of cats. They have finally banded together to make their demands, which has proven disconcerting to all humans involved.

You may find Connie in the following ways:
Facebook: Connie Suttle Author
Twitter: @subtledemon
Website and Blog: subtledemon.com

Demon Lost

Demon Revealed

Demon's King

Demon's Quest

Demon's Revenge

Demon's Dream

God Wars Series:

Blood Double

Blood Trouble

Blood Revolution

Blood Love

Blood Finale

Saa Thalarr Series:

Hope and Vengeance

Wyvern and Company

Observe and Protect*

First Ordinance Series:

Finder

Keeper

BlackWing

SpellBreaker

WhiteWing

R-D Series:

Cloud Dust

Cloud Invasion

Cloud Rebel

Latter Day Demons Series:

Hot Demon in the City

A Demon's Work is Never Done

A Demon's Due

Seattle Elementals Series:

Your Money's Worth

Worth Your While

BlackWing Pirates Series

MindSighted

MindMage

MindRogue

MindMaster

Black Rose Sorceress Series

The Rose Mark

Rose and Thorn

Black Rose Queen

Queen of Thorns and Roses

Future Wars Series

Buffer Zone

Black Zone

Lion and Raven Series

Raven, Red

Exile, Ancient*

Other Titles from SubtleDemon Publishing:

Malefactor

Transgressor

Underhanded*

by Joe Scholes

*Forthcoming

CHAPTER ONE

*V*erillium
Royal City, Kingdom of Vorus
Jessil

I should have known.

Father wasn't yet cold in his tomb when Nessil called for the tappers to come for me. As the daughter of the King, I'd been protected. Loved, even, as playthings often are. Once the tapper placed a controller beneath the skin on my neck and connected it to my brain and spine, I'd be consigned to life as a drudge, a broodraiser or, worst of all, a drone in Nessil's army.

"You will wait here," Verlin, Nessil's best friend and new Prime Minister, ordered me to sit in an antechamber, already undergoing renovations to reflect Nessil's tastes rather than Father's. I was instructed to wait docilely among the scents of fresh paint and sawdust for the worst thing possible to happen to me.

Nessil didn't have the courage to face me himself in the matter; he'd sent someone else to do it for him, just as he always did. Verlin sneered as he commanded me to wait; his expression as ugly as his heart but far easier to see. Nessil wouldn't hold Verlin back as Father had; there was no need to hide his debauchery from the King any longer, now that Nessil held the title.

We were siblings, Nessil and I, although I'd been born first. He was male and therefore the heir. I'd spent most of my life staying out of his way, as he had a talent for blaming someone else for his own mistakes and bad judgment.

Even my mother had been controlled, although Father sometimes gave her a bit of freedom by turning off everything except the will to argue or run away. She'd been born into an aristocratic family, found to be a suitable match by Father's physicians, the controller had been placed and her remote placed in Father's hand.

From then on, she was his to command—to bear his children. I found the thought of following in my mother's footsteps more untenable than going to the military.

That's why I climbed out the window of the vestibule, dropped two floors to the ground *and ran*.

Three weeks later, my hands were red and raw from scrubbing pots, pans and floors in the kitchens, located in the lower bowels of the castle. Nobody expects to single out a drudge from other drudges, all acting like programmed wood or metal toys for boys to play with.

No—we were invisible. I could only hope that Nessil had given up looking for me, thinking I'd died or something.

My plan, and a very poor one at that, was to run and keep running. Something, however, made me turn around and go back to the castle. I couldn't explain what it was, exactly, that convinced me that leaving the castle was a bad idea.

Therefore, I'd hidden myself in a kitchen filled with controlled servants, copying their silence and obeisance as well as I could.

Until Verlin entered the kitchen one afternoon and decided to haul one of the drudges away to slake his lascivious thirst.

I tried to go about my duties.

Really.

But when the drudge uncharacteristically fought back, Verlin shoved her away, flinging her body against the hot oven door another drudge had just opened. Without thinking, I rushed to the woman's aid as her skin scorched and hair burned.

Verlin grabbed my hair before I could pull the woman to safety; that's how I ended up being dragged up endless palace steps and thrown onto the floor of Father's study, which Nessil had taken for his own.

"Well, Balver won't take her now—not since she's been in the kitchens for three weeks and available to anybody walking in," Nessil's boots came into view as Verlin held me down, my cheek pressed hard against the new rug on the study floor. My eyes watered from the scent of fresh dyes—Nessil had been quite busy removing evidence of Father's rule.

Wait—he'd said *Balver. Lord* Balver. Old, bandy-legged and smelly Balver. Nessil had gone looking for the worst possible place for me to serve as a breeder and broodraiser.

"She hid well enough in the kitchens—I say send her back there," Verlin suggested.

"No—she liked it there or she wouldn't have stayed," Nessil pretended to be wise. "Let's give her to the army, instead. As a punishment."

"Sound decision," Verlin grunted, removing his knee from my back. "Stay down, drone; the tappers are on the way."

CHAPTER TWO

*E*astern Sector Three, Verillium
       Drone Jessil

"Eat," he commanded. Only a small part of me remained, and I couldn't hate the one standing over me now. I'd been ordered not to hate him or any other man.

A bowl of food was shoved in front of me, on a portable table inside a large tent. Others sat at the table with me, all gobbling food after being ordered to do so.

My stomach rumbled and ached, although I'd forgotten what those things meant. My past was also lost; I only recalled waking in a city of tents, being forced to do exercises, dress like all the others and run long distances, until many of us dropped.

How long I'd done this, I also couldn't remember. Lifting the spoon beneath my hand, I dipped it into the bowl and place a portion in my mouth. The taste of it I didn't know. It didn't matter what I thought of it, good or bad. I ate as commanded, until the bowl was empty.

"Rise. Single file formation. Walk to the training ground."

"They're getting through the black zone," one man said to another as I followed the drone ahead of me out of the tent. "These will probably be called up half-trained."

"We don't have magic or proper armor," the other said. "Even with training, these drones will be worthless against the pigs Cjerl hired."

"Try convincing the King of that," the first snorted. Soon enough, I was too far away to hear more of the conversation.

Dust rose beneath my feet—I should have known what that meant, but I didn't. Regardless, it made me want to sneeze. I forced myself not to do so. Sneezing or attempting to speak without permission resulted in stripes across backs—that much I remembered with clarity.

"Change in schedule," the trainer barked at us as we lined up in designated rows. "Today, you learn how to fire weapons. You will only fire weapons at assigned targets, unless instructed otherwise."

"Yes, Trainer Rade," we spoke in unison, just as we'd been ordered.

"You will learn to fire weapons quickly," he went on.

"Yes, Trainer Rade."

"Bring the weapons," Rade shouted at his male assistants.

Weapons I'd never seen before were pulled from large metal boxes, and each drone was handed a rifle and shown how to hold it. Failure to do so would be met with a punch or worse—Trainer Rade would pull the remote from his pocket and give the foolish drone a jolt to the brain.

That I remembered well enough.

"Hand here, other hand here," an assistant placed the weapon in my grip and repositioned my hands. I held the weapon once he took his hands away, without moving. Moving without a command would certainly bring out the remote.

Trainer Rade received the last weapon. "Put the weapon against your shoulder like this, to carry it properly," he demonstrated the move. The drones followed his example immediately. "Now, single file march after me."

Raising more dust, we fell in behind him as we'd been taught, walking toward a distant field we'd never gone to before. Large piles of straw, with cotton-filled cloth bodies tied to them, waited for us to aim our weapons and shoot.

"You have three days to learn to use your weapon," Trainer Rade

5

shouted at us as we lined up many steps away from these targets. We stood still, unmoving, waiting for further instruction.

We jerked and jolted in our seats as the transport hauled us across rough terrain three days later. Perhaps in another life, I'd know what season it was, or why the hot wind dried the sweat on my skin in an eyeblink as we rode along on hard benches in the canvas-covered back of a transport.

With no idea where we were going, the others around me stared straight ahead, as if seeing nothing—noting nothing. Occasionally, I glanced through a small tear in the canvas, watching dry fields with dead crops pass. Was that significant?

I couldn't remember.

The transport dipped and swayed dramatically, throwing the drone to my left against me. Neither of us made a sound—we'd been ordered to remain silent. Should I have understood what caused the vehicle to do that?

Probably, but the idea left me quickly enough, and I was back to staring straight ahead, like all the other drones around me. My throat felt as dry as the ground we passed over—I struggled to remember the word for what I felt.

Thirst.

Yes. I was terribly thirsty, but there were no water barrels or canteens on the transport. We were at the mercy of the men who ran the training camp, and only ate or drank when they allowed it.

Some things the remote didn't override—or couldn't. *Thirst.* I would remember that word and tuck it away in a hidden part of my mind. That hidden place was very small, but word by word, it was growing.

The remote couldn't find that place—the trainers wouldn't know of it either unless I revealed it to them.

I would never do that willingly.

Once that hidden place was overflowing, I would know the name I sought—the name of the one who sent me here. I was determined to remember that more than anything else.

And, once I knew it, I would also know how to deal with that knowledge. The sound of a massive explosion, followed by the sliding screech of the transport coming to an abrupt, rocking halt, tore me from my crippled thoughts.

"Get out," Trainer Rade's head appeared in the gap between canvas curtains at the back of the transport. "Collect your weapons from the weapons transport three vehicles down. Hurry. The enemy is attacking."

The enemy.

I had no idea who that really was, although that word had been mentioned often during training, along with other names I had trouble recalling.

The others around me were already leaping from the transport and running toward the weapons vehicle. I was the last one out, and I shouldn't have been. I was also the last one to receive my weapon from Rade's assistant trainer, settling it in my arms as instructed and running after the others, toward the front vehicle. Another blast occurred, tossing two transports and those inside them into the air.

There was no screaming or flailing—the bodies weren't whole as they sailed outward, before dropping awkwardly to the ground. Dust and smoke obscured my vision as the first trainees ahead of me knelt, pulled their weapons into positions and began firing.

I couldn't see what they were firing at—were there targets ahead? We'd only been instructed to fire at targets before. Trainers were shouting at trainees as weapons spit bullets and shells like metal rain.

Rain.

Yes. Another word. No rain caused dry ground. Why was there no rain? How long had there been no rain?

"Kneel and fire," Rade shouted at his trainees. Without stopping to think or argue about the others ahead of us, I knelt and positioned my weapon as I'd been trained to do.

The explosive that hit those ahead of us flung more body parts into the air. I only heard one scream as the ground suddenly erupted beneath our feet.

My scream.

Mine.

Fire erupted. We would burn to death. I recalled the scent of flesh burning but couldn't remember how or why.

More fire bloomed, but it moved abruptly away from me. Why? Fire ate whatever it could, living as long as there was fuel to consume.

How did I remember that?

A terrible boom shook the ground around me, while the dust and dirt crumbled downward, leaving me in a hole I felt too helpless to crawl away from.

As if a giant hand had scooped out a hollow beneath my body, blocking all sight of the battle going on all around.

My weapon had been knocked from my hands earlier, during the first explosion. I hadn't thought to search for it after the fire came.

Now, I was in a deep hole while a battle raged above.

Another explosion shook the ground, flinging dirt and dust into my hole and covering me as I pulled my body into a protective crouch, hands over my head.

When had the bullets stopped? I couldn't say when it was that I'd last heard one of our weapons discharge against the enemy. Were the others dead? If that were true, then we'd lost the battle. Why was the enemy still bombing us? Why was I still alive?

Why?

Bombs had shaken the ground before. This time, a roar caused it to rock, knocking me one way and then another inside my hollow. I must have cried out, although the sound of the terrible roar drowned all but the vibration of my own voice.

Then, everything turned black.

I was only aware for a moment or two. But in that short time, I understood all of what I heard. A female voice came to my ears as I stared up at the roof of a cloth tent. I knew it was cloth; it rippled and popped while the wind blew against it.

"I wonder what he intends to do once he's lost all his troops," the woman snapped. I didn't recognize her voice—I'd never heard it before.

"It doesn't matter what he does. He'll lose his life and the planet," a man snorted. "I only wonder if he'll figure that out before or after they kill him."

"Awake too soon, eh?" A face appeared above mine. Green-gold eyes lightened as a strange man smiled. When he tapped my forehead with a gentle finger, sleep claimed me.

～

Cassie

"If Ver'Dak is allied with Cjerl, he's certainly hiding himself well," Kear sighed.

"That's his biggest and best trick," I told the youngest of the Blackmantle brothers. "Ver'Dak's motto is, *if you can get somebody else to do your dirty work, then you only have to kill one rather than thousands to get what you want.* Right now, he has all of Cjerl's army to play with, plus a wizard or two he's smuggled in, no doubt."

Kear, like his four brothers, was a fifth-level Karathian warlock, and well-versed in all the spells Cjerl's hired wizards were lobbing at King Nessil's forces. Nessil was so oblivious about battle tactics that he wouldn't know to pick up a rock to defend himself.

As for Cjerl, he wasn't much smarter, but Ver'Dak had recognized the opportunity that Cjerl's better trained and equipped forces presented. Cjerl had competent leadership guiding his army, and conscripted both male and female troops.

With Ver'Dak's hidden influence in Cjerl's actions, combined with help from mercenary wizards he'd found somewhere, it was only a matter of time before Nessil's all-female army was destroyed and his kingdom overrun.

Neither Nessil nor Cjerl were evolved enough to know they lived atop a planet rich in an unmined quartzite that would be more than useful in manufacturing the latest and best information storage devices. The local name for that quartzite was copelis, and nobody living on the planet understood its importance.

Ver'Dak hadn't missed it—I'd bet the total worth of the planet on that. Then, with a bit of trading among criminal elements, he could set himself up to be the king of information storage, and no doubt he'd parlay that into owning or enslaving the entire known universes.

Frankly, I didn't give a damn if Ver'Dak killed Cjerl and Nessil. What I did care about was the subjugation of the women born on the planet, no matter what kingdom they belonged to.

We'd saved a few from the latest attack on the convoy carrying barely-trained female troops to the western edge of the black zone. The black zone was a mysterious, lightless strip between Cjerl's and Nessil's kingdoms which served as a barrier between the two factions.

Long ago, it was spelled by wizards or some such—before that talent was outlawed and infants with the ability were put to death, effectively eliminating the power from a people in desperate need of it now.

It truly was a black zone—held in deep, eternal twilight, where shadows and trickery became more evident—and more deadly—the farther you ventured inside.

"The man's awake," Denevik joined Kear and me inside my tent. "Karzac says he'll transport him to Le-Ath Veronis if he doesn't prove helpful."

"Shall we go ask questions, then?" I lifted an eyebrow at Denevik.

"Yep. I'll be interested in what he has to say." Denevik cracked his knuckles, as if he wanted to punch Trainer Rade before he even said anything.

As do you, a small voice reminded me. The only thing Rade had going for him—and the only reason Karzac healed him in the first place—was that he'd never forced himself on a woman. As for any other male on the planet with the inclination, I couldn't say that was true.

Denevik took the lead; I followed and Kear fell in behind me. He wanted to hear what Rade had to say just as much as I did. And, with a truth spell, he'd be forced to tell us what we wanted to know.

"Well, that explains a lot," Kear blinked at me over a cup of coffee. We'd brewed it over a small, solar-powered camp stove moments ago. Denevik had stayed near the tents where our two guests were now asleep.

"Pretty tough life to live when you're in just as much danger as the trainees you teach," I agreed. Rade preferred men, and in his kingdom, that meant a death sentence. He'd built a façade about himself—one so impenetrable that his associates considered him one of their roughest trainers.

"What about the girl?"

"Her name is Jessil. Zaria says she won't give that, or the memories associated with it, back to her just yet—for her own sake. Rade didn't know her name either, but he might recognize the one given to the new King's sister."

"We have to call her something."

"I know. Got any ideas?"

"She's a princess," Kear sighed. "Or should be. Actually, she ought to be Queen, rather than the puffed-up coward who sits the throne."

"I agree. Shall we give her a princess name—in another language, of course."

"I've always like Keela," Kear grinned.

"You've been talking with Bleek, haven't you?"

"Maybe. Who wants to know?"

"Because Keela is a Blevakian term for a royal female heir," I pointed out. "All right, we'll call her Keela."

"We still getting reinforcements?"

"Last I heard," I shrugged. "I just hate the part of it where we present ourselves as Nessil's troops to fight Cjerl's encroaching army."

"We're special forces, remember?" Kear grinned. "We strike in secret and retreat. Cjerl won't know what hit him, and it'll piss him off so bad he may cross the black zone himself."

"And we'll hope that Ver'Dak comes with him. In the meantime, we'll have two more troops to fight with us; we just have to convince them that the former King set this up without anyone being the wiser."

"What about you? Will they understand that a woman is a co-commander, here?"

"Maybe they will when we tell them we've removed Keela's controller. Her missing memories will be an unfortunate side effect. A thinking soldier is far better than a drone any day."

"What will we call ourselves? The King surely named us," Kear said.

"How about Dessil's Rogues?" Denevik pulled up a camp stool and joined us around the stove.

He'd named the former King—and Jessil's father.

"Sounds reasonable," Kear agreed, warming his coffee with power. "Who's watching our newest rogues?"

"Vik and Dave," Denevik smiled as he poured himself coffee. "They just ate, so they offered to take the watch."

"Well, we certainly can use all the High Demon help we can get," I told Denevik. He winked at me in reply. If we were forced to go into the black zone, two were better than one at keeping the spells from harming any of us. We also faced the possibility of finding more of Nessil's troops who'd been abandoned by their clueless monarch—more female drones who had no idea what to do or how to keep themselves alive without a remote-wielding male in charge of them.

Controllers. One of the worst things ever created. And, as this planet didn't belong to either Alliance, they'd skated past any opposition to the practice of enslaving others. Zaria figured that a certain rogue god had his name all over this.

Add that to the fact that Ver'Dak had made his way to Verillium as if he'd had a road map, and that certainly pointed in Liron's direction. Liron was gone, but his unholy brood of half-Krelk had been unleashed upon the universes after his demise.

Ver'Dak was undoubtedly whispering in Cjerl's ear and lending a hand in his war against Nessil. Before then, Cjerl hadn't been able to cross the black zone, and neither had Nessil's father—or his fathers before him.

Whomever had set the black zone in place was wise, with a clear eye to the future—until Ver'Dak's interference. Dessil hastily built his army to combat what Cjerl was lobbing his way, and thus began the conquering and destruction of his half of Verillium.

Already, Cjerl claimed more than fifty miles of Nessil's lands—at the shortest point. He held more than one-hundred-fifty at the longest point. Nessill didn't have the troops, weaponry or the knowledge to contain the entire border outside the black zone.

That's where we came in. We were the strike force, assigned to eliminate Cjerl's troops encroaching on Nessil's lands, hoping to draw Ver'Dak out without alerting him that we were anything other than a band of rogues set up before Dessil's death.

Likely, too, Cjerl and Ver'Dak had Sirenali slaves with them, to hide him from the most powerful among us. That meant we had to find him the old-fashioned way—by sight or scent.

A werewolf would be assigned to us, but Winkler and Lissa were looking carefully for a suitable candidate. I wondered who it would be and when he or she would arrive.

As if he were tuned to my thoughts, the werewolf appeared wearing a huge grin, Falchani leathers and two blades strapped to his back.

"Sursee," I dipped my head to him. He'd taught me bladework, handfighting and too many other disciplines to name—in case fire wasn't safe or called for.

"Cassandra Rath," he dipped his head to me.

"Welcome to Verillium," Denevik rose to shake Salidar DeLuca's hand.

Keela

"Where am I?" I spoke to the roof of a tent, believing I was alone.

On a comfortable cot with a clean blanket.

I had no memory of this, or how I arrived. In fact, memory was like a ghost I chased as I struggled to bring any part of my personal history to mind.

"You're on the edge of enemy territory, east of the black zone." A man's face appeared above me. I didn't know how close his head was to mine until another man joined him. *Far* above him, actually.

"If you're experiencing trouble with your memory, it's because of the controller," the tall man informed me. "We removed it, but sadly, we can't replace what it may have taken from you."

"Who are you?"

"I'm Dave," the shorter one grinned. "This is my brother, Vik," he pointed upward with a thumb. "Do you remember your name?"

I searched what little I had, before shivering. "No," I admitted.

"We'll call you Keela, then. Until you get your own name back. You're lucky we found you after Cjerl's forces bombed your unit. Only two of you survived—all the others were killed."

"Cjerl." I said his name flatly. "I recognize that name, all right."

"Most people do, only they add a few descriptive terms to it, and none of them are complimentary."

"Why are you out here? You're not dressed as the King's troops."

Dave turned toward Vik. They laughed and bumped fists.

"We're the King's Rogues," Dave turned back to me. "We don't meet the enemy head on; we sneak in behind the lines and eliminate as many as we can."

"Nessil isn't that smart," I snorted, before catching myself and wondering how I knew that.

"We agree," Vik said. "We're Dessil's Rogues. Nessil doesn't know about us."

"You're still working for the old King?"

"We uh, like what we do," Dave shrugged. "And it serves a purpose, does it not?"

"Who else survived?"

"Someone named Rade. He didn't have a controller."

"Rade," I hissed his name as I recalled shouting *Yes, Trainer Rade*, too many times to count.

"Don't worry, he's not in charge here, and he won't ever be," Vik crossed arms over his chest.

"Are you in charge?"

"Hells, no," Dave laughed. "That would be Cassie and Denevik."

Cassie

"Feel better?" I asked Rade, who'd awakened and now sat up on his cot. He'd slept through the night after Karzac placed a healing sleep.

Denevik, at my side, carried a breakfast tray for the former military trainer. He'd told me that it was better if Rade didn't see another woman in a subservient position. Therefore, he carried the tray for me.

"I'm surprised I'm not dead," Rade turned his head to blink at me. Clearly, he was confused by a woman speaking directly to him without being ordered to do so.

"That's not how we think," Denevik corrected. "Here, you're equal to everyone else. That includes the women."

"Women are weaker," Rade turned away.

"Then why are they serving as troops in the King's army?" I snapped at him. "Wouldn't it make more sense to send the stronger ones out to fight the enemy? Or, is it that on the battlefield, all troops will get mowed down by larger, better equipped forces, no matter how they identify?"

"Here's your breakfast," Denevik dropped the tray onto a small, folding table beside Rade's cot. "I suggest that you never accuse Cassie of being weaker unless you're prepared to defend yourself. I, for one, will not ask her to hold back if she decides to pound you into pulp— because she can."

"Eat," I said. "We can discuss all your prejudices later."

Denevik and I walked out of the tent, leaving Rade to contemplate his continued existence.

~

Keela

I wrapped the blanket around myself and followed the scent of food. The moment I left the tent, a guard fell in step behind me. I stopped in my tracks.

"Go on, you're heading in the right direction," the man told me. Hesitant, I took another step, and then another, expecting at any moment that a hand would fall or that a whip would lash out to cut my skin. Neither of those things happened.

"We don't need a tray—she brought herself to get food," the man said.

"Rajeon, find her a chair," a woman ordered as she pulled a skillet off a small stove and set it aside. "We'll have your breakfast on a plate in a minute," she told me.

"Want tea?" The man she'd called Rajeon asked after I sat on a camp stool.

"Yes. Please," I breathed. I couldn't remember when I'd last had tea, but then my memory was full of holes and unreliable.

Rather than telling the woman to bring tea, he went to the pot and filled a mug with honey-brown liquid and brought it to me. "Clare makes good tea," he said.

"It smells so good," I said, sniffing the steam coming off the mug.

"Drink up," Clare said, placing meat and eggs on a plate. "We may have to move soon; two of our scouts are still out, looking for signs of Cjerl's forces."

"Scouts back," two men appeared from the dry brush surrounding the camp, making me jump. I almost spilled tea on the blanket; it sloshed but I moved with the liquid to prevent losing even a drop of the precious liquid.

"This is Chazi, and that's Bekzi," Clare introduced the men who were obviously brothers. "This is Keela," she introduced me.

"Good to meet," Chazi grinned.

"Same," Bekzi said.

"What did you find?" Clare asked them.

"Need to move," Chazi said. "Soon. Wizard and Mask with unit."

"Eat," Clare reminded me as I stared at the brothers. "I'll go tell the others," she walked toward the tents.

Had I heard correctly? Cjerl had spell-weavers working for him? What was a Mask?

"What's a Mask?" I blurted before I could stop myself.

"They—hide others," Bekzi explained. "Not see easy. Have to get close."

The brothers had a clipped version of speech, belying the intelligence in their eyes. I studied them for a moment—their eyes were somewhat strange, but didn't hamper their sight, apparently.

"You not worry. Eat. Need food," Chazi made a motion with a hand to encourage me to finish my breakfast.

"We have a few extra things," Clare returned with clothing in her arms. "There's a bucket of warm water, soap and a cloth in your tent, if you'd like to wash up after you eat."

"Thank the skies," I mumbled and stuffed cooked eggs in my mouth.

"The wide tires allow us to go easier across rough terrain," Dave explained as I followed him around the last of three transports. Long and wide, each transport could carry several people, tents, gear and supplies.

"Where did all the food supplies come from?" I asked, peering into the open hatch of the transport.

"Hmmph," Dave said. "The enemy is well-supplied. We can take whatever they have once we infiltrate their camps and do away with the troops. These transports are theirs, too. Our tracks will be no different from their tracks if they come across them."

I wore the clothing and boots Clare supplied; the shirt and pants were multicolored to blend in with the rough bush country around us. The boots were far better than the ones supplied to drones in the King's army. I'd been given socks, too, and that was a gift beyond price.

"We'll be ready to leave soon; we're waiting for two more to get here."

"Who?"

"Morrett and Yandiveri, although Yandiveri prefers to be called Yan."

"Each of you have a purpose, don't you?"

"Yes," Dave grinned. "I'm in charge of every transport and piece of equipment. If I can't fix it, then it's beyond repair."

"What about Vik?"

"Vik is a warrior, as are Denevik, Cassie and Salidar. All of us can fight, but those four lead the charge. Clare is a weapons expert—she shoots with deadly accuracy. Yan can infiltrate any enemy camp without being seen. Rajeon is a master of disguise. Kear and Morrett— they provide special services to keep us concealed."

"What about me?" Suddenly, I felt inadequate.

"I think we'll put you with Clare and Salidar—to teach you how to handle weapons properly, and to fight with your hands when necessary. Salidar trained Cassie, so you'll learn from the best."

"What about Rade?" I'd seen him loading tents into one of the transports alongside Rajeon, but gave him a wide berth. I had no intention of getting close to him—or speaking to him—ever again.

"He'll learn the same things, but you'll be switching off with your teachers, since you don't have a comfortable past."

"You have that right," I mumbled.

"The only reason we didn't turn him out when he woke is that he's not a rapist."

I blinked at Dave. Until then, it hadn't hit me that among these people, no male had treated a female as chattel to be abused at their whim. The males were also warriors, right along with the women.

Drone wasn't a word to be used within this group; I understood that in a way I couldn't explain. I hoped Rade understood that, too.

"They're here," Vik leaned around the back of the transport. "Load up, we'll move out quick. Cjerl's troops are heading this way."

～

"They usually move at night, so this is different," Vik explained as we bounced and jostled along a track meant for animals to travel. "We think they're getting bolder because of the lack of training your unit had when they hit it with the first bomb. When they're lobbing bombs, the best way to react is getting the hells out of their way."

"That's how any normal person would react," I admitted, rubbing the back of my neck where the controller had been. Already it was scabbed over, but it had left remnants of its presence behind, represented by the gaps in my memories.

"They hadn't thought that much ahead," Vik growled. "Nessil must truly be a fool. You can only throw so many bodies at the enemy before you run out of that precious resource."

"I suppose he thinks those males he's protecting are going to learn how to reproduce on their own," Dave leaned around Vik and grinned.

"He's killing his future. Already, males outnumber females by a ratio of six-to-one," Rajeon observed. "Only sending women and girls to fight the enemy has destroyed their numbers and ensured the eventual demise of all his people."

"And yet the people still prefer to birth males," I said, before wondering where that thought originated.

"You mean the males prefer their female slaves to birth more males," Clare said quietly. "Every female wearing a controller is a slave."

"Don't let the King hear you say things like that," I huffed. "He'll have you killed."

"I'd like to see him try," Rajeon cracked his knuckles.

"Where does Cjerl get his spell-casters?" I asked, changing the subject. "I thought all of them died out after the black zone was created."

"Died out is such a misleading statement," Vik sighed.

"I know they were killed," I hunched my shoulders and stared at the toes of my new boots. "I just don't remember how I know that. But," I lifted my head and leveled a gaze at Vik, "you're saying that Cjerl has spell-casters at his command. Where did they come from?"

"That's a subject to discuss on another day," Dave said. "We're about to change directions to avoid another enemy unit. Hang on, everybody—we have missiles incoming."

I followed Clare's lead as she grabbed a belt attached to the wall of the transport and locked it to a clip on the other side.

The ground shook beneath the vehicle as an explosion occurred not far away. I was glad for the tight belt—it kept me in my seat when the next bomb detonated even closer.

CHAPTER THREE

*K**eela*
"I had no idea transports could move that fast," I said as we climbed out of the vehicles to set up camp.

"You can thank Dave for that," Clare said.

"I did some tinkering," Dave shrugged.

It had taken more than two hours to get away from the bombing; as if we were racing away from the entirety of Cjerl's army, rather than merely two units of it. Nessil had certainly underestimated his enemies and had no idea how far past the black zone they had come.

"Some of us will be going out tonight—to deal with what was chasing us," Rajeon said. "Sal will stay here and show you how to handle a weapon properly."

"What about Rade?" *Was he getting to go with them?*

"He'll be here, learning fighting tactics from Vik. Don't worry, neither of you will be asked to go on a raid unless you want to and can defend yourself. I will say this, though. It's in both your interests to learn fast and do what you can—a lot is riding on all this."

"I know." I hung my head—the fate of the entire kingdom rested on whether the King's army could hold Cjerl's forces back, and so far, all he'd done was lose his troops to a bigger, better-trained force.

"I have a question," Rade's voice made my head jerk up.

"What's that?" Rajeon turned in his direction.

"How are they getting through the black zone?"

"They're not going *through* the black zone," Rajeon frowned at Rade. "They're going over the black zone, using their power wielders."

"I wish we had some, too," I said, bitterness in my voice. "We can't fight Cjerl's forces—we have no magic."

"How can you be so sure?" Kear joined our conversation. "Have you ever tried?"

"All magic wielders were killed in the past—you should know that unless you've been living in a cave all your life," Rade snorted.

"I've actually lived in a cave during part of my life, but it wasn't so bad," Kear grinned. "We fixed it up nice."

"What would you do if you discovered you had what you call magic?" Cassie approached and handed Rajeon a pistol. "This one fires rubber bullets," she told him, giving him a small carry-case she also held.

"Fight the enemy," I shrugged, answering her question. "Lives and the survival of our Kingdom depend on it."

Kear turned toward Cassie, who lifted an eyebrow at him. He offered her a slight smile before turning toward me. "Do you know what the Book of Light and Darkness is?

"Forbidden—and all copies destroyed," Rade answered before I could open my mouth.

"What if I told you not all copies were destroyed?"

"That's—unheard of," Rade exploded.

"You sound like you're afraid of words written on paper," Cassie said.

"I'm not, I," he floundered for words.

"You have no idea, because somebody in the past condemned it, just as they condemned the people with power, and destroyed all of it —isn't that right?"

"They were evil! They created the black zone," Rade snapped.

"Uh-huh," Cassie's fists went to her hips. "Like you know anything about any of that. For somebody who's also forbidden to exist, I'd expect you to have a little more understanding than this."

"You like other men, don't you?" I stared at Rade.

"It's none of your business," he spat.

"I don't condemn you," I told him. "Those laws are stupid and should never have been written. That type of law—it teaches many to hate and gives license to torture and kill on the basis of accusation alone. No law should be permitted to do that."

"And who do you think you are?" Rade hissed, sounding close to tears. "The King himself?"

"I don't know who I am," I replied softly, feeling small. "The controller saw to that."

"I don't want to be forced to separate you two, but I will," Cassie said. "Rade, there's not a thing wrong with who you are, and there's nothing wrong with Keela, either. Here, you're equals. If you can't bring yourself to deal with that, then we'll send you back where you came from, and we won't bother to save your life next time."

"Aren't you tired of hiding?" I asked him. "Don't you want to be with people who see your worth as yourself, rather than having to constantly hide and be afraid?"

Rade refused to answer.

"I'll give you three days to think about it," Cassie told him. "After that, if you don't think you can handle equality, then I'll certainly send you back."

"I'll go put up my tent," Rade hunched his shoulders before turning to leave. I watched him walk away. He was uncomfortable; I could read it in his posture. A part of me wanted to help him. Another part failed to understand why he continued to punish himself.

"You can't really help them until they accept the idea that they need it," Cassie placed a hand on my shoulder. "Many will fight that truth to the bitter end." The moment she touched me, I saw fire in my mind. Blinking, I forced the image away. My controller-affected brain was playing tricks, and it terrified me.

～

Cjerl's Palace
  Royal City, Kingdom of Sorvus
  Commander Jek

Cjerl's new Prime Minister, who called himself Lord Tekar, leaned down to whisper in the King's ear while I stood before the throne, feeling tired, angry and betrayed.

I'd agreed to meet with an envoy from the new King of Vorus, only to watch as one of Tekar's magicians destroyed the entire party before I could approach them.

Except for one survivor—who was sent back with a message.

There will be no treaty.

Only death—for all in the Kingdom of Vorus.

What Cjerl planned to do with an empty Kingdom, with the dead piled and rotting across its lands, puzzled me greatly. He had no use for more land. He needed to tend to his own lands and people, rather than sending out more and more of them to die at the hands of the outlaws on the edges of the black zone. So many were starving because Cjerl had conscripted too many farmers and their sons and daughters to fight, rather than considering what those left behind would eat, were there no crops planted.

Tekar, however; I didn't like the gleam in his eyes whenever he mentioned taking Vorus.

He had secrets, that one.

"Commander Jek," Cjerl finally noticed me.

"I am at your service, my King," I dipped my head to him, as I'd already bowed when I arrived earlier.

"Very good. It has come to my attention that these outlaws you reported in the past are gaining momentum and harrying our troops. I am reassigning you to deal with these threats. Take twenty suitable for stealth warfare and track them. One of Tekar's magicians will accompany you."

He meant the magician would keep an eye on me and report everything to Tekar, who would bend what he heard into whatever he wanted the King to hear. I was being relieved of my duties as

24

Commander of Cjerl's armies. I wondered who Tekar would choose as my replacement.

"It will be as you say, my King."

"You are dismissed," Cjerl motioned with his hand. Turning on my heel, I left the throne room behind. Soon enough, I walked out a side door of the castle—the one closest to the Royal Guard's barracks. He hadn't said there were restrictions on whom I could choose to make up the twenty.

Two were among the King's guards, and they, like me, had lost much of their admiration for the man who sat Sorvus' throne.

"Commander, wait," a voice called out, stopping me in my tracks. Already, the magician had found me—no doubt with the infernal magic he held.

"What is it?" I rounded on him, before blinking. This one—I hadn't seen him before and frankly, he was much younger than the others. Barely into manhood, if that much.

"I was sent to you," he trotted in my direction, his magician's robe parting and flying about his thin body as he ran.

"Your name?" I frowned at him.

"Nakleer, Commander, but most people call me Nak." He arrived at my side; I expected him to be panting and out of breath.

He wasn't.

"Well, Nak, since you're here, we're going to ask two guards to join us, then I expect you to get us on the other side of the black zone before nightfall. I have eighteen more men to choose, and enough vehicles and supplies to gather to sustain us for a month."

"I can do that, sir."

He was being respectful? I certainly hadn't expected anything of the sort. "Good," I replied. "Come on, then. We have to hurry."

As good as his word, Nak had us on the other side of the black zone long before nightfall, where Lieutenant Bern was already waiting. I knew, just by the expression on his face, that we needed to get away from the main camp and soon, or we might not survive the night.

Word had come from Tekar, apparently, and my Second-in Command, Skur, was already asserting his authority among the King's troops.

"I took the liberty of making choices, Commander," Bern said softly as he fell in beside me. "We've packed your tent and gathered supplies and three vehicles. We're ready whenever you are."

"Nak," I turned to my magician. "Can you detect poison in food?"

"Yes, sir," he replied, his eyes widening in surprise. "Do you think?" he began.

"I think a lot of things. Come on, we need to eat and get out of here."

"Yes, sir."

~

Nakleer

The transports were far from comfortable, but they held everything and everybody. Nobody poisoned our food when we ate at the main camp, but Commander Jek was worried about some kind of attack. Therefore, I obscured our vehicles and left a wizard's trail behind us— after disabling the trackers on both vehicles.

Trackers were for those who wished to be found. I doubted Jek wanted anyone in the regular army following us. The King had devised a suicide mission for the Commander and his chosen crew. Both Jek and I wanted to know why, but I didn't voice my concern. Jek didn't trust me, and he was right not to.

The others weren't sure what to make of me, either, so I kept a shield up, just in case. My duty was to make reports, and that's what I intended to do, until the Commander and his troops were officially dead.

And I with them.

~

Keela

Salidar set up a log, which bore a rough outline of a man drawn in white chalk for target practice. Instead of a rifle, he'd given me a pistol, first, showing me how to hold it properly. Then, he explained which parts of the body, if hit, would result in a kill, and which ones would only wound an enemy.

I'd been taught none of this by Rade; I wondered if he knew any of it himself. "You'll be carrying a pistol for close work, and a rifle for long range," Sal told me as I held the pistol in both hands and fired at the log.

I didn't even hit an arm, when I was aiming for the center of the chest. "Try it again," Sal said, instead of shouting at me like Rade and the other instructors had. The second bullet nicked a crudely drawn shoulder.

"Make the adjustment and try again."

~

Nakleer

My wizard's trail warned me of the incoming missiles; the King wasn't wasting any time in killing Commander Jek.

My job was to make the attempt appear successfully fatal.

My wizard's trail was quite long, and at the end of it, a duplicate location signal was implanted in the spell.

We were two miles ahead of the spot where the missiles detonated, which resulted in a brief shaking of the vehicles. Still, it caused the Commander to curse under his breath. From the look in his eyes, I could tell he understood the explosion was aimed at him.

If he asked me, I'd tell him what I'd done. For now, he kept his fears to himself.

Closing my eyes and reaching out mentally, I removed the wizard's trail and the location signal, allowing the King and his troops to believe their mission was a success. From this point forward, we'd be shielded from scrying eyes and on our own.

For a short time, at least.

Mission accomplished, I received the message. *Tekar is practically dancing in his seat in Cjerl's study.*

Cjerl studies?

It's a misnomer. Cjerl goes in there to drink. Tekar does—whatever it is Tekar does. Mostly he gloats over getting what he wants with very little effort.

Just remember to stay away from his touch, I said. *We don't know what could happen. Did somebody send the one I replaced to a dungeon somewhere?*

Sure did. I figure he's being stared at and questioned even now.

Be careful. I don't trust anybody in that place.

Don't worry. Servants are invisible.

Says you.

I have Zaria's medallion. Keep your wits about you—you have to sleep sometime, remember?

Yeah. Thanks, Pauly. I'll keep you posted. You do the same.

Cassie

The goal was to go in without employing power and eliminate or transport the ones we found. Cjerl had scouting groups, and they were well-equipped with weapons, vehicles and sometimes, a wizard or warlock.

This group had weapons, a Sirenali and a wizard. I was grateful that between Morrett, Denevik and me, we could hide ourselves, neutralize the enemy's power and keep our small group safe. Bekzi and Chazi, both in lion snake form, had dropped back to slither in the grass next to us, in case one of the two power-wielders was a power sniffer. There was a safe perimeter surrounding Morrett, Denevik and myself, and we didn't want to slip up even a little to alert the enemy to our presence.

I was also grateful that Kear could mute any sounds we made; Zaria said it was necessary on this mission. Ver'Dak had upped his game after his brother Je'Dik's death, no doubt.

My main concern this time was the Sirenali in the camp—were they there of their own free will—or were they slaves, like so many others we'd seen? Too many of those had their tongues removed, and, because of the means employed to create them, they were also sickly and had limited lifespans.

Morrett understood that far better than any of us. He'd been enslaved for centuries, beaten, starved and used by his master to hide from the powerful, which enabled his master to commit evil deeds.

We're here. Surround the camp, Denevik announced. He and I would take opposite sides of that circle, while the others would spread out on both sides as evenly as possible.

Take the wizard, I nodded at Kear, who dipped his head in acknowledgement. From what we'd seen so far, the rogue wizard was probably a second-level or a strong third. I wondered which house he came from; getting that information could put us on the track for identifying others who'd fallen into Ver'Dak's thrall.

I'll take the Sirenali, Morrett sent.

That left twenty troops for the rest of us. These would be elite troops—the best Cjerl had to send. They had to survive long enough to send valuable reconnaissance to the regular troops, after all.

We were about to see who would live and who would die.

King's Palace, Vorus
Nessil

Verlin was so incensed by the message sent by Cjerl's forces—conveyed by one of our own—that he dispatched the man before I could ask questions.

"Clean up the blood and get the body out of here," I ordered a servant, who rushed to pull the body toward the door of my study. Streaks of blood were left on the floor as the foolish female tugged and dragged the messenger away.

"Get help, then have her beaten when they're done," I waved an angry hand at Verlin, who'd caused this mess in the first place.

Verlin shouted, bringing two more females rushing in. Without glancing in my direction, they lifted the body together, turning it face up so the blood wouldn't drip onto the floor as they carried him away.

Another female drone ran in, a stack of cloths and cleaning supplies in her arms. She set about clearing up the mess Verlin's poor decision left behind. Once the last drone was gone, I spoke.

"You should have waited until I was done with him," I snapped. "I wanted answers, and he's beyond that, now."

"My deepest apologies," Verlin bowed low. "I have made you angry. How may I appease you in this?"

"Go find the information I seek. How close is the enemy? How well are the troops doing against Cjerl's forces? I don't trust anyone who expects me to believe he has the might to destroy all of Vorus."

"Who will act in my place while I am gone?"

"Cawlin, of course."

"Excellent choice. I shall return the moment I have the information."

Cawlin was Verlin's toady cousin, and afraid to do anything that didn't pass Verlin's inspection, first. In this, he was the best choice I could make. I could trust Verlin; therefore, I could also trust Cawlin.

"I shall visit with your Generals in the field, first," Verlin bowed to me. "Before I leave, I shall also inform Cawlin that he is to serve the King."

"Very well. Send Cawlin to me after you've spoken to him. I have letters to write, and I wish to send two to the Generals."

"I will wait for your messages," Verlin replied and strode from my study.

"One last thing," I called out, bringing Verlin back through the door, an inquisitive expression on his face.

"What is it, my King?"

"I wish to hear whether Jessil has died. If not, you'll see to that, I hope?"

"With great pleasure, my King."

I didn't call Verlin back this time. If my drone sister were still among the living, Verlin would derive the last bit of service from her before she died.

∽

Cassie

He thought to attack me with his fists, after I knocked the pistol from his right hand with a well-placed kick. Punching at me with his left, I caught his fist in my right hand before it reached my face. He followed quickly with a second, harder, right-handed punch. Capturing the right wrist in my left hand, I released a bit of my fire, burning his skin and making him yelp in pain and terror.

"Want to stop now, or shall I do your face and genitals next?" I asked him pleasantly.

"Please don't," he begged, fear in his eyes and voice.

I released him, then. He fell back with a cry of pain, dropped to his knees and then huddled over his injured hands.

"This one is wanted by the CSD," Kear drove the terrified wizard in my direction.

"We can send the whole lot to them," I shrugged. "If any of them need to go elsewhere, they'll take care of it. Where's the Sirenali?"

"Here." Morrett pulled the youngest Sirenali I'd ever seen toward me. "Can't speak, of course," Morrett didn't bother hiding his disgust.

How old are you? I sent to the frightened boy.

I don't know.

"I'd say maybe seven," Morrett sighed.

"He needs to go to Quin. She'll know what to do," I shook my head. "Ask her for a report after she's seen him."

What will happen to me? The boy was afraid—the fear washed off him in swiftly increasing waves.

"I wish I could go with you, where you're going," I told him. "You'll be fed and cared for."

Will I have a bed? Of my own?

His sending made my breath catch. These fools had been using him for—I couldn't bring myself to finish the thought.

You will have a bed of your own. What's your name?

They call me meat.

That isn't your name. Queen Quin will help you choose a better name. "Denny, can you get him to Quin?"

"Of course." Denevik stepped forward, pulled the boy into his arms and disappeared while I stared in anger at the wizard and the one who'd attacked me.

"Well, I see a familiar trend here," I snapped at both. "Rape may not be a crime on this world, but it sure as hell is where you're going."

"There is no other world," the one at my feet scoffed. The wizard giggled at his statement.

"That's too bad, then, because you're about to be proven wrong. Kear, will you do the honors?"

"With pleasure." He and the two prisoners disappeared. All the other troops were dead; some by suicide when they saw what they were up against, others by clumping together and lobbing handheld bombs.

Denevik had dealt with the bombers by taking flight and dropping into their midst. They never had a chance after that.

Dave and Rajeon destroyed or disabled the tracking beacons on the two vehicles, while Bekzi and Chazi gathered weapons and supplies.

"Not a bad haul," Dave sounded satisfied. "Everything's ready to move whenever you are."

"Load up, then, and we'll head back."

～

Avii Castle, Le-ath Veronis

Quin

Queen Lissa was with me when Denevik arrived with the young Sirenali. The moment I saw him, I knew he'd been abused.

He was reluctant to leave Denevik's arms; somehow, the ancient High Demon had made him feel safe.

They called him meat, Denevik's sending conveyed disgust.

"You will be safe here," I told the boy as Denevik set him on his feet. "Are you hungry?"

He looked up at Denevik, who smiled at the boy. "He's hungry," Denevik confirmed. "He also wants to know if he can touch your wings. He's never seen anyone with wings, before."

"Of course," I held out a hand. He came to me, his steps tentative. I placed an arm around his shoulders and opened a wing for him to touch. While he ran a shaking hand down my red primary feathers, I gave him as much healing as I could.

We'll be fine, I sent to Denevik. *Although you will always be important to him. This is imprinting, in a way.*

Then I'll visit him after the mission is over, and we can discuss his future.

I'll tell him that while he eats.

~

CSD Prison Facility
Campiaa
Teeg San Gerxon

"He can heal in a normal, humanoid fashion. He deserves those burns Cassie gave him," Kear explained as he and I studied the man inside the shielded cell. A physician had treated his burns already and wrapped his hands.

"I'll question the other one first, although this one probably knows more. I don't like laying compulsion if the prisoner has been medicated."

"You know who the other one is?" Kear asked.

"I only heard the term wizard, before heading this way fast."

"That's Jevonn Hirdess."

I drew in a breath. "You think the Hirdess Clan," I didn't finish.

"That remains to be seen, but it would make more sense than the entire clan dying in a bizarre murder-suicide, wouldn't it?"

"This puts too many worrisome things in a different light," I shook my head. "There are some first-levels in that clan, and perhaps a master wizard. Does Zaria have this information?"

"She does now," Zaria appeared beside Kear and shook her head at the prisoner inside the cell. "Shall we pay wizard Jevonn a visit?"

"I think that's wise," I agreed. If he weren't obsessed, Zaria could read more in his face than I might get with compulsion. If he were obsessed, we could end up with nothing.

"Down this way," I led Zaria and Kear through a well-lit hallway, lined with shielded cells on both sides until we reached the one that held Jevonn Hirdess.

"He's a low second-level," Kear described Jevonn's talent. That was still very strong, as only a first-level and a master wizard were stronger. Kear was a fifth-level Karathian warlock; their power-designation system was the opposite of the one classifying wizards.

Wizards went from fifth-level, which was weakest, to first-level, and then gained Master status if they went beyond that. Few did.

As for warlocks and witches, their weakest level was first-level, while fifth-level was strongest. There were plenty of jokes concerning both, and Kear had probably heard all of them.

Tapping the control panel beside Jevonn's shielded cell rendered the shield invisible, allowing us to see the wizard held inside.

Jevonn was angry, now that he could see us as well as we saw him.

"Well, he's pissed," Zaria drawled, sounding so much like my mother it was uncanny. I was still getting used to having a half-sister nobody had known about, but there were times when she did things or spoke a certain way that I would have known she was related anyhow.

"Is he obsessed?" Kear asked, hope in his voice that the answer would be no.

"He is," Zaria shrugged. "But my money is on the Hirdess clan being all over Verillium right now, and all of them under Ver'Dak's thumb."

"That could mean they've been under his thumb for more than thirty years, then," Kear grumbled. "Everybody thought they were dead, too."

"Maybe the Lyristolyi drug was involved," I hunched my shoulders as I watched Jevonn flop onto his cot and turn his back to us.

"I doubt there's a *maybe* involved in that statement," Zaria sighed. "This really screws things up."

"What do you suspect?" I turned in her direction. Zaria's mind always worked a dozen steps ahead—at the very least.

"It's too horrible to comprehend," she said. "Until I find out more, I'll keep it to myself."

"What are you going to do next, then?" I asked.

"I'll have a meeting with Cassie and the others. Are you ready to go back, Kear?"

"Sure. Will you keep me posted on what happens to Jevonn?" he asked me.

"Well, he's already dead. According to the official records, anyway," I shrugged. "Before we turn that into a fact, I'll ask Kevis and Karzac to do a full workup on him."

"You think he may have gotten the drug?" Kear's eyes widened in surprise.

"I don't know what to think, but Zaria does."

Zaria gave me a tight smile in return, letting me know I was on the right track.

See ya, she sent, then she and Kear folded space.

Keela

Salidar and I were having a cup of tea with Vik and Rade after a satisfactory target practice session when the others returned from their raid. They arrived in two captured vehicles filled with supplies and weapons.

Rade shifted uncomfortably on his camp stool when Cassie hopped out of the lead vehicle first, a grim smile on her face.

He couldn't accept the fact that a woman could be a leader; he'd been raised to believe that women were drones or breeders, nothing else. I wanted to feel sorry for him but squashed that idea quickly.

After all, he'd been one of the trainers that sent me and my fellow drones against Cjerl's forces without proper training or the ability to think for ourselves. He knew we'd die quickly—and most of us had.

He and I—how strange it was that we were the only survivors.

"Do you know how to drive a vehicle?" Sal spoke unexpectedly, making me jump.

"Women—drones—aren't allowed," I replied.

"Tomorrow, Dave and Vik will teach you."

Rade responded by an indrawn breath that resembled a hiss.

I was so surprised I almost dropped my cup of tea.

CHAPTER FOUR

*E*astern Sector, Vorus
    Verlin

My body swayed with the movement of the vehicle. From my seat opposite the driver, I looked through the dusty, insect-gut-covered glass, frowning at the rough road ahead of us.

Most of the rough track was dirt or gravel, lined on both sides by untamed brush, weeds and tall grasses. This was a new experience, since I'd never been this far from the palace.

"I'll tell the King that he should increase taxes, and force the locals to build better roads," I said.

My driver—a trainer returning to the camps, glanced briefly at me before looking away. He wanted to say something and chose to bite his tongue. Too bad; I wanted to work out my frustration on somebody, and he'd do well enough.

He was my driver, however, and unless I wanted to learn how to drive the vehicle on my own, I was forced to sit beside him on this worthless mission. After all, when the messages arrived for the King regarding the front, they were always good news—that we were beating back the enemy successfully, and to please send more drones.

Until the most recent message, however, which informed us that Cjerl was crossing onto Nessil's lands and intended to kill us all.

More drones were required in this, no doubt. I didn't care how many drones died and needed replacing—they were nothing more than meat to fuck, in my opinion.

The messenger that I'd dispatched; his words were the only ones that had painted an uglier picture of the ongoing war. His life was worth nothing, yet Nessil punished me for taking it, and that rankled.

For five days we'd driven over uneven roads, eventually passing fields that bore no crops. Were the farmers shirking their duties? I considered asking the driver to stop in a village along the way but didn't—the faster I got this mission done, the faster I could return to the palace.

As for sleeping arrangements, there were mattresses in the back of the transport, where a second driver was now asleep. He was our night driver, and, as I was sleeping when he drove, I'd had no conversation with him, either.

"Why are there no crops growing?" I blurted as we drove past another field that should have been filled with vegetables or grain.

"Drones called to serve in the King's army. None left to tend the fields," came the gruff reply.

"That's untenable," I snapped. "Drones should be coming from elsewhere."

"What elsewhere?" The driver finally displayed irritation. "We've already cleared out the Eastern, Western and Southern sectors. The fields closer to the Royal City supply the Royal City exclusively, and the Northern sector isn't easy to navigate to collect drones. You'll have to target it soon enough, though."

"Why?"

"Because there aren't any other drones."

"That's a lie."

"You'll see the truth of it soon enough, Prime Minister."

～

Dessil's Rogues Camp
 Eastern Sector, Vorus
 Cassie

"So far, we haven't found any bone dust, but that doesn't mean it isn't all over Sorvus," Denevik answered Zaria's question.

"I have eyes and ears in Sorvus, but he hasn't found anything, either—not yet," Zaria hunched her shoulders as she held the cup of hot tea we'd provided. The morning had dawned crisp and cool, indicating that the fall season was establishing a foothold on this portion of Verillium.

It wasn't a good thing—for Vorus' troops, anyway. Already, Nessil, and Dessil before him, had destroyed too many of their own subjects for the kingdom to recover—not for generations, if ever.

Cjerl showed no sign of pulling his army back during cold weather; just the opposite, actually, after Zaria told us that the prisoner, whose hands I'd burned the night before, had information that Cjerl intended to increase his attacks.

No doubt Cjerl had received reports that Nessil was running out of female troops, and few males had any training at all. At this point, all he could do was throw conscripts' bodies at Cjerl's forces, until he destroyed his own kingdom and died for his shortsightedness.

"I know what you're thinking, and we can't interfere the way you'd like to," Zaria snapped me out of my thoughts.

"Then what do you suggest?"

"Maybe a short trip—to the North," she said. "Just you, Clare, Keela and I."

"That—sounds interesting," Rajeon said with a frown. He didn't say it, but he felt concern for Clare.

"She'll be fine," Zaria told him. "Who wants to get Keela and bring her in?"

∼

Northern Keep, Vorus
 Yolanna

We'd wakened from our long sleep three days earlier, only to learn what idiocy had occurred during those centuries.

"The courtyard has been cleared," Mey walked into my chamber, disturbing my thoughts.

The keep itself was spelled against time, dust and the elements, but the courtyard and outer wall had fallen to ruin.

At least the stasis spells on the food had done their job—we had plenty to sustain us until we could replenish, but a swift scrying of the land showed that only the King and his Royal City had enough to eat; rationing was established in all four sectors due to the war.

I couldn't bring myself to call the man sitting the throne a King. His concerns were for himself, for the most part, and the ones he sent to the front lines he cared for not at all.

Had we made a mistake, taking such a long sleep?

"Things are so much worse than I ever imagined," I told Mey. "Thank you for clearing the courtyard. Has the wall been lifted?" Much of it had fallen to ruin while we slumbered, even with the spells against decay.

"The others are lifting the wall, now. The keep should be intact by the end of the day. When do you think she'll arrive?"

Mey had finally arrived at the question she truly wanted to ask.

"I feel," I lifted a hand helplessly. How could I explain what I felt? That so much needed to be done in so little time, it could prove impossible. I felt responsible for not seeing this in the past. This was my failure, and the fate of the planet now lay in ruins, along with my miscalculations.

"Where is Neek? Is he helping the others lift the wall?"

"He is, but I can ask him to report to you afterward."

"Please."

"Yolanna," young Gia rushed in, breathless from running up too many steps.

"What is it, child?"

"There are four at the gate, asking to come in."

"Four?" My heart thumped painfully in my chest. "There should only be one. Males?" I thought to ask.

"Four females," Gia panted.

"Mey, come," I told her, and transported both of us to the gate.

Keela

I stared through thick, iron bars at two women on the other side of the enormous gate. Beyond that gate, I could see a courtyard and a massive, stone keep behind it. So much had happened is such a short time.

Only moments before, we'd been in the Eastern Sector of Vorus, where fall had come, although the summer's heat still drained the soil of moisture. Now, we stood outside an ancient keep in the Northern Sector, where winter was beginning to establish itself.

In fact, snowflakes, small and swirling as they rode the winds, blew all around us while we waited. Zaria, the new one, appeared to be in charge of this journey, what little there was of it. Knowing I needed time to think and process, I stood, numb with cold and trepidation, as the women on the gate's other side studied us in return.

"You," the elder of the two women pointed directly at me. "What's your name?"

"I can't remember my name," I answered truthfully. "They call me Keela. I don't know what that name means, but it's all I have."

The woman's shoulders sagged; her face looked as if it had aged in the space of a moment. "Not good," she muttered. "Not good. Mey, open the gate. Can't you see she's freezing?"

Cassie

"We won't interfere with your plans," Zaria replied to Yolanna's question. "The fate of the planet rests in your hands. We're here for the interloper—he doesn't belong and is a threat to all worlds. Your vision was true—when you saw it. Ver'Dak's father, on the other hand, arrived and—things changed."

"The girl has no training," Mey mumbled. "How can we proceed, when she needs time and teaching?"

"We can buy you that time," I told her. "We have been harrying Cjerl's army, hoping to draw Ver'Dak out of Sorvus. We attack him there—he'll destroy the entire planet. He already has a plan in place if he discovers it's us he's fighting, rather than rogue bands of troops in the King's army."

"That's terrifying," Mey breathed.

"It's a fine line we all walk," Zaria explained. "Do what you must; we'll try to do our part to hold Cjerl and his overlord off while you do it."

"Will the girl cooperate? Do you know?" Yolanna asked.

"I hope so. I'm leaving Clare here so she'll have a familiar face, and Clare can send your concerns to Cassie and me. If I do that, however, I'll also have to ask a favor—for Clare's mate to join her here. He has talents that even you may find unusual."

"Is he safe? Around women?" Mey demanded.

"Absolutely. You have nothing to fear from Rajeon, although if anyone thinks to attack," Zaria shrugged.

"He can protect us while we work?" Yolanna demanded.

"In ways you've never imagined."

"Then I say yes."

～

Eastern Sector, Training Camp
Verlin

"We've been forced to move back six times, now." The General, who acted as the training camp commander, didn't like my objective and critical opinion of our current location.

"Forced back?" Crossing arms over my chest, I glared at the man. He was clearly lying to me. "All our reports say exactly the opposite."

"Then you've been lied to. Repeatedly," the General spat.

"I'll have you up on charges the moment I return to the Royal City."

"Then I'd say it was a foolish notion that you could handle this on your own—without guards," the second-in-command, who was a lower-level general, drawled. "Your blade and knife are next to useless here—we have pistols and rifles. Try to kill either of us; you'll be shot by three trainer-marksmen who have their weapons aimed at you, ready to shoot you down. A messenger will carry news of your heroic death on the battlefield to the King."

My fingers touched my sword hilt, but a heavy hand from behind grabbed my wrist so hard I was forced to let go. Before I could protest, both my hands were cuffed behind my back, while the second-in-command removed my sword, scabbard and knife.

"Here, you mean nothing to us. Our lives are at stake. And, from this point on, so is yours. You'll be sent out with the next crop of trainees—no fully-trained troops have been sent to the front for more than a year, and the attacks are coming far faster than we can train," Commander General Shif snapped at me.

"You can't force me to go," I hissed as I was hauled away by two guards.

"Even if we have to place a controller, you'll go," he called out. The guards were compelled to stop while I heaved up everything I'd eaten during the day.

Cassie

"How far back did we go?" I asked Zaria after landing in the same tent we'd left moments earlier.

"Fifteen years," Zaria's shoulders sagged. "That keep was destroyed by Cjerl's and Ver'Dak's forces eight years ago."

"I'm not going to ask anything else," I held up a hand as a shudder shook my body. "Only Ver'Dak has enough power to accomplish that."

"I know." Zaria pulled in a slow breath, to steady herself.

The evil in the world often wore people down, and, on this world, there'd been far too much evil already. I could only hope that the power-wielders we'd visited were able to read the signs and save themselves when the time came.

Clare and Rajeon were left with Keela and had instructions to contact Zarigar if an emergency arose. He'd know how to handle things, should the timeline shift and place the Northern Keep in danger too soon.

Clare and Rajeon would continue training Keela with weapons while Yolanna and the others provided a different sort of training. Her fate lay in whether, and how well, she learned her lessons.

"Nak is currently heading in the opposite direction," Zaria interrupted my thoughts. "In two days, change course and arrange a meeting. I think it's time we had a come-to-reality moment with Cjerl's former Commander, don't you?"

"I'm ready to start the revolution from within," I shrugged.

"Good. There's somebody else we should arrange to meet—from this side. Who knows? That one could prove to be a real eye-opener."

"I suppose Morrett can keep the peace in camp if it proves necessary," I said. "Yan can help."

"Don't singe them too much," Zaria offered a weary smile. "I should go; I want to ask the fool in Rylend's dungeon a few questions before he's dispatched for crimes against both Alliances."

"The one Nak replaced?"

"That's the one," she confirmed. "I'll let you know if he tells us anything important."

"Will we get replacements for Clare and Rajeon?"

"Yes. Let me think about who to send, okay?"

"Thanks."

Queen's Palace, Le-Ath Veronis
Lissa

"We need at least two, and one of those ought to be a cook," I smiled at Wolter, who'd accepted vampirism at the end of his normal life. Tony offered his blood for the turn; which resulted in Wolter's ability to walk in daylight and eat normally.

I'd been surprised at Tony's careful training during Wolter's first five years as a fanged resident of Lissia. He could defend himself very well, protect if necessary, use all sorts of weapons and cook pretty much anything.

He'd even taught Tony a few things in the kitchen and that, in itself, shocked the hell out of both of us.

"I hear young Pauly is working in the enemy's palace," Wolter voiced his concern.

"He is. Don't worry; Zaria and Zarigar are both keeping tabs on him."

"Do you know who else is going?"

"Not yet. Zaria is still considering that assignment, although I have a feeling that Jett Riffler may be a consideration."

"I would like working with him—very much."

"I doubt he'd agree to go without Nari and Tiri, though, so there's that."

"Maybe we should make more room, then," Wolter chuckled.

King's Palace, Karathia

Zaria

"His power is so weak, it's almost not there. It's probably the reason they sent him out to die with the others—he couldn't block a missile in his dreams," Rylend shook his head as we stared at the prisoner in his dungeon.

"But Nak can," I said.

"That was a good move," Rylend dipped his head in agreement. "He makes his parents proud."

"Sounds like he makes his uncle proud, too."

"He's been here upon occasion. I may or may not have taught him a thing or two."

I didn't bother hiding my smile. Erland Morphis had taught his son well—and had probably taught Ry the tricks he'd passed on to Nak. Grey House wizards only learned self-defense as a short course. Ry knew all the tricks, thanks to his father, Erland.

"Well, we're looking at a thief and a murderer," I said, bringing both of us back to the subject at hand. "He's loosely connected to the Hirdess Clan, so no surprise that he's with the others on Verillium. They thought so little of him, they didn't bother to obsess the boy."

"He's twenty, and not the sharpest knife in the drawer, as Mom says."

"I have mixed feelings about getting rid of him," I said. "Because of his intelligence level. That has hampered him all his life, and the things he's done have always been to please others, while they kept their hands clean."

"That does change things up a bit," Ry rubbed his jaw as he considered this new information. "Too bad we can't start from scratch with him."

"What if we can? Eliagar has been looking for a project."

"You're going to *Change What Was*?"

"No. Eliagar can remove the memories—and start with a clean slate. If it doesn't work out, then we either institutionalize him, or," I shrugged.

"Separation of particles," Ry blew out a breath.

"It would be the kindest thing to do for a tortured soul."

"They should never have awakened what little power he has," Ry grumbled. "Anyone with any sense would have known not to. I doubt he's even up to a first level's talent—as warlocks measure ability."

"Eliagar can suppress that, too." The idea had only occurred to me after Ry assessed the boy's ability.

"Good idea. Take him back to that level, and he'll never know of it."

Eli? I sent.

"I'm here," he appeared beside me, all nine feet of him, smiling widely.

"Here's a project for you, if you want to take it on," I indicated the boy inside the cell.

"What's his name?"

"Genk." I said the name, although it left a bad taste in my mouth. Among wizards, the name was an insult.

"You want me to erase that, along with all the bad times, troubles and the awakening of his ability?"

"If it's something you want to take on."

"I believe I'm the one uniquely qualified to handle it," Eli told me. "If there are problems, I will let you know."

"Thank you, Son."

"You are welcome, Mother."

Northern Keep

Keela

"A trickle of water is easy to divert, and something we teach our beginning students," Mey began. The night before, I'd met with Yolanna alone. She'd placed her hands on my head and that's the last I remembered until Mey woke me for breakfast.

Now, I watched, half fearful, as she moved a finger, causing a trickle of water in a fountain five feet away to move aside, as if an invisible conduit were directing it.

How did this place exist?

I'd asked myself that question so often, it had worn a hole in my brain. All of this—all these people—were outlaws. They should have died during the purges. Yet, here they were—and here I was, listening while Mey insisted that I had something in me to move water.

"Take a deep breath and release it, then focus on the water."

The deep breath was no problem. Focusing on the water definitely was. "This isn't working," I muttered.

"Hmmph. It took me a week to do anything. Keep focusing on the water. Yolanna says *be the water*, whatever that means." Mey patted my shoulder and walked away. "I'll come for you when the midday meal is ready."

"No problem," I frowned at the water. "They'll know soon enough I can't do any of this."

~

Training Camp, Eastern Sector
   Verlin

The first indication that the enemy was nearing came in the form of shaking ground and a noise so loud it deafened me. "Get off your ass or we leave you behind," a trainer hauled back my tent flap to shout at me.

Just then, another detonation came, causing me to fall while attempting to stand. With hands cuffed behind my back, I rolled over before coming to my knees, then stood quickly before the next missile hit.

Nessil didn't have bombs or projectiles this powerful, and fear began to gnaw at my innards. Cjerl really was coming to take us; we'd been so content to sit in the Royal City and believe we were holding him back.

"Come on," the trainer held up a key. I turned so he could unlock my cuffs. "If you make it out of this mess alive, I'll be much surprised," he grunted as the cuffs dropped to the ground and another missile hit, closer this time.

"Go on—follow the others." He took off running toward a line of transports; I ran after him. I can't really say when it was that the enemy hit us as we raced away in the transports—I only recall blurred vision as everything turned upside down, followed by terrible pain.

And then nothing.

~

Le-Ath Veronis
   Eliagar

"The official word is that your parents and other members of your family died in a terrible attack," I told the young man. He lay in a hospital bed provided by the Lissia Medical Center. "Do you remember that?"

"Uh," he reached toward his forehead but never touched it. "I don't remember," he blinked at me. "What's my name?"

"We can't say for certain, but it may be Zak."

"Zak?" He blinked again, considering the name. "I like it. Maybe it is my name."

"Good," I smiled at him. "I'll be working with you in the days to come, to help you recall what you can, and to assist in your recovery."

That stopped him for a moment, as he slowly considered those words. "Was I supposed to die, too?"

"I'm sorry to say, yes, that was the objective. Thankfully, someone managed to keep you alive, and here you are. Don't worry about such things; there is food coming, and lessons later. Do you remember reading?"

"I—can't read. I don't know how I know that," he was momentarily confused.

"I think you can," I said. "Are you willing to try?"

"Yes," he beamed, and that was that.

Eastern Sector, Vorus

Verlin

"Well, well. Look who's awake." Blinking brought a face into view.

A drone. "Don't touch me," I hissed. No drone was taught healing skills. They cleaned up after a healer, and they certainly didn't speak unless directed to do so.

"Somebody needs his manners readjusted," the drone crossed arms over its chest and glared—*glared*—at me.

"You're not Prime Minister here, Verlin," it snapped.

"Did I hear that someone needed adjusting?" A man appeared beside the drone.

"Yan, allow me," another man arrived, who studied me with a deep frown.

"Morrett, he's all yours," the one called Yan nodded respectfully to Morrett.

"First," Morrett began, "you will not refer to Cassie," he indicated the drone beside him, "as it, or drone, or anything other than her name or her rank, which is Commander of this unit, or she or her."

I struggled to sit up as his words took hold of my mind—and stayed there. I couldn't force them out no matter how hard I tried.

"Next," Morrett began again, "you will be respectful to all within this unit. None here are your underlings. You will follow orders, learn what is taught to you and will not be a nuisance. Also, you will not attempt to escape. And, if you say anything that isn't polite or helpful, I will remove your ability to speak until you agree to cooperate. Is there anything else to add?" He turned toward Cassie.

"All females will be addressed appropriately," he said after lifting an eyebrow in her direction. "Here, no woman, girl or child is beneath you. They are not your servants, and you will look after yourself. Never again will you force yourself on any female."

"Or I will remove your dick for you," Cassie said, studying her fingernails.

"He doesn't believe you can," Yan told her.

"I know. This isn't the first thing he's wrong about, and it probably won't be the last." She turned and stalked away.

"I should probably tell you now that her father is the God of War," Yan informed me with a smirk. "The only reason he isn't here defending his daughter is because he's not needed. You've been healed of your injuries, only because she thinks you may become useful. I'd suggest not making her believe otherwise."

"There are no gods," I croaked as Yan and Morrett left me lying on my cot.

"Try us and see for yourself," Yan replied before he and Morrett walked out of my tent.

∾

Northern Keep

Keela

When more than two hundred women, young and old, arrived at the gate, they were accompanied by a man Clare and Rajeon called Zarigar.

"What's going on?" I whispered as Clare stood next to me, watching while they walked through the gate to be welcomed and fed by Yolanna and the others.

"This is the last of Nessil's troops—the training camp has been overrun and Cjerl's forces are heading toward the Royal City," she told me, her voice soft.

"These are drones?" Uttering that filthy word made me shudder and hug myself.

"Not anymore. That problem has been dealt with."

"Like mine was dealt with?"

"In a similar fashion," Clare agreed. "All of them would have died without a certain amount of—intervention."

I dimly recalled my first—and last—battle. How fire had somehow walked over my hollowed-out hiding place and routed the enemy. Something about that memory now niggled at my brain.

Fire.

It wasn't a thing, after all.

It was a who.

"Where are the commanders and trainers?" I brought myself back to the present with an almost-shudder.

"Cassie didn't find any of them worth saving. They fell to Cjerl's forces."

"Vorus is lost, then." Tears stung my eyes as the women, some so weak they had to be held up by their companions, shuffled through the keep's gate.

"It's not lost yet," Clare straightened her shoulders. "You, however, need to learn your lessons, and learn them well and swiftly."

"I can't even move water," I mumbled, feeling embarrassed. "I don't know why everyone thinks I have it in me."

"Cassie and Zaria see much more in you than you see in yourself. If they say it's in you, then it's in you."

"Which of us is wrong, then?"

"You are. Come on—these women need our help, and we ought to talk to Zarigar about food and supplies. When they're back on their feet, Rajeon and I will begin training the ones who want training. We'll teach them combat techniques, weapons and other things they should know."

"You sound like Cjerl is on the other side of the planet, rather than at Nessil's doorstep."

"Do you think Nessil should be spared?" She turned toward me, then, a hard glint in her eyes.

"Nessil is a fool," I sighed.

"Yes. That's what I thought." Clare walked ahead, leaving me standing still. After a moment, I ran after her. There was a plan in all this; I understood that, now. The saving of Vorus would not include Nessil.

Or most of the others, unless I was very, very wrong.

CHAPTER FIVE

Royal Palace, Vorus
Nessil

The man trembled before me as I waited for the message.

"He's afraid he'll die when he delivers the news," Cawlin ventured in a whisper.

"Say it," I snapped at the messenger, making him jump.

"Cjerl's forces," he swallowed hard. "On the way. Ours are dead. All of them. In a single battle."

"That's not possible," Cawlin stood, making the messenger cower. "Where is my cousin? Verlin was among them."

"All. Dead." The messenger dropped to his knees when his legs would no longer hold him up.

"How far away is Cjerl's army?" I demanded.

"Be here. Two days at most."

"What is your command?" Cawlin asked, his voice a quaver.

"Evacuate the city," I rose and waved a hand. "Bring the Commander of my guard. Quickly."

A terrible boom made the palace shiver. Dust and debris rained down from the rafters above us.

"They're here," the messenger whispered before he fainted.

~

Eastern Sector Camp

Verlin

"Vorus is officially destroyed, as of ten minutes ago," Yan set a plate of food beside my cot. "Enjoy your food."

"But," I said as he turned to leave. "What about?"

"Nessil is dead. The palace is destroyed, as is the Royal City. For now, you're the city's only survivor."

"What are we going to do?" I hated that my voice sounded so small.

"Well, we know where Cjerl's forces are. Maybe it's time to visit Cjerl, who's still in Sorvus—where his forces aren't."

"What good will that do? We're all dead men walking," I muttered. Nessil was dead, leaving me Prime Minister of—*nothing*.

"Speak for yourself, *Prime Minister*." Yan left my tent without another word.

~

Cassie

All around me, everyone else prepared for the move. In a single sweep by Cjerl's forces, all our plans had turned to dust. We now depended upon a secondary, weaker plan to combat Ver'Dak's dark plotting.

We'd pack Verlin's tent last of all. He'd cooperate or I'd send him to suffer the same fate as Nessil. The only thing we waited for now was Nak's arrival, with another twenty who'd either fall in line with our newest strategy or be left behind. I wouldn't know for sure whether any would be suitable; I'd have to meet them, first.

"Nak and his charges are two miles away," Zarigar appeared inside my tent as I packed my things in a duffel for transport. "I'll take you to Sorvus after they arrive."

"Great. What about Pauly?"

"I can retrieve him now, if you like."

"I'd prefer him with us rather than where he is."

"I'll go now while you're waiting for Nak."

"Thanks."

Zarigar disappeared, only to reappear moments later with Pauly beside him. "What's going on with Cjerl and Tekar?" I asked him.

"Cjerl's drinking in celebration. Tekar is suddenly sly and coy."

"Because Cjerl's days are numbered, no doubt," I nodded at Pauly. "Got all your stuff?" I frowned at the half-empty duffel at his feet.

"Most of my clothes were in the palace laundry, and I really don't want them back."

"What did you have to clean up?" I asked after watching Pauly shudder.

"Blood, of course," Zarigar waved a hand. "I was happy to take him away from such reprehensible people."

"She was a kitchen slave," Pauly sighed. "Somebody got their nappies in a bunch, so she was an easy target."

"This planet is really starting to piss me off," I huffed. "Bastards."

"We are here for a reason—or so Mother and Grandmother tell me," Zarigar smiled grimly. "We will see this through."

"Yeah. I hope it's worth it in the end."

Nakleer

The drivers of our transports believed they were traveling southward. Instead, they were heading due west, toward the location where Cassie, Denevik and the others camped. I'd been informed already of Nessil's death and the destruction of the Royal City, effectively placing Vorus in Ver'Dak's greedy hands—wherever he was.

Cjerl only believed himself in charge, until Ver'Dak no longer had a use for him. After all, why fight an entire planet, when half of it would willingly destroy the other half, and cut your work down dramatically?

How long before Ver'Dak's wizards were turned against Cjerl and Sorvus?

Nak? Pauly's voice sounded in my head. *Cassie says cut the engines now.*

With little effort on my part, our lead vehicle developed an engine failure, causing the transport to lurch and stop several times before dying in the midst of waist-high brush and thorns. Only one path ran ahead of us, and that was to the camp.

Good to hear your voice, I told Pauly. *I take it you've been collected from that hell-hole?*

Zarigar came to get me.

Good. We're stopped, now, so Cassie and the others can come get us any time.

She says to keep a shield up; they're on the way.

Commander Jek

We didn't hear or see them—suddenly, they were among us, taking weapons away before we could flinch.

"We don't intend to harm you—unless you try to harm us," the woman told me.

Tall, dark-haired and apparently in charge, she studied me in particular before turning to our wizard, who should have protected us.

"Even if I wanted to put a spell on her, which I don't," Nak informed me, "it wouldn't work."

"Will someone explain what is happening?" I snapped, feeling trapped and out of sorts.

"This is Cassie, that's Denevik, Kear, Yan, Vik and Dave." Nak ended the introductions by naming the shortest warrior I'd ever seen in my life. I didn't say anything; Dave looked as if he were more than familiar with the weapon he aimed at me.

"The Royal City of Vorus is destroyed and its king is dead," Cassie informed us. "That doesn't mean we've been defeated. We're not here on Nessil's behalf. We're here on Verillium's behalf."

"You have to take one side or the other," Chuk, formerly of Cjerl's palace guards, demanded.

"No, we don't," Denevik shrugged. I didn't want a fight with that one. He and Vik were the tallest of our captors, and both were so well-muscled and forbidding, they looked as if either could twist my head from my shoulders and laugh while they did it.

"You really ought to look at the bigger picture, here, or Verillium and all its people will die," Cassie said. "We're going to build an army to take it back from outside forces. It's your choice whether to stay here, waiting for Cjerl's army to find and kill you, or come with us and stand with troops from both halves of Verillium. My advice is to take the latter option. Should you choose to stay, you'll die in three days because Nak is coming with us."

"I've been shielding you after disabling the transports' trackers," Nak turned toward me. "Cassie thinks there's some value in all of you. If she hadn't asked me to protect your convoy, you'd be dead already."

"You're not from Vorus," I spoke my realization aloud. "You don't have a controller."

"No."

"I pity the one who attempts to change that," Vik mumbled.

"You can't be from Sorvus," Chuk pointed out. "Cjerl doesn't place women in command positions."

"Not from Sorvus, no. Just like the one who whispers in Tekar's and Cjerl's ear is not from Verillium, neither are we."

"The theory that other worlds exist is only speculation, according to my studies," I said.

"Your studies can be updated, if you choose to come with us."

"And if we change our minds?" Chuk demanded.

"Then we will set you free, after we suppress the memory of where you were and with whom," Yan said softly.

"What's in it for us?" Binn, who stood behind me, asked.

"Training, regular meals, a comfortable place to sleep and the satisfaction that you gave your best to protect your home world," Vik replied.

"He and another instructor can teach you forms of hand fighting that you've never heard of," Cassie explained.

"How long will we have to build this army and train it?"

"A year, if we're lucky. After that, who knows?" Cassie shrugged.

"I think I would like to try this," Binn sighed. "I doubt Cjerl will be pleased when he finds us wandering his newly-conquered lands, when we should already be dead."

Turning toward my men, I studied them. "Those who want to stay?"

Two hands were raised; Gil and Lunn, the transport drivers, weren't interested.

Two out of twelve wasn't a majority. Did I force them to go, or let them stay and wait for Sorvus' army to arrive?

"The rest of us are going. Do you wish to reconsider?" I asked both.

Gil turned toward Lunn. Before they could reply, both jumped, as if struck by a serpent.

"Uh, we'll go," Lunn stuttered, as if he were in shock. I had no idea what happened, but whatever it was, it had changed his and Gil's minds.

"All right. Our camp is not far. Gather your belongings, leave your vehicles and come with us. We'll eat before we transport away from here."

"What about our weapons?" I asked.

"Leave those, too. We have better where we're going."

Sirena

Randl Gage

"The plain, the mountains and the high valley have been recreated. I'll move the keep intact with everybody in it and leave a duplicate in its place." Zaria sat beside me in the palace kitchen. "You can keep the changes in topography, or we can return the area to its original state afterward."

"Wasn't much there to begin with," I told her. "We'll take a look."

"This was the only way out of this mess," Zaria sighed. "Unless we want things to go straight to hell with no rest stops in between."

"Hey, Zaria," Dori walked into the kitchen carrying an empty coffee mug. "What's up?" She grinned at both of us.

"Oh, this and that," Zaria teased. Dori knew very well why Zaria was here.

"How's Cassie doing?" Dori filled her mug from the coffee maker.

"Pretty well, considering she has a planet filled with stubborn idiots to deal with."

"People do get set in their ways," Dori saluted us with her mug and walked out of the kitchen.

"I love her," Zaria laughed. "You're perfect together."

"You don't have to tell me that," I agreed. "What's next on the agenda?"

"Looking for Ver'Dak, what else?" Zaria said, pushing her barstool away from the island. "There must be clues, but I can't find them. He's hidden himself so well that locating him may prove impossible. If that's the case, we may all be screwed."

Zaria disappeared, leaving me with my mouth agape. Where the hells could a half-Krelk hide, that not even Zaria could find evidence of him?

Cassie

In Rade's mind, he believed we'd been traveling three days before reaching our destination in the northern sector of Vorus. He'd gone quiet after being told that King Nessil had fallen, along with the entire country.

In fact, all of our guests believed it had taken three days to reach the valley beyond the first set of mountains, thanks to Morrett.

They'd never know they no longer stood on Verillium's soil—unless someone told them or Morrett removed the obsession.

"Others will join us to train," Denevik informed our company. "Rade, you will learn new tactics and handle new weapons, although you will attend the advanced classes."

"Does this mean the laws of Vorus are no longer in place?" Rade ventured.

"It does mean that. A new set of laws has been drafted that will treat everyone fairly and equally. If anyone fails to recognize a fellow inhabitant as someone who deserves the same rights and freedoms, that one will be released to fend for themselves."

"No matter what?"

"No matter what. If you're attacked as if those rights don't belong to you, your attacker can rely on being put on trial, facing the possibility of banishment—or worse."

"That doesn't mean you should provoke them; all misbehavior should be reported to a trainer or senior officer. A decision will be made on a case by case basis," I said.

"Will there be others from Sorvus in the ranks?" Jek asked.

"Many," I confirmed. "I hope everyone sees this as an opportunity to save Verillium, rather than destroy it."

"In the meantime, we'll sort you into barracks, and take you on a tour of the training grounds," Denevik announced. "And, there'll be a simple interview for all of you before tonight's mealtime."

"Interview?" Lunn asked.

"To find your strengths," I shrugged. "Nothing to worry about."

Will they freak if they find out they have latent gifts for wizardry or such? Denevik sent.

Some, maybe. I already have my eye on a couple. I'm sure Kear does, too. Zaria will make the determinations on whether their power should be awakened if they have the gift.

Has the Northern Keep been relocated?

Tonight, when everybody inside it is asleep.

Probably for the best.

"Kear and Yan will guide you through the training grounds and the barracks," Denevik announced. "We'll see you during the interviews, and at dinner afterward."

～

Sirena

Randl Gage

Chief Markus and Jincus stood before me. "You're saying Cassie and Denevik need trainers for Verillium's troops?" Markus asked.

"Yes, although most are so raw, they don't qualify as troops yet. They need to learn discipline, along with all the other qualities a good soldier needs. Cassie wants regular reports on who is or isn't suitable for the job."

"This is about taking back their planet, isn't it?" Jincus observed.

"In a nutshell, as Zaria says. Travis and Trent have already volunteered, as has Zanfield. Jett, Nari and Tiri will also help."

"What about Miz and his sister?" Markus asked. "They've been whispering together lately. I suspect something's up on the technical front."

"We're wondering how much technology to offer—this is a delicate situation, and, if our mission is successful, any survivors on Verillium will be inundated with offers from tech companies to buy the raw copelis quartzite for information storage."

"That means they need lessons in technology, then," Markus nodded.

"Those two—with Sabrina's help, will bring some of the trainees with the proper aptitude into the current century—as the Alliances measure time. What do you say? Want to take this on?"

"I will," Jincus agreed, while Markus dipped his chin to indicate assent. Markus had a light in his eyes—he was looking forward to the assignment.

"Good. Report to Cassie at the Northern training camp in the morning. Have fun," I added as they turned to leave.

"On it, boss," Jincus turned back with a grin.

∽

Cassie

Zaria narrowed her eyes at Verlin, studying him for an extended length of time before sending the message—*He has talent.*

He's also a murdering, asshole rapist, I countered.

What is your recommendation?

Burn the talent out of him, tell him what you did, and then force him to serve those at the castle who will learn how to use what they have. Let him know what it's like to have a controller.

The idea has merit, but first, we should take him on a journey. Morrett and Denevik should come with us.

For backup?

Of course not. To protect Verlin from ah—others.

This sounds intriguing.

Yep—Verlin is about to switch places, and he isn't going to like it. If he doesn't learn his lesson in this life, we'll have no further use for him.

CHAPTER SIX

*V*erlin

I awoke from the worst dream of my life, only to discover that I'd also wakened in the worst place I'd ever been. I recognized it because I'd been there a handful of times, for food—and *other things*.

"Get up, you filth," the castle cook shouted, forcing my body to jerk and rise, like that of a puppet on a string. "Breakfast won't make itself," Nard continued. "Get to work."

I couldn't stop myself from falling in line with two dozen other drones, who, after sleeping in their food-stained clothing, now marched toward the massive kitchen at the bottom level, following Nard's orders.

All of them were tapped and controlled. Why was I here with them? Only a few men worked the kitchens, and they were all in charge of the drones.

As if my hand and arm were weighted, I struggled to lift both to check the back of my neck. Stifling a yelp, I allowed my hand to drop after encountering the familiar nub—the one indicating an implanted controller.

How? Had my captors done this to me? Wait—that was a dream. I had to find Nessil. Struggling again, I attempted to step out of line, only to discover that my body wouldn't cooperate with my brain.

Or that my mouth wouldn't open to tell Nard that I didn't belong on his crew. Didn't he recognize me? He barely glanced in my direction as I passed him by, my eyes begging him to release me from this imprisonment. I knew nothing about cooking or cleaning.

My feet veered to the left along with three other drones, heading for the ovens, which had already been warmed by another set of drones. While my mind screamed at my body to stop, I began to make bread in tandem with the other three. My hands, feet and body knew the rhythm, even if my mind did not.

Glancing briefly at the drone who worked beside me, I saw her eyes were dead. Would mine end up that way, too?

Had Nessil ordered this fate for me?

Why?

Turning back to watch my own hands, I finally noticed what I should have long before then; that a scar was missing from my right hand—one I'd gained while practicing bladework with Nessil years ago.

Closer scrutiny made my heart thump so fast I worried I'd die from it—the hands were smaller than they should be—the nails unkempt, and calluses where there should be none.

More terrified than I'd been before, I swiped a hand over the polished stone surface of the counter before me.

The face staring back was vaguely familiar, although I couldn't place it.

That wasn't what frightened me most.

The face staring back at me was that of a drone; one whose eyes looked as dead as those of the drone beside her.

"Get back to work," Nard slapped me viciously across the face after my hands stopped moving.

I wanted to kill him then and there—mutilate his body while the entire kitchen watched. Mentally raging, my hands obediently went back to their task, a spate of shouted curses held unwillingly behind my teeth.

The pain of the slap had stung my skin and my pride, while my body continued working as if nothing had happened.

"Let me see," a gentle hand touched my cheek. Turning slightly, I saw her.

How was she here? Was I dreaming about the past? Jessil lifted a damp, clean cloth and wiped my cheek. When she drew it away, the cloth was stained with blood.

My blood.

"I wish I had medicine," she whispered. "Too many die because they get no care. I know this means nothing to you," she looked about her, as if watching for someone to strike her as well. "It means something to me," she added, "and I'd stop it if I could."

She moved away, then, leaving my line of vision while my hands were buried in dough for breadmaking.

Jessil. She was dead—killed in her first skirmish, along with her fellow drones. I'd asked the Generals about her when I'd traveled to the front—the same front where I'd almost perished.

Except for a strange intervention.

Now, I found myself a drone in Nessil's kitchens, living in a female body. Nothing more than an obedient pair of hands, connected to a belly that rumbled with hunger, even as those same hands prepared food for others to consume.

Keela

I was beginning to hate water. The only time it obeyed me was when I poured it into a glass to drink.

I crept closer to the fountain, hoping that distance was the factor in moving the falling element aside.

Still nothing.

I'd made attempts while standing, sitting and kneeling, none of which made any difference. Although, sitting on frozen flagstones held its own kind of hazard, I discovered. I hadn't felt warm since I'd tried it two days earlier. The cold of the mountain itself had invaded my soul, and I was helpless to cast it out.

Sleet hit my shoulders as I cursed under my breath. Why wasn't the fountain frozen over? Maybe ice would be simpler to move about, because it was stationary. Frowning, I concentrated on moving sleet, which fell heavier upon my head. Nature laughed at me; ice pellets ticked and bounced off the flat stones beneath my feet.

"You should probably go inside," Clare arrived to herd me toward the keep. "I hear this will last for about an hour before turning to snow."

"I'm never going to get this," I said, turning to gaze into her eyes.

"You have a ton of baggage to overcome before you allow yourself success in this," she replied cryptically.

"Baggage?" I wasn't sure she knew the meaning of the word, or the proper use of it.

"Mental baggage," she tapped the wool hat she wore with a mitten-covered hand. "Come on, let's go inside and get tea. You look half-frozen."

"I wish I was only half-frozen," I mumbled. Thick socks and leather boots had done nothing to keep my feet from the numbing cold; I walked on pins and needles as I followed Clare to the nearest doorway.

~

"Try this." Someone set a mug of tea on the table. Looking up, I had to blink twice before my brain accepted his image as real.

Trainer Rade had brought me tea.

Pulling out a chair opposite mine, he sat there, his face revealing an emotion I'd never seen in him before.

"I have it, too," he began. "Or so they tell me. I can't get water to move to save my life. I'm sorry, by the way. Someone handed me a book to read last night—a history book. I had no idea." He moved uncomfortably on his chair.

"No idea about what?"

"About the power we've inherited, and that there's no difference between a male's or female's strengths when it comes to using it. You have what you're born with. I was shown last night what's possible—by the strongest wielders at the keep. Both of them are women."

"I can recall a recent time when we were nothing more than drones to you," I countered, sipping tea and eyeing him over the brim of the cup.

"I know. These two—they've never been drones. Nobody here has ever been a drone." He shuddered, as if shaking off the lies he'd been fed for decades. "So many dead in battle—deprived of any wit to save themselves."

"I still can't recall most of my past—thanks to a controller," I muttered.

"If I knew what your past was, I'd tell you. They only sent us fresh bodies, to train as well as we could before they were sent out to die."

"It wasn't nearly enough," I pointed out. "I've learned more from Clare and the others in only a few sessions, than I ever learned from Nessil's trainers."

"I know." Rade's eyes dropped as he admitted what we both understood. "I should have gone out with my trainees."

"You'd be dead," I handed him more truth.

"Yes. I know that, too. I can't help but think you came from a good family—you can read, write and speak well enough."

"A good family that had no qualms about sending me to the army?"

Rade hunched his shoulders. "It is often done as a punishment for wrongdoing; whether real or imagined I cannot say. Sometimes, rumors came with the trainees."

"Nothing about me, though?"

"We received nothing, spoken or written."

"I'm losing hope that I'll ever recall my past—or move water at my command," I sighed.

"At least we don't have to live in fear where we are," Rade told me. "I've already met others," he didn't finish.

"Who are no different from either of us," I filled in the words. "And we don't have to let those—*things*—rule our lives any longer."

"You were right to say the laws are wrong," Rade nodded. "Wise words, and much appreciated." He rose and stretched before giving me a tentative smile. "Friends?" he asked, extending a hand.

"Friends," I agreed, clasping his hand with mine. "Maybe we can become frustrated together, next time we attempt to control water."

"I'd like that."

I watched Rade walk out of the keep's kitchen, more relaxed and confident than he'd been when he arrived.

∼

Verlin

Six long, torturous days passed, while my hunger grew, along with the anger that festered in my brain. A controller kept it from spilling over; otherwise I'd have murdered the cook's assistant the second time he tripped me and laughed about it.

Both times, and more times than that for the drones about me, a hand lifted us up, setting us on our feet with a kind word whispered in our ears.

Jessil had done this for a very long time and was practiced at it; she always waited until the perpetrator turned away or was distracted before helping. If she hadn't—the thought struck me then.

Somewhere, Nessil and I—my former self, anyway, were looking for her. She'd hidden in the castle kitchens for three weeks, unnoticed.

Just as I'd never noticed her in the past.

She'd been beneath me, but off-limits while her father lived. That protection ended the moment the old King died and Nessil took the throne.

Jessil, out of necessity, was practiced at playing the invisibility game. I, on the other hand, was a fool. I hadn't forgotten how she'd been found—or my part in it.

Yes, I was a fool—of the monstrous, malicious variety, and only now was I beginning to understand.

∼

Cassie

"It always starts out bad, then pulls together," Travis and Trent flanked me as we watched new troops drilling from the edge of a wide, flat field. Trainers shouted at those who lagged or turned in a wrong direction.

We planned to visit Verillium again to gather good candidates to fill this army, but we'd stopped by the training field to see how things were going after four days of instruction.

Most of the newest trainees would be pulled from certain death when their battalions were hit by Cjerl's forces—which involved traversing time.

A few others would be taken from Cjerl's own lands—before he starved and taxed them to death or pulled too many family members away to serve in his army. That act alone left too many farms without enough hands to do all the work.

Randl offered to help; he, Dori, Zanfield and Perri had already left for Cjerl's kingdom. Randl would choose those we could rely on to save the planet, rather than their own, puffed-up King.

"How was target practice yesterday?" Trent asked, his eyes following Jincus' trainees. "Who knew that a junk dealer would make such a good drill instructor?"

"Target practice went well enough; the weapons they're training with are far more reliable than the ones provided by Nessil's army."

"Just call Nessil's weapons crap—that's what they are," Travis snorted. "Nessil only spent on Nessil. Everything the army had was provided by Dessil, and most of that from five years ago, before he became addled and listened to an altered version of the army's success."

"Just as Nessil did. I wonder how long ago Cjerl's wizards interfered with the messengers?" I asked.

"I'd say Ver'Dak is responsible for that," Zarigar appeared before us. "I've come to carry you from time to time and place to place—so you won't be too tired to choose wisely," he smiled down at me.

"I like that idea," I told him, smiling back.

"Shall we go, then? We'll be vetting troops during training, then collecting those you want when they face their deaths at enemy hands."

"We're ready," Travis and Trent chorused.

We were gone in an instant.

Randl

"Wow," Perri breathed. We watched as a brother and sister, fraternal twins, tossed heavy bales of hay onto a mule-drawn wagon driven through the field by their father. Both were tall, with wide shoulders and enough muscle to impress anyone.

"Zaria tells me that these three were killed because their father refused to allow them to take his son and daughter for the army," I told her and Zanfield. Dori already knew; we'd talked about coming here first after learning of the atrocities committed against this particular family.

"Then they went to the house and killed their mother and two younger sisters," Dori took up the tale. "Raped and murdered them."

"Sick," Perri hunched her shoulders. Zanfield subtly reached for her hand and squeezed it.

"We'll take care of that, love," he whispered low.

Perri had suffered abuse for years at the hands of her uncle. He was dead now, and nobody mourned his passing.

"Here they come," I said, as the vehicle carrying Cjerl's military enforcers drove rapidly onto the field, rolling over cut hay and stopping in front of the wagon. They startled the mules and prevented the wagon from moving forward.

"Shall we?" I asked my crew.

"Oh, yes," Dori muttered before turning to ocelot. Her back claws tossed hay in the air behind her as she raced toward the enforcers, who'd climbed from their vehicle and proceeded to argue with the farmer while his son and daughter hung back.

Our turn, I sent to Perri and Zanfield. Dori had already

incapacitated the lead enforcer after climbing his torso with a single leap and knocking him to the ground.

Two other enforcers fired their weapons at Dori, only to learn they no longer worked. Perri folded Zanfield to the scene—I was already there.

∼

Cassie

My shoulders slumped—only seven out of eighty-five trainees were suitable. The others had been controlled since the age of two and would never climb out of the pit they'd been forced into. With no memories of ever having made a decision in their lives, they'd cower on a battlefield without a controller.

Dearest, they will surely have a better life after this one, Zarigar told me. He knew I was frustrated, just by the set of my mouth.

Let's go pull our seven from the battlefield, then, I replied, as Travis and Trent shook their heads—they'd reached the same conclusion. *You know this is Liron's fault,* I added.

I do. He arrived and found an easy way to weaken the population, making them ripe for takeover by one of his half-Krelk children.

Zaria made Liron's death far too painless for my liking.

While I understand your viewpoint, I also understand hers. It is our way to deal out death, Zarigar sighed. *Otherwise, we become those we punish.*

Yeah. My shoulders slumped another notch. *I sure don't want to be the next Liron.*

Let us hope there is never another, Zarigar said.

Yeah.

∼

"Looks like Randl had better luck than we did," Travis nodded as we watched the last farm family herd milk cows into a barn in the foothills below the Northern Keep.

"I had to promise them help with their animals and crops, but they're here and their children are willing to serve in our combined army," Randl appeared beside Travis. "We have plenty of volunteers looking for work here on Sirena. They'll arrive tomorrow."

"We could only find slightly more than three hundred former drones, and a handful of trainers or officers worth saving," I told Randl. "Tomorrow, if you're willing, we can visit the farms in Vorus."

"I say we go back farther in time," Randl suggested.

"How far back?"

"Let me make some split-time decisions."

"Sounds good to me."

~

Cjerl's Palace, Sorvus

Cjerl

"I was told never to go to Vorus," I argued with Tekar. "I admit, gloating over my enemy's demise would be enjoyable, but I was warned. I was told to never leave the palace, you know."

"When were you warned?"

"When I was a child, I think. It doesn't matter. My mother said she was warned as well, when she was small. No King of Sorvus should ever leave the palace. Not even to visit Vorus' Royal City, which now belongs to me."

"Bah," Tekar dismissed my fears. "I know as much as any soothsayer. Besides, what is left to harm you? The country of Vorus is no more, except as an extension of your own lands."

"But the black zone," I continued my argument. "I will not cross it, no matter what you say."

"Did the warning counsel against that as well?" Contempt for me—and my beliefs—dripped from Tekar's tongue.

"I will not go, and that is the end of the matter. Leave me now—I must consider how to deal with my new lands."

"But you need my advice, my King, on how to do exactly that."

He was correct, but I didn't want to give him that satisfaction.

"Leave me. Have wine sent. I will consider the expansion of my kingdom for a few hours."

I intended to get extremely drunk, but Tekar didn't need that explanation. He wasn't a fool and would know my intention already.

"Very well," Tekar huffed. Flipping his robes to convey his irritation at me, he fled my study, his spine straight and fury in every step.

"I will not go to Vorus, even to see Nessil's head stuck on a pole," I muttered to an empty room. I was warned, and that warning I would not ignore.

~

Tekar

"Have wine sent to the King's study," I flung at a guard in the hallway. My robes billowed behind me as I strode toward my chambers. Fuck Cjerl. I had my orders, and those orders were to get him out of the palace at all costs.

His death lay outside it, just as he'd said. My death would come here if I failed to convince the King to leave this place. More subtlety was surely required, but time slipped away from me with each passing day.

The rest of my evening would be spent in the Royal Archives, researching family journals and histories. Something in those records had to exist—*or perhaps could be created*—to convince the King to travel to Vorus. Both thrones on Verillium were required to be empty, with no living heirs, before the planet could truly be taken. Nessil was dead already, as was his drone sister.

Cjerl needed to be dead, and the swifter it occurred, so much the better.

For me.

~

Avendor, Distant Past

Leare

The gishi fruit I held in my hand was tiny—nothing like its larger, tamed descendants. These grew haphazardly along the river's course, which would one day flow through SouthStar, the home of Strength.

His was the domain least hidden among the Three. Wisdom and Love hid their homes, although Love's mates could find their way to her private planet. Wisdom's home only he and the Shining Ones could reach, and the Shining Ones had to ask permission to be ferried in by Wisdom himself.

Unless he summoned one of us.

I'd dallied long enough after receiving his call. He had a mission for me, and I was concerned it would take me back to Verillium.

I answer, I sent to Wisdom, while pocketing the gishi fruit. In moments, I was *Pulled* away from Avendor's past, to land in Wisdom's library. Lifting the gishi fruit from my pocket, I set it gently on his desk.

He'd know where I'd been. It would remind him of whom I would answer first, should an alternate call be sent.

Wisdom and I—we had an uneasy truce between us, and he understood better than anyone just how fragile it truly was.

~

Keela

"Don't be discouraged. You have talent; Yolanna says you're filled with it," Mey patted my shoulder. "Come now, time for your midday meal."

"At least the snow stopped falling." I stood with difficulty, my body complaining from being in the same position most of the morning. A small area had been cleared an appropriate distance from the fountain, so I could make my futile attempts, and someone with power had even warmed the flagstones for me.

None of that made a single bit of difference. Somehow, my will and my talent were disconnected, and I had no idea how to bring them together.

Rade and I had asked to make our attempts together, only to learn that it was forbidden for students to do so until both had achieved their goal and unlocked their ability.

Therefore, Rade would take my spot in the afternoon, while I attended to my studies—mostly consisting of the types of spells and castings I should be able to perform, once I made a connection with my talent.

Which could never happen, in my case. Hunching my shoulders, I followed Mey toward the castle. Once inside I'd hear, no doubt, that someone had succeeded where I'd failed.

My stomach growled as we entered the keep and the scent of fresh-baked bread reached my nose. Wondering whether a spell existed to shut out conversation over a meal, I continued to follow Mey to the dining hall.

"Mind if I sit here?" He was about my age, with dark hair and a wry smile. I'd chosen a small table in a corner to consume my meal, hoping nobody would pull out the chair opposite mine to sit and eat.

"Chair's yours," I shrugged, keeping my eyes on the stew in my bowl.

"Name's Pauly," he stated. "And I know exactly how you feel."

"Nobody knows how," I snarled, jerking my head up to lock eyes with him. Immediately, I backed down. There was something in his gaze—and the sympathy there, that told me he did know.

"You have power—I can feel it," he said as I continued to stare. "There's probably a reason why it isn't answering you at the moment, but it's definitely there."

"Hey, man, mind if I sit?" Someone else set his food adjacent to Pauly's. Then, without waiting for permission, he dragged an empty chair over from a nearby table.

"This is Nak, my best friend," Pauly introduced us. "He's already gone through training. He keeps me out of trouble," Pauly grinned.

"I can't even move water," I confessed, feeling embarrassed.

"Then stop worrying about moving water. Try something else instead," Nak shoveled a spoonful of stew into his mouth.

"What else is there?" I demanded.

"Now that your power is awake, anything could be on the menu. They're asking you to move water, because there's no danger involved," Pauly explained. "To you or the water. Imagine what would happen if somebody told you to concentrate on creating a landslide instead, and it happened on the second try?"

"You could be crushed before you figured out how to stop it," Nak told me. "There are other safe tasks besides moving water, that don't involve freezing your ass off outside," Pauly went on. "Unless you already know how to create a warming spell, so the cold won't distract you."

"I thought Nak was the one who finished training," I frowned at Pauly.

"He is. All I have to do is copy everything Nak—or another power wielder—does."

"Pauly's different," Nak explained. "But we're not allowed to say exactly how. What we can say for certain, is that sniffing power runs in his family. If he says you have it, then you have it."

"And you have it—in plenty," Pauly grinned at me again. Somewhere in him, and I couldn't say how, was a deep well of pain that he'd hidden until he could deal with it. At least he had a good friend who didn't mind that he was different.

The other thing I noticed?

Neither of them considered me less than they, because I was female. Rade had come around, but there were still some male trainees who were uncomfortable around the women learning the same lessons.

"I hear we're getting a few more trainees tomorrow," Nak scraped the bottom of the bowl with his spoon. "Pauly and I will size them up when they arrive."

"You're part of the training staff?" I breathed the words, only now realizing their truth.

"Yeah—we were asked to help out," Nak grinned this time. "So we're helping out. Flower in your assigned pot and all that."

While I finished my stew, I considered why these two had chosen my table, rather than someone else's. For most, it would be a coup to sit with instructors, especially those who were capable of entertaining conversation.

Actual conversation was sadly lacking in my life—what little I could recall of it. "You look troubled," Pauly said.

"I keep wondering who I was—before I was controlled," I sighed. "All that is gone and I can't bring it back."

"Maybe someday, when you least expect it, you'll have it again," Nak soothed. "For now, don't let it worry you. You're here and you're safe."

Tears pricked my eyes—had a man ever worried about my well-being before? Had anyone been concerned about my safety when I was sent to the front to die?

"I thank you for your words." I stood, struggling to keep from choking on a sob. Lifting my bowl, I carried it toward the table where it would be collected to wash.

Everything will be all right, Pauly's voice sounded in my mind. *Keep your head high and your hopes alive.*

Verlin

My life had narrowed to a long but limited set of duties, often interrupted by tripping, slapping or another brutal game played by the male kitchen helpers. The head cook had forbidden them from causing a ruckus in his kitchen, but his eyes weren't everywhere or every *when*.

I would have lost what little was left of my sanity, had it not been for Jessil. Until I found myself trapped in another body in Nessil's kitchens, I hadn't realized what a kind word or deed meant after a stinging slap or yet another shove to the floor, followed by rude laughter.

My bruises, cuts and other physical marks were bad enough; the wounds across my heart and soul were far worse. The cruelest thing, however, was the controller, which kept me dancing to the male puppeteers' commands in the kitchen. With no way to fight back or speak in my defense, I was helpless and I knew it.

For the first time in my life, I understood what the controller was for—the subjugation of living, thinking beings.

And then the day came. The one I knew would come, only I had no understanding of how I could be in two places at once. Busy at the sink, washing dishes, I turned to see what the sudden hush and the rush to open a path were all about.

Until I saw myself approaching.

Prime Minister Verlin. How puffed up with self-importance I'd been. The anger on his—*my* face—was terrifying. I knew what he—*I*—wanted. Except, I hadn't expected to reach for—*me*. I was away from the sink in a moment, willing my body to flee.

I couldn't.

When Verlin grabbed my hair to pull me out of the kitchen, someone else shouted at him to stop.

With a new target in view and a careless swipe of his hand, Verlin knocked me toward the hot stove opposite the sink. Skin sizzled, and pain forced a cry from my throat. Jessil pulled me away before the burn became worse.

Verlin—*I*—grabbed Jessil by the hair and yanked her to her knees, before dragging her out of the kitchen while cursing and leveling accusations the entire time.

Tears of pain—physical and emotional, dripped down my cheeks, until everything went dark.

CHAPTER SEVEN

*L*eare
"You were highly recommended, and able to teach in daylight hours," Cassie answered my question—why I'd been chosen rather than a vampire to instruct native Verillians.

She led me toward the classroom building not far from the training grounds while she spoke; I followed carefully. "Only a few will learn history, and with your qualifications, you can teach the history of both Alliances, as well as the history of technologies," she continued.

"I can do that easily," I agreed. "I can also make suggestions on which fighting skills and tactics work best, if they're needed."

"We have plenty here who already know that sort of thing," she waved away my offer.

Perhaps someday, she and I would talk of war, and how many battlefields I'd been instructed to watch—and how many commanders' conversations I'd listened to. I could recount battle plans and their execution verbatim, and then describe what had gone right or wrong with all of it.

There were also things she and I ought to discuss, but here and now was not the place or time for those conversations. Willing myself not to sigh, I stepped inside the door of the hasty construction, where a utilitarian classroom waited for me.

"You have an assigned room in the officers' building, and are invited to have meals there, unless you wish to visit the keep on the mountain. Either place has good cooks, if you want to satisfy your curiosity."

"I may visit the castle for the evening meal, then," I said. "I have been interested since I learned of its existence."

"Your call. And, as Lissa sent you, I assume you know not to tell anyone where you are or what you see or do?"

"Of course. I have guaranteed discretion to those who sent me," I said. "And I guarantee it to you as well."

"Thank you. This is your classroom," we stopped outside an open doorway. "You'll have to teach in the beginning using paper and ordinary writing tools. Books have been provided. I'm grateful you can speak the language."

"It is closely related to other languages, which I have also mastered," I agreed amiably.

"Supplies are down here," she continued walking along the hallway, then stopped outside a locked door. "Here's your key," she handed me an archaic, metal device which would open the door. "Paper, pens, pencils and research books are inside the supply room. Your first students will arrive tomorrow morning at nine bells. You'll be teaching three classes a day. Keep me apprised on the fastest and best learners—we may authorize a fourth class to teach them an advanced course."

"Will I have any students from the castle?"

"Yes. We've divided those who need your help into three groups— they'll join the troops chosen to attend."

"Very well. I will design my courses to include power wielders."

"Good idea. I think they'll be avid listeners if you include their kind in the history lessons."

"Thank you."

"Just—don't go overboard on the power thing. All right?"

"I will restrain myself."

"I'm sorry I'm overloading you with the *don'ts* right now. This is new for me, and it isn't new for you. Therefore, I apologize."

My eyes widened in surprise—nobody bothered to apologize to me.

For anything.

"I hope I make you proud," I responded. "I will do the best job I can."

"I know you will." She smiled at me, and that was another rare occurrence. "Come on—I'll show you to your quarters."

Keela

Another day was almost gone, and I'd wasted it grunting, huffing and cursing softly, as the water ignored my commands and maintained a steady course from fountain to bowl and back again, in an endless loop.

At least I was inside the keep, in a small chamber where a fountain was set up. I learned it was powered by sunlight—or the battery that ran it was powered by sunlight, anyway.

Nevertheless, I was grateful that Pauly and Nak smiled and greeted me when I took a seat at their table during the dinner hour.

Someone else arrived shortly after I did, and he introduced himself as Leare, a new history teacher who'd just arrived.

"You'll be in his class," Nak told me after his eyes lost focus for a moment. I'd learned that the mental speaking that he and Pauly could do was called mindspeech. They said that I might also have it, when I learned how to employ my power.

"The history class is in a building not far from where the troops are training," Pauly said. "Nak and I may be selected to transport the students from the keep to the facility and back again."

"Not everyone will attend this class," Leare said, breaking a piece of bread and putting butter on it. I watched his hands as they performed this normal task—his fingers were long and fine, but somehow, I knew he'd done hard work with them in the past.

"Have you ever served in battle, Master Leare?" I asked him. He studied me for a long moment before answering.

"Yes," he said, and the answer, short as it was, told me it was a final answer and no more questions were welcome.

Nodding, I went back to my own plate of food.

"How was your day?" Nak asked.

"Same as yesterday," I mumbled. "Complete failure. Water appears to be my nemesis."

"How long have you been at it?" Leare lifted an eyebrow.

"Days. Even Rade got a response today, and that was extremely discouraging."

"Rade?"

"Former trainer for Nessil's army," Pauly replied softly. "He has talent, but nothing like Keela does."

"Ah." Leare went back to his food, taking his last bite and chewing thoughtfully. "Well, I suppose I'll see you tomorrow," he offered a wry smile before rising and carrying his plate to the collection table.

"He came highly recommended," Nak sighed. "I wish I could sit in on his classes."

"Why can't you?" I asked. "It would be nice to see a friendly face there."

"I'll check with Cassie," Nak grinned.

"Good. I'm worn out, so I'll see you tomorrow," I told my companions. I wanted a bath before bed, and if I didn't go soon, there'd be nobody in the bathing suite to warm the water for me.

"Someday, I'll do it for myself," I said quietly as I dropped my plate on the collection table.

Leare

A conundrum—how to help the young woman without drawing attention. Even the powerful ones stationed here hadn't guessed at the problems assailing her.

A focus.

Yes.

That's what she needed, and it could be provided easily, although it had to come from someone other than me.

That, in itself, would require further reflection. I needed an ally—one who could keep this secret for as long as it was necessary to keep it. The survival of a planet and its people rested upon it.

I would consider this—and make my choice carefully.

Nakleer

"We get to stay for the lecture in the afternoon, when Keela is in history class," I fist-bumped Pauly. "Cassie says it's a good idea for her to feel comfortable."

"And we can help her when it passes from pen and paper to comp-vid," Pauly grinned.

"Right as usual," I laughed. "I think she'll love a comp-vid."

"We have to take things slow—the object is to allow them to accept things naturally—in an orderly progression."

"Yeah. The ones chosen to attend the history classes are the ones who'll be most accepting of the fact that they're not alone in the universes."

"I'd really like Keela to see Avii Castle with us someday," Pauly sounded wistful.

"Quin would love that."

"We have to get Keela through this, first," Pauly pointed out.

"Yeah." The weight of that responsibility settled onto my shoulders, like an unwelcome burden. We had no guarantee that she'd survive this.

Or that *we* would. Considering the enemy we faced, things could go wrong in a nanosecond.

"It's a mess, isn't it?" Pauly sighed.

"It's that—to the forty-third power."

Leare

The heavy, ornate chain didn't matter; I left it in the crypt where I found it. The gem-carved pendant hanging from it is what I took. Had things happened differently, perhaps it would have passed through the generations to its intended recipient.

With a sigh, I shook my head at the dust, animal droppings and cobwebs cluttering the crypt. It was so old, it was buried beneath layer upon layer of wandering topsoil—as was the massive building above it, slowly sinking its way into obscurity.

The amber-colored focus, roughly the size of a child's fist, lay among the remains of the one who'd borne it last. It took much longer than it should have for me to reach out with power and lift it from its cage of rib bones.

I'd already chosen the one who'd hand this to Keela—after hanging it upon another chain, of course. That item would come from a particular jewelry maker. Slipping the pendant in my pocket, I folded space—and bent time.

~

Pauly

"It's called a focus stone," Professor Leare explained as he handed the delicately carved necklace to me. "Long ago, early power-wielders needed a focus of some type—a wand or other item, to assist in their spells and such. It may not help at all, but I think it may be worth a try."

The pear-shaped, amber-colored pendant, carefully carved with the image of a sun on one side and two moons on the other, covered half my palm as I studied it. The attached gold chain hung freely off my hand, although its workmanship was more than worthy of the pendant it held.

"If it works for her, I suggest she wear it at all times, including in the bath. A quick wipe will keep it clean," Leare explained.

"If she believes it works, whether it actually works or not, perhaps it will help," I nodded my head before stuffing the necklace in a pocket.

"Exactly my thinking. It's an old relic that I collected. I feel it may better serve Keela, rather than sitting somewhere collecting dust. Don't tell her it came from me or at my suggestion—I don't wish to show favoritism among my students," he added.

"Understood. Thank you, Professor. I'll give this to her later."

Turning, I headed for the door before folding space back to the keep. If things worked out, I could give the pendant to Keela at dinner. I'd read about the focus stones, wands and other accoutrement that early wizards, witches and warlocks used in the distant past.

Besides, if Keela believed it could focus her power, perhaps things would go smoothly for her. At the moment, she was getting more discouraged by the day as those around her revealed their talents.

"I've read about those," Nak breathed as Keela accepted the necklace at dinner, running fingers over the delicate carving before settling the chain over her neck. "My father says there was something of the sort that belonged to an ancestor, but he described it as being carved out of jade."

"It's beautiful," Keela smiled. "Thank you for thinking of me."

"I hope it works for you," I told her. "If it doesn't, it's still a nice piece of jewelry."

"I'll try it tomorrow." She tucked the pendant beneath the tunic she wore. I thought it wise not to let anyone else know she had it—she apparently thought the same.

Keela

Rade joined me for breakfast the following morning. "How are your lessons coming along?" I asked him.

"Power or mundane?" He grinned self-consciously.

"Both."

"I'm still working with water. Sometimes it does what *I* want it to, other times, it does what *it* wants to do. I really enjoyed Master Leare's class yesterday. I've never been taught anything about history, much less that of historical warfare and how it has evolved."

"It makes sense, too," I agreed. "Everything has a beginning."

"When he said that some things have been lost to time and forgetfulness, I felt a chill," Rade sighed. "As if we need to know those things, and we'll never know them."

"Can you imagine?" I mused. "That sometime, far in the past, two friends sat at a table, discussing what was lost to time before them. It makes you want to find someone from those times and ask them questions—but that's impossible," I sighed. "They're dead."

"You're right." Rade appeared glum. "Master Leare says some things are recorded in books, though. Do you think he knows where to find them?"

"We can ask, I suppose. I wouldn't mind reading before bed. It might take my mind off disobedient water trickles."

Rade ducked his head to hide a smile.

"You two ready to start your day?" Nak and Pauly walked past us, carrying empty plates toward the collection table.

"Oh, we're almost late," Rade breathed, stuffing the last piece of bread in his mouth.

I dipped up the last bite of eggs on my plate—I didn't want them to go to waste.

"We'll see you later," Pauly chuckled before following Nak.

Yolanna

"If Keela doesn't master her concentration soon, we'll have to proceed with training the others on more advanced spellwork and leave her behind," I told Mey.

"But," Mey objected.

"She can't be the one. There's no way she'd be this incompetent if she were."

"What can we do, then? The time for saving Verillium draws close. If we don't have the proper one," Mey's words faltered.

"The proper one may be dead, and we just haven't learned of it, yet."

"But what about those who brought her?"

"They've made a mistake. Mistakes happen all the time. Their intent was good, their judgment flawed. Who is the best student we have among the new trainees?"

"Nettle and Bette are too close to make a proper distinction," Mey admitted.

"Then tell them they'll have classes with me every morning beginning tomorrow. If Keela hasn't shown us anything by then, we'll place her with the servants. Inability is inability, no matter how you look at it."

"I'll see to it," Mey's words conveyed her defeat.

"No trainee has ever taken this long, before. We both know this, Mey."

"I know."

~

Mey

Yolanna had completely reversed her initial evaluation of Keela, and I didn't understand it at all. The Keep's Mistress had developed a noticeably harder stance on many things since Keela's arrival, and that also didn't add up.

I'd known Yolanna for years, and I'd never seen this kind of behavior before. Perhaps it was because we faced difficulties now that we'd never seen in our long lives, but still it concerned me.

Even so, I was determined to work with Keela as much as I could, in the hopes that she'd connect with her power soon and prove Yolanna's opinion unfounded.

~

Keela

"How are we progressing?" Mey arrived just as I was settling onto a small rug to begin my fruitless, water-manipulating exercises.

"So far, nothing," I admitted, my cheeks heating in embarrassment.

"Clear your mind," Mey settled on the rug beside me. "Forget what has come before. Today will be the day," she smiled. I blinked—desperation was hidden behind that smile. My final test was today; I felt it as surely as I felt the rug beneath my hand.

Drawing in a shaky breath, I closed my eyes for a moment. Would the pendant help me, as Pauly said? Did I need to touch it? Ask it questions?

Help me, I focused on the carved, amber stone.

Opening my eyes, I concentrated on the water falling in a thin trickle out of the fountain in the room's center.

Mey's gasp made me draw a breath—there was movement in the water, but not what I intended. The stream of it split, going in two directions at once, both splashing outside the bowl meant to catch them.

~

Eventually, even Yolanna came to witness my success. By that time, the water was obeying better; it moved right or left as I mentally commanded it.

"Much better. You will join the class with most of the others tomorrow," Yolanna shook her head, as if she'd given up hope that I'd ever reach this goal. "Mind you," she added, "you'll have to keep up with the others, or give up your training altogether."

With that threat hanging in the air, Yolanna turned swiftly, her robe swirling about her as she stalked out of the room.

"Come," Mey pulled me to my feet. "You have books to read before classes begin tomorrow morning."

No pressure, I mentally scolded myself. All I'd needed was a focus, just as Pauly said. If he hadn't given me one, I'd likely be changing sheets and washing dishes before the day was out.

What had Yolanna meant when she said *most of the others?*

I was destined to find out, and it wouldn't be good for me—or most of the others.

~

"Yesterday, we spoke of battles fought on Verillium," Master Leare began his lecture. "I know a few of you have heard rumors or perhaps have read books alluding to other worlds. That is what we will cover today. Nak, will you assist me in this?" he asked.

"I will," Nak rose from his seat and walked to the front of our classroom.

"Nak is working at the keep, helping the instructors, as many of you know already," Master Leare explained. "He is fully trained as a power wielder, so he will create an image of Verillium and its sun, including the moons and all four planets surrounding your sun."

I gasped with the others as the room darkened and an image appeared before us—the sun in the center, with the four planets and their moons, except for Hidral, the smallest planet, which had no moon of its own.

"This is your solar system," Leare said. "Nak, show them what is outside this system."

The images shrunk before us, bringing in more stars. Those stars—many of them had planets orbiting them, too.

"Not all those planets will support life," Leare went on. "Some do, however. Those that are in the proper place, with the proper type of atmosphere, will support life, and most of those do."

I gaped and gasped that entire lecture, as I learned things I'd never thought to learn, including things I'd never imagined before.

~

"I heard you're coming to the common classes tomorrow." Rade grinned as he sat at our table for dinner. His enthusiasm made me feel better.

"I heard that, too," Pauly said as he and Nak joined us. "Congratulations."

"I was about to wash out," I admitted, feeling embarrassed again.

The focus helped, didn't it? Pauly grinned, this time.

Yes, I attempted to answer him.

Hey, it works, his grin widened. *You have mindspeech.*

She has mindspeech? Nak joined the conversation.

Apparently, I do, I answered him.

Thank the stars.

Do they need thanking?

Maybe not. It's just a saying, Nak cut into his sliced beef and gravy.

Rade? I sent to him. He jumped in his seat as if he'd been stung by a wasp.

What? His eyes were round in shock.

We have mindspeech, I crowed.

"Keep it to yourself—it's advanced stuff around here. Frankly, nobody else needs to know about it, either," Nak informed us.

"Use it sparingly," Pauly cautioned. "An ill-placed message can disturb important work, you understand."

"Understood," Rade agreed and began eating. *But isn't it amazing?*

I stifled a laugh and turned to my food.

The following morning, I learned that I'd been holding up regular classwork on more advanced spells and such. Today's lesson was lifting rocks. I thought it would be easy after I'd finally dealt with water the day before.

I was wrong. Rade lifted a palm-sized rock after three tries. They set a larger rock before him while I struggled with the same small rock I was first given.

Black looks from other students were cast in my direction as the morning faded away. All of them had larger stones to work with at this point; mine remained the same. When the instructor set us free for the midday meal, the other students rushed past me. Two bumped me rudely on their way out.

That was uncalled for, Rade sent as the last student, a tall, sturdy young man, elbowed me aside to reach the door.

Maybe I do belong with the servants, I replied. *I know how to wash dishes and stir the soup or make beds.*

Don't say that, Rade argued. *How many of these can use mindspeech?*

No idea.

Let's ask Nak and Pauly, Rade sighed aloud. *Come on or they'll eat it all.*

Dejectedly, I followed Rade to the dining hall, although my appetite had vanished.

❧

Eliagar

"Zak, hold your fork like this," Lexsi instructed while I watched. I'd taken him to the High Demon palace, where Lexsi showed him how to make eggs the way he preferred for breakfast.

He was determined to do everything right for the Crown Princess, and immediately moved the fork into the proper position.

"Now, taste your eggs," Lexsi, who'd helped cook the eggs, dipped into half what they'd prepared together.

"Mmmm," Zak nodded his approval.

"Very good—you know not to speak while you're eating," Lexsi praised him. "But that sound is always a compliment to the cook."

"He is reading," I said while they ate breakfast. "And he's growing stronger with each day's passing."

"Good for you," Lexsi smiled at him.

"Will you teach me how to cook other things?" Zak asked Lexsi, pausing between bites.

"Of course. Whatever you'd like to learn. I have a comp-vid book, too, that you can read. It explains basic cooking terms, which are accompanied by vids."

"Really?" Zak was more than pleased. "Yes. I want to read that."

"You know how to access definitions for the words you don't know," I said. "This may improve your reading skills quickly."

"Thank you, Eli," Zak said politely. "Thank you, Lexsi," he dipped his head respectfully to her.

"You are very welcome," Lexsi smiled at him. "Before you know it, you'll be a master cook."

"Will I?" He turned a questioning gaze in my direction.

"That is up to you," I replied. "Becoming a master cook requires much devotion. What you put into anything usually determines what you get out of it."

"I want to become a master cook," he decided, before finishing his eggs.

Wait until he hears about firefighters and starship captains, Lexsi sent to me. I turned my head to hide a smile.

She was right. Zak was in his twenties, but because of his upbringing, or the lack of a proper one, anyway, he was still innocent in many ways. I was taking things slow with him, so he could adjust.

My hope was that one day, he'd be prepared to rejoin proper society and contribute in his own way.

Whether it was as a cook, firefighter or starship captain—or something else, I had no idea at the moment, and, as I was enjoying the teaching and companionship, I didn't bother to *Look* into his future.

Leare

The focus had helped get Keela past the first obstacle of her training, but then she immediately ran into difficulty with the second stage.

All the others in her class were ahead of her in that respect, including her friend, Rade.

Mentally cursing about what was known and not known regarding the history of power wielders on Verillium, I greeted the afternoon class and began the day's lesson.

~

Pauly

"I just can't figure out what the problem is. The focus seemed to work with the water, and then nothing for lifting the rock," I shook my head. "If they could only see what I see in her," I shrugged my shoulders.

"We know the power is there. Yolanna's ability can't compare with that," Nak agreed. "I've asked Zaria about it. Zaria knows what we know, but she can't figure this out any better than we can. We're all stumped."

"And the no-interference thing is holding us up, no doubt," I grumbled.

"That's what Zaria told me. She says that Keela must be trained the way Verillium trains power wielders. The whole thing sucks, as Gran Lissa says."

"Nettle and Bette have already started shunning most of the other trainees, too, since Yolanna singled them out for private lessons."

"Yolanna thinks she's doing the best thing for Verillium. Unfortunately, we disagree with her."

"I hope they can handle the wizards Ver'Dak plans to set against them when the time comes. If not, Verillium is lost already."

"I need a drink," Nak said. "Want to join me?"

"You got something stashed?"

"Not here. I'll let Randl know we're about to pop in and raid his liquor cabinet."

"You do that. I need to get away from this place for a while."

~

"Well, I see our idea wasn't an original one," Nak breathed as we walked into the room set aside for after-dinner drinks at Randl's palace.

93

Already, most of the army instructors were there ahead of us, drinks in hand. "Come on, we have plenty," Travis waved us over to the bar at the far end. "Pull up a stool and have a drink or three with us."

"What precipitated this mass abandonment of the training site?" Nak grinned.

Trent, standing behind the bar, passed glasses of bourbon to both of us.

"Probably the same thing as you," Travis tossed back his double and slapped his glass on the bar for a refill.

"We keep running headlong into the non-interference thing," Trent supplied the answer. "Sure, we can train them on weapons and fighting skills, but most of them have no idea where any of this equipment is from, who made it or who we really are."

"Yeah—we're disenchanted with the Verillium method of training those with power," Nak set his empty glass down for a refill. "They have no way of gauging actual power. Pauly could tell them all day long what some of them have, and they wouldn't believe him for a second."

"To living in the dark ages, my friend," I tapped my glass against Nak's refilled tumbler.

"Second that," Travis clinked his glass with mine.

"All the way around," Zanfield arrived with his empty and got a refill. "Damnation, this job is harder than I thought it would be. Jincus is having nightmares about it."

"I thought Jincus always slept like a log," Trent observed.

"You see the problem," Zanfield downed his drink.

I couldn't stop the laugh; didn't even try. Nak grinned and fist-bumped Zanfield.

Verlin

I became aware as the body I now occupied stumbled up the palace stairway to Nessil's study. Ragged breathing, a stitch in my side and a terrible dread engulfed me.

I knew what was about to happen and wanted to turn around and run.

Like my time spent in the kitchen, I was encased in a body which refused to obey my brain.

"Message—from the front," I gasped to the guards outside the door.

The door was opened, I was announced and subsequently shambled into the presence of the King—and his *Prime Minister*.

Me.

Verlin.

I cursed myself mentally as my mouth delivered the message I'd been instructed to convey.

Verlin, sword in hand, moved swiftly.

Darkness fell.

Again.

My subsequent days of suffering could not be numbered, or sufficiently describe in the measure of pain and humiliation I suffered —by my own hand. Cruelty was synonymous with Prime Minister Verlin; those in the palace who still had their minds intact growled and hissed curses at his back.

Perhaps it would have been a mercy to die on the battlefront, a victim of Cjerl's more advanced troops, rather than waking in this endless cycle of abuse and frequent deaths.

Mercy.

I would have begged for it if I could speak the words. My body and tongue were controlled, like most of the other servants about me and therefore, my suffering was borne in silence.

CHAPTER EIGHT

V erlin

"Welcome back." She stood over me, as she'd done once before.

I cowered. "Please," I begged. "No more. Kill me and end this suffering."

"Ah. So, you know what suffering is, eh?" Her tall, angry companion now spoke. "We ought to send you back as a drone in Nessil's army, so you can feel what real suffering might entail."

"Denny," she cautioned her male companion.

"I think he may have learned his lesson."

She'd arrived—the one who'd set this in motion. She terrified me.

"Tell me—if you saw Jessil again, what would you do?"

"Ask her to kill me—I deserve it."

"You want to die that badly?"

"I don't want to remember my past," I mumbled.

"Isn't that the point—what you've learned from your past? What you shouldn't do the next time?"

"We don't need a broken Verlin," the one called Cassie knelt beside my bed. "We need a determined Verlin. One capable of doing the right thing from now on."

"I owe Jessil." Tears stung my eyes. "She's dead. How do I repay that debt?"

"By looking out for her in the future?" Cassie appeared thoughtful.

"Did you not hear me?" I hissed while tears fell. "She's. Dead."

"She'll never trust him, looking the way he does," Cassie rose to her feet and turned to the other woman. I listened in disbelief. What part of dead did they not understand?

"We can fix that," the other one said. "Easy. Verlin will be the only one to remember who he was. What name would you take for yourself, if you could change it and your appearance?"

"Sorrow," I stated flatly.

"Hisan?" She turned to Cassie.

"Hee-san?" I rolled the word on my tongue.

"It means grief and suffering—in another language," Cassie explained.

"Then that is my name."

"Now, for your face," the other said.

"Give me scars," I pleaded. "To resemble those on my heart."

"Scars." She sighed before light formed around her.

"You have scars," Cassie told me when I could see again. "Burn scars on your face, and a deep, knife scar across your throat." The other woman was gone.

"Deserved," I said, hunching my shoulders.

"Come on—you have catching up to do. Remember, from now on you are Hisan, the determined one," she said. "When you see her, you'll know her as Keela, rather than Jessil. You will not call her anything but Keela. The controller you ordered affected her. She can no longer recall her early memories, and those include her name, her parentage, her brother, or Verlin, who is now named Hisan."

Keela

Classmates whispered as he walked into the room to join our lessons. They were rude, in my opinion. The man had clearly been burned and almost murdered, if the scars on face and neck told me anything at all.

Had he been wounded in battle? I couldn't imagine that a criminal of any sort would be welcomed into this classroom. That could prove disastrous.

"Welcome, Hisan," Neek, our instructor for the day, greeted the newcomer. Neek's near-shudder told me how he viewed Hisan—revulsion shone in his eyes.

This would give an example for the other students in my class—on how the newcomer could be treated. Was he not wounded enough already? Why would they consider adding to that burden? Sadness washed off him in waves; how could they not feel it?

Soon enough, Neek began the lesson, working with some students who were lifting stones large enough to be called boulders. I still struggled with the same small rock from the day before.

Help me, I begged the pendant—something I hadn't done the day before. Slowly, and wobbling precariously, the stone lifted from my workspace.

Even Hisan had better luck—he'd raised his small stone on the first try, while I struggled to lift the stone a second time.

Neek took the stone away before I could lift it again and set a larger one in its place. Not far from me, Rade was working with his third stone—and lifting it easily.

Why was this so hard for me? Feeling exhausted already, I began to concentrate on lifting the larger rock.

Surprise widened Hisan's eyes as Rade and I set our trays on his table. Everyone else gave him a wide berth—as if coming close to his scars would affect them in some way.

"I'm Keela, this is Rade," I introduced us to the newcomer.

"You sure you want to associate with me?" Hisan mumbled, before stuffing food in his mouth.

"Why wouldn't we?" Rade asked.

"Are you sure you want to associate with me?" I returned Hisan's question with one of my own. "You probably know already that I'm the worst student in the class."

"Look, Nettle, it's the broken one, the scarred one and the nebble," Bette swished past our table, with Nettle close behind. She'd just insulted all of us, her slur aimed at Rade the worst of them.

"Look, it's Bette, who'll die face-down in pig muck," I snapped back. I had no idea where that had come from; it escaped my mouth before I could stop it.

"Like you'd know," she half-turned to sniff before leaving to find a table for herself and Nettle. Nettle looked cowed as she slumped along behind Bette—that told me volumes about which of them had come out on top in their private lessons.

"Don't mind them," I reached out to pat Rade's hand. "They'll get theirs, someday."

"That doesn't help us in the meantime," Rade ducked his head and went back to his food. The insult Bette leveled at him stung; I could feel his pain and anger while he ate.

"Hmmph," I replied.

Hisan had stopped eating after I'd flung my words at Bette, and rather than staring at her, he'd blinked at me. He was still staring until he came back to himself and went back to eating.

"Are you in the late afternoon history class with Master Leare?" I asked him.

He nodded and kept eating.

"Good. Nettle and Bette are in the middle class, so we don't have to see them again until dinner."

"Will Pauly and Nak eat with us again?" Rade asked.

"I hope so. I'd like to see Nettle and Bette belittle anyone while they're here."

"Pauly and Nak?" Hisan sounded curious.

"They assist with some of the training—in the advanced classes," I explained. "They also transport us to Master Leare's classroom, which isn't far from the army training grounds."

"Not only that, but they attend the classes with us—they're interested in the subject and Master Leare is a good teacher."

"They're friends," I said. "I enjoy having conversation with them. I can't recall ever having friends or conversations before."

"Keela is still searching for her name," Rade said. "Perhaps if she recalls that, she'll remember whether she had good friends in the past."

"I wish I had been your friend before," Hisan mumbled, setting his fork on his empty plate with a sigh. "I had a knack for picking those who aren't such good friends. I will regret that forever." He touched the scar at his throat, as if it still pained him.

"I am guilty of using that word—the insult Bette used—in the past," he confessed to Rade. "I have since learned better. You have nothing to fear from me."

"We have combat practice after this," I said, changing the subject. "At least I'm doing better in that class."

"Keela is one of our best at hand fighting," Rade complimented me. "She is swift and cunning. Masters Drake and Drew are quite pleased with her progress. I've had to relearn so many things," Rade grumbled.

"What did you do before you came here?" Hisan asked.

"He was trainer Rade before," I said.

"Forced to toss weapons into untrained hands and send drones to their deaths, there at the last," Rade sighed. "I still have fears that Cjerl's forces will climb these mountains and kill us before we're capable of giving him a good fight."

"Is that your desire? To give him a good fight?" Hisan asked.

"It is."

"Then we stand together, brother. Cjerl has much to answer for."

Leare

A new student joined the class; they called him Hisan. That wasn't his given name, but I'd never reveal that.

Instead, I gave him notes to catch up on the previous lectures, and then, because he'd understand better than most in the class, I began to discuss more recent history on Verillium, including the use of controllers and an all-drone army, both of which were major mistakes.

There was no discussion as I walked them through the division of Verillium into two kingdoms, the introduction of the controllers, and a King who didn't want his friends to go to war.

"Any questions?" I asked as class was nearly over.

Hisan lifted his hand.

"Yes, Hisan?"

"What about the black zone? You never explained what it is or how it happened. You only say it came into being to divide the kingdoms."

"The black zone's existence can only be explained by the black zone," I answered.

"But," he protested.

"Think about it," I said. "In fact, I assign all of you to think about it, and write your thoughts for a final project in four months. Answer these questions, in your own words—what is the black zone, and how was it created? You're dismissed."

I watched them file out of the classroom, talking amongst themselves. The assignment would only be given to this class.

I had my reasons.

Keela

"There are no books in this library—or any other library—that mentions the origins of the black zone," Nak told us at dinner. He and Pauly welcomed Hisan into our group, and when we asked them about the black zone, they had no answers, either.

"I've always heard that if you wanted to kill yourself, walking into the black zone was a good way to do it," Rade said.

I turned in his direction, knowing without a doubt that he'd considered doing just that.

Nebble was a vicious word—the worst insult one could level at Rade, and might have ended in a death sentence, had someone with authority accused him of it.

I'm glad you're still here, I sent to him.

How do you—wait, never mind.

I'm confident the laws will change, Pauly told me. *It will take time, though.*

If I were in charge, they'd change right now, I returned.

I know that about you, he said. *Keela, the Just. Hisan, the Determined. Rade, the Stoic.*

Nicknames?

Why not?

What's your nickname, then?

Pauly, chosen son of Ironsmith, he said. *The Ironsmith name carries a lot of weight. My adoptive father is an honorable man.*

And Nak?

Nakleer, wizard of the first level.

Sounds important.

He is important. He may become a master wizard, someday.

I have a question.

Go ahead.

Why are two important people sitting at this table—with us?

Because you're friend material. The others aren't. You talk about things other than your instructors and your classmates. It's refreshing.

We enjoy our conversations at this table, Nak joined in. *We're friends, right?*

Of course. I enjoy my days more when I know I have this to look forward to.

"We're something to look forward to," Nak bumped his fist against Pauly's and both grinned.

"What just happened?" Hisan asked.

"Fist-bump, dude," Pauly held out his fist. Hisan, after thinking about it for a few seconds, bumped his fist against Pauly's.

"What does dude mean?" Rade asked.

～

Commander Jek

I'd been exempted from many of the basic training courses by Travis and Trent, after they'd assessed my level of training. I was assigned to advanced weapons courses, and hand-fighting with an experienced instructor.

Salidar put me on the ground more often than a grass-bounder leapt across it during a lifetime.

I was also asked to help guard the perimeter around the farms down in the valley twice per week. When I saw the young farmer attempting to sneak past the boundary, heading for the keep higher up, I stopped him and used the communicator to summon Commander Travis.

"What's this about? You've been instructed to stay on your assigned property after nightfall," Travis paced inside the farmer's kitchen.

"I only wanted to see the keep—it's so mysterious," farmer Clawd replied.

I didn't believe that was the reason.

Neither did Travis.

"Stay on your property from now on," Travis snapped at the man. "I don't care how many women are inviting you to dally farther up the mountain. This is for your own safety, understand? We have guards posted around these farms for a reason."

"Cjerl will never make it up this mountain," Clawd refuted Travis' words. "Nessil's dead."

"Cjerl may not come himself, but others could. Try this again and we'll send you back to Sorvus where we found you."

Clawd swallowed hard at Travis' threat before nodding his acceptance.

"Good. I'll have eyes on you from now on," Travis said before stomping out of Clawd's farmhouse.

"He's right, you know," I snapped at Clawd. "Show some sense, man. We live in dangerous times."

Turning on my heel, I followed Travis out the door.

Keela

"Where am I?"

"You're in my workroom. It's a dreaming, Granddaughter."

The woman claiming to be my grandmother looked far older than the memory I had of my father's mother—before she died.

"I'm not that grandmother," she smiled at me. She wore a sturdy, canvas work apron, short boots and a plain, ankle-length dress with long sleeves. Her hair, pinned back in a neat bun, was silver-threaded auburn.

"What's a dreaming?" Curious, I studied the stone craft of the room we stood inside.

"Only a few will ever hold the talent," she said.

"So, this is a dream?"

"It is a dream—with a side-serving of reality."

"I don't understand that."

"You're here to learn, and we can only interrupt your sleep for short periods," she told me. "Call me Iris when you're here. That will do well enough."

"What will I be learning?"

"How to use what you have. Your power is weak where you are. No, you shouldn't attempt to change that—you're safe and well taken care of. I and a few others will teach you what you should know when the time comes—and your power is connected again."

I still didn't understand, but as this was a dream, I felt it was useless to argue with a wisp in my imagination. "All right," I agreed. "Can I move rocks in my dream?"

"Hmmph," Iris expressed disdain. "Are they still beginning with that old cow dung?"

"I—guess," I hesitated.

"Come with me and have a seat. I'll teach you how to find your power."

"You're quiet today," Rade told me at breakfast.

"Trying to wake up," I told him. "I had weird dreams last night."

"Shake it off, we have class this morning." Hisan didn't bother looking up as Bette, with Nettle right behind, bumped into his chair on her way to get a tray of food.

"She'll get both of them killed if she's not careful," I huffed. "Full of herself, that one."

"I heard she's from Sorvus," Rade whispered. "Never wore a controller. Looks down on everyone who did. Calls them weak."

"Hmmph," Hisan snorted.

"Where did you hear that?" I asked Rade, although I knew his words were truth when he spoke them.

"I heard rumors last night," he shrugged. "I usually wait until the last minute to shower before bed."

My breath caught and I went still. He was afraid of being attacked by the others. Had this happened his whole life?

"So you overheard something, then," I remembered to breath.

"Yes. I was drying off when I heard the door open. At first, I thought they'd come to find me, so I did my best to hide. These were from Vorus and thought they were alone, so they started talking. Bette hasn't made any friends here, and Nettle is too afraid to say otherwise."

"You think this will start a smaller war between Sorvusi and Vorusi?" Hisan asked.

"It could. We're supposed to get along—according to Yolanna and the other instructors. We're here to learn how to fight to save all of Verillium—not take sides again. Our teachers have no idea what's going on behind their backs."

"We could talk to Nak and Pauly," I began.

"We don't have solid evidence," Rade held up a hand. "I can't identify those I overheard last night, and as far as Bette insulting us or bumping into your chair—that's not enough for punishment, and it's her word against ours anyway."

"All of these people are supposed to be adults," I sighed. "I guess they're too old to grow out of any mischief they've learned so far."

"People can change, but they have to want to change," Hisan observed. "Watch yourself, Keela. Bette has it in for you, for no real reason that I can see."

"The bullies always pick on the weakest targets," I scraped my chair back and stood. "I'll see you in the classroom." Stalking toward the collection table with my plate, I was determined to avoid Bette from now on.

~

Pauly

"I've heard you've been showing favoritism," Yolanna thumped a hand on her desk. Nak and I'd been called into her study early that morning, before breakfast.

"What?" Nak exploded in disbelief.

"Having meals with trainees," Yolanna snapped. "I've heard multiple reports of it."

"They're not our trainees," I said as evenly as I could. "They don't answer to either of us and aren't in any classes where we assist."

"It sets a bad example, and I won't have it," her voice rose. "From now on, you will not fraternize with those three, or I'll have you dismissed."

"Very well," Nak's anger was near the boiling point. He could kill the old bat with a look, but that wasn't why we were here.

"Come on, Nak," I said. "We have work to do."

~

"Multiple reports, my hindparts," Nak growled as we made our way to the advanced levitation class for our morning duties.

We both know Bette is behind this, I sent. *I'll let Keela and the others know why we can't have meals with them from now on.*

Too bad we can't bend time—we could sneak away and have private conversations without the jealous bitch watching.

Well, that's not in our repertoire, I agreed. *Not yet, anyway.*

Nak leveled a curious gaze in my direction. The wheels were turning, however. *Forget it*, I said. *I have no idea whether it would work anyway.*

"Worth a try," he stuffed hands in pockets and lightened his steps.

Cassie

Where the hell could Ver'Dak be? Denevik asked in mindspeech. We'd gone through Cjerl's palace twice, looking at every servant, page and anything else that moved. I imagined Tekar, Cjerl's Prime Minister, would be obsessed.

He wasn't.

That didn't mean he wasn't influenced, somehow, by the still-missing Ver'Dak. He had an agenda, that was plain to see, and there was only jubilation in him that Vorus was conquered and Nessil dead.

"Tekar's tried repeatedly to convince Cjerl to leave the palace. He wants the King to gloat over Nessil's head on a pole in Vorus," Zaria joined us at the pub where we sat in Cjerl's capitol city. "Cjerl refuses to leave."

"That's rather odd, don't you think? That he'd conquer a country and then refuse to go there?" I asked.

"It's not like it's another planet," Denevik turned his mug of beer. Neither of us wanted what we ordered—it smelled awful and tasted worse.

"With his wizard servants, he could get there and back in no time," I agreed with Denny's assessment. He reached a hand across the table to squeeze my fingers.

"Are all his wizards in Vorus?" Denevik asked Zaria. "They're not here."

"I suppose. Do we want to check on that?"

"If all of them aren't there, and they're not here, either, then Ver'Dak has them stashed, no doubt."

"We have other problems beside missing wizards," Zaria said. "Yolanna's training protocols aren't up to the standards we're used to. She's personally training two, neither of whom are Keela. Keela is having difficulty reaching her power for some reason, and now Pauly and Nak are prevented from befriending her, because of the aforementioned two—who feel it's their right to bully the others."

"That sucks," Denevik frowned.

"Yes, it does. If they have any hope at all of fighting off Cjerl's army, they need Keela's power. Right now, they're doing everything they can to turn her away. Yolanna threatened to make her a servant if she couldn't perform to their standards."

"If I didn't know better, I'd say Ver'Dak's hand was in this," I grumped. "Cripple the one who has a chance against you and subvert those around her to keep it that way."

"I can't drink this swill," Denevik pushed his mug away. "Let's go look for rogue wizards in Vorus."

The stench is horrible, I sent to Zaria while covering my nose with my collar.

I've already blocked it, she told me. Denevik blew smoke beside me as we surveyed the pile of rubble that used to be Nessil's palace.

Cjerl's forces had blasted it to the ground with too many left inside it. They were all dead, now, whether they were killed in the blasts or died trapped under heavy rocks afterward.

Likewise, the walls around the palace now lay in ruins, and perhaps a half mile away, Cjerl's army had settled, their tents and Sorvus' flags flapping in the afternoon breeze.

We'd shielded ourselves, invisible to the scavengers from that same army, who crawled across the rubble like ants searching for food.

These were treasure hunters, hoping to find something of value from the wreckage. I doubted their commanders knew they weren't tending to their duties.

Or that they cared.

Shall we visit the camp? I asked. I'd do anything to get away from this mess.

Let's go, Zaria said and transported us to the nearest edge of a sea of tents.

"Seven wizards, and there should be many more, by my calculations," Zaria sighed as we sat in Randl's kitchen, having decent beer and wine. "Pauly said he counted as many as sixteen once, and, by listening in, determined there were more elsewhere."

"Then Ver'Dak has a hidden base—either on Verillium or close-by," Randl walked in with Dori. "I wonder why he's making himself so scarce. Liron's spawn aren't usually this demure—about anything."

I snickered at his choice of words—demure couldn't be used in any context when describing Krelk—half or whole.

"Pauly also said that Cjerl won't leave his palace because of some kind of warning or a prophecy," Zaria told us. "Whatever it is, and whoever said it, it forbade the King from leaving, or he'd face his death."

"Well, it may or may not be true, depending," Randl offered Dori a glass of wine.

"I was thinking the same—fifty-fifty," Zaria nodded.

"You think there are records of the prophecy in his palace? I wouldn't mind checking on that and who the prophet was," I said. "Just to see whether they were a credible source."

"Pauly may have an answer," Zaria replied. "If you can find anything, let me know. I'm going to check the nearest solar systems to Verillium."

"He'll have Sirenali or their bones, count on it," Randl said.

"I know. I'll take Nari, Tiri and Jett with me. Their talent could tell me something."

"Need a ship?" Randl asked.

"You got one handy?" Zaria grinned at him.

"Sure do. BlackWing XII needs a new project."

"I'll give them one." Zaria disappeared.

Pauly

Yolanna won't let us have meals with you. Says it's favoritism or some such nonsense, I sent to Keela after history class was over.

Bette is behind this, she replied. *I just know it.*

I think so, too. If you or the others need to talk, or just want to get together, we may be able to do it behind Yolanna's back.

I don't want you to get into trouble, and I don't want to be sentenced to cleaning up after everybody else.

We're good at hiding things, and that includes people, I told her. *Besides, we can always talk this way—she didn't forbid that.*

Because she doesn't know about it. Thanks for letting me know. She sounded depressed, now.

Don't let this get you down—all right? Nak and I are still here.

All right.

Leare

I understood what had happened; Pauly and Keela were having a silent conversation while walking out of the classroom.

Yolanna's will was bending to a student's, and that shouldn't be. I would certainly find the student in question, to determine whether she bore watching. A single, malevolent student could destroy the entire plan, splitting these survivors into factions. Should that happen, they would never stand together when facing Cjerl's army.

I'd heard rumors of planned field exercises, combining the talents of the power-wielders and the army.

Their focus should remain on defeating the enemy, rather than whose side they chose among students and trainees.

Time to open my ears to hear everything from certain students and teachers. Bette would be among the first chosen.

Travis

"Jek, we're going to give you command over your own company," I explained. He'd given me a concerned look when he stepped into my small office near the barracks. "You know what to do already, and we could use your help with training. We're elevating some of your men to higher positions, too, to help other trainers. You and they will be welcome to have meals in the officers' mess, unless you're assigned to supervise during mealtimes."

"That—is welcome news," Jek sighed.

"Take a seat," I offered him a chair. "Give me your observations on the trainees and their progress. Do you see any troublemakers? You have a unique perspective from seeing them after training exercises."

"I have a few names," he nodded. "I can write reports for you, if you'd like."

"Sounds great. Here," I rose from my desk. "There's paper in the top drawer. Write your reports and leave them here for me to read."

"Thank you, Commander Travis."

"I'll see you in the officer's mess for dinner?"

"Of course, Commander."

Keela

"Well, that's fucked," Rade didn't mince words when he learned about Pauly and Nak being forbidden from eating with us. "This just proves they have it in for us."

"Unfortunately, you're right," Hisan spoke softly. "I've seen this type of behavior before. The predator maneuvers to separate its prey from the herd and any protection provided by it. We're learning fighting skills, but that won't do anything for us if somebody throws a boulder in our direction."

"Too bad we don't know any protection spells," Rade complained. "I hear that's advanced work, and by the time we get to that point, we'll already be tossed out."

I drew in a breath as I recalled my dream. Iris had shown me a simple spell, and in my dream, it had worked. Here, I knew without a doubt it wouldn't work for me.

Would it work for Rade and Hisan?

"There's something we can try," I told them. "But we need to find a secure place to do it, so we won't be seen."

"I don't know of any place like that," Rade said.

Pauly does, I sent. *But we have to be careful—we can't be caught doing any of this*. I had no idea how I knew that, but I knew it as surely as I knew anything.

Nak nodded as I explained the self-protection spell to Hisan and Rade. In my dream, Iris said it should be one of the first things taught, rather than the last.

"You think it will work?" Rade asked Nak, who leaned against the wall with Pauly. They'd found an empty room for us and set a perimeter spell around it so we'd know if anyone came this way.

"It's sound enough," he agreed. "Let's see if your power is up to the task."

"Hold your hand above your head and form light," I said. Rade and Hisan did as I asked, although Hisan's light was slower to appear than Rade's.

"All right," I said. "Now, make your light strong. Feed your will into it until you know it is as impenetrable as steel. Then, drop your hand, leaving the shield in place."

"Here," Pauly pulled one of my hands out and set a soft, fuzzy ball in my palm. "Test their shields with this."

The ball bounced off Rade's shield and came back to me. Hisan's was softer, but it held. "Yes," Rade pumped his fist in the air. "We made a shield."

"A soft shield," Nak frowned at them. "The more you practice this, the better it will get. The object is to get it to repel steel, stones or bombs. Work on this for another half hour, and we'll call it a night."

"You do have lofty expectations of us, don't you?" Rade grinned at Nak.

"Lofty expectations? No. Saving your life? Yes."

CHAPTER NINE

*P*auly

"It's dusty as a tomb down there," I told Cassie, who'd arrived in my small sitting room to ask about the books, scrolls and other writings in Cjerl's palace. "I was afraid to touch anything—most of it is so fragile, it may turn to dust in someone's hand unless they have power to hold it together."

"Maybe I'll ask Nefrigar to help me, then. He's had plenty of practice with ancient texts."

"Good idea. If anybody can hold it together, a Larentii can."

"How is Keela doing?"

"Still struggling, although, and I have no idea how she did this, she taught Hisan and Rade how to shield themselves last night."

"Where did she learn how to do it? You have to know something before you can teach it in spellwork."

"I know. I was afraid to ask her. Nak says that Yolanna is grumbling about leaving Keela with the other students; she wants to send her to the kitchens."

"How long do you think she has before that happens?"

"Maybe two or three days. Keela can barely move a small stone, still, while the others are lifting huge rocks."

"Something is off about all of this," Cassie fumed. "She has plenty of talent and power. She just can't connect with it, for some reason."

"I want to try an experiment," I spoke hesitantly.

"You want to pull power from her?"

"It would tell me, at least, that it's really there."

"Wait until Denevik and I can be there, in case it has to be neutralized."

"That sounds like a plan," I heaved a sigh. "Wild, uncontained power could cause some damage."

"Tomorrow evening?"

"Sure. After dinner. We can get her out of her room then, with nobody the wiser."

～

Cassie

"She's first in her hand fighting class," Clare said. "It's true that she struggles with the other lessons, but I just feel she's blocked, somehow. As for Yolanna, Rajeon and I have already run into that interference. We were told to back away from the students after I started encouraging Keela."

"What an old battleaxe," Rajeon described Yolanna. "Doesn't seem to care even a little if some students bully others."

"When I first met her, I didn't get that vibe, but things have certainly gone off the rails," I mused. "Here's what I think. If Yolanna decides Keela shouldn't have a place with the students, then we put her in a special detachment with the army."

"You'll have to send Rade and Hisan with her. Those three stick together."

"Interesting, but noted," I said. "I'll talk to Zaria about it."

"If Keela goes to the army, I want to follow her," Rajeon declared. "I'm not needed here."

"I'm with Rajeon," Clare said. "We'll be of more use with the army."

"That gives me an idea," I tapped my chin as I considered things.

"What idea is that?" Clare was curious.

"Remember when we gave everybody the choice if they had power —to either train to learn to use it, or to stay with the army and not employ it?"

"Yeah. So?"

"There are a few who stayed behind. How about we train battle mages—on the battlefield? The choice will still be theirs, but some didn't want to exchange the outdoors for the indoors, you know?"

"Now you're talking," Rajeon began to nod with enthusiasm. "I can get behind that."

"Me, too," Clare nudged Rajeon with an elbow. "Keela can go through the classes—we can say she's monitoring, and, if anything else comes to her that she can teach, well," Clare's eyes brightened at the prospect.

"We just have to get her away from the—what did you call her again? The battleaxe? I'll let Pauly and Nak know what's in the works; they'll go with Keela, one hundred per cent."

"Oh, yeah," Rajeon nodded. "Just say the word and we're out of here."

∼

Keela

"Ah, you're here," Iris hugged me in my dream. "I see the shield exercise was a success—you've taught it to others."

"I still don't understand that," I told her.

"Don't worry; if you learn something here, you can pass it on to others. You'll know who needs it and who doesn't. Wait until you see what we're going to do today."

"What's that?"

"Holding spells," she smiled. "Come. We have much to do."

∼

"Do you think they'll complain if I take a mug of tea to class?" My dream the night before had been so intense, I felt weary enough to drop.

"Only if you can hide it from Mey. I hear she's teaching this morning," Rade said.

"I don't think I'll be in class much longer," I sighed. "I haven't been able to handle a palm-sized rock, and they're past impatient."

"If they send you to the kitchens, I will go with you," Hisan growled. "I was told we had a choice where to serve. I will serve where you are."

"Same here," Rade declared.

"Rade, you can't mean that," I whispered emphatically. "You have a chance—both of you do—to be more than common kitchen help. This is about fighting an enemy, not being stubborn to make a point."

"Already, you've been more help to us than our instructors have—they haven't taught us to protect ourselves—but you did."

"We practiced last night," Rade informed me. "We're getting pretty good at it," he proudly stated.

"Actually, I have something new to show you," I leaned down and kept my words low. "After dinner tonight. I'll contact Pauly again."

"Come on, finish your tea and let's go or we'll be late," Hisan urged.

Lifting my mug, I emptied it and hoped it kept me awake enough to concentrate on moving a small rock.

Yolanna

"You can't sweep into the classroom tomorrow and remove her in front of the others," Mey argued.

"I can and I will. She's an embarrassment. I have no idea why those who came with her thought she was special. I can't believe I fell for that."

"We both thought she was," Mey mumbled.

"Well, we were wrong. The worst of the other students can lift a rock the size of her head. It's time to winnow, and it starts with Keela."

"All right, but if this blows up in your face, don't say I didn't warn you."

"What is that supposed to mean?"

"Nothing, Yolanna. Nothing at all." Mey turned and walked out of my study, her posture stiff and anger in every step.

Keela

"What's your theory about the black zone—have you thought any more about that?" Rade asked as we walked toward the gathering room, where Nak and Pauly would transport us to our afternoon history class.

"I thought about it before going to bed the night he made the assignment, but I fell asleep trying to come up with an idea," I replied.

"I have nothing," Hisan said. "All I know is that it's a death trap if you walk into it."

"Oh, look, Nettle, it's no talent and low talent," Bette rounded a corner before we reached our destination.

A large book was hugged to her chest—they'd been given reading material, while the rest of us slogged through water and rocks.

"Can you even read that?" I snapped at her.

"I can read fine," she flounced past, with Nettle silently trailing behind.

She couldn't, in fact, read fine—I knew it in my soul. "Good luck with the holding spell," I called after her. "It's tricky."

"Good luck in the kitchens," she shouted after stopping abruptly in the hallway.

"At least I know what to do, there," I shouted back, my voice echoing off the stonework surrounding us.

Trouble? Nak and Pauly walked past us, pretending to ignore the shouting match.

Just Bette causing trouble as usual, and you know I can't keep my mouth shut around her, I returned.

Nak snickered; Pauly punched him on the shoulder.

Come on, Pauly said. *We have a history class to attend.*

❧

Leare

Yolanna intended to send Keela to the kitchens during class the following morning, to embarrass the girl.

For no reason.

She walked in with Rade and Hisan, as usual, with Pauly and Nak following in a knot of students close behind.

This wasn't her fault, but I was at a loss to prevent it, unless a miracle happened in between.

"Good afternoon, class," I greeted them after they took their seats. "Today, we'll discuss what the black zone has prevented until recently. Can anyone give an accounting of that?"

"Until twenty-three years ago, it kept Vorus and Sorvus from warring against one another," a student in the back raised his hand to speak.

"True enough," I agreed. "Does anyone else have other ideas?"

Keela raised her hand.

"Yes, Keela?"

"Trade. Exchanges of ideas, technology, travel, intermarriage, too many things to count," she shrugged.

"Very good," I nodded at her. "So many things that could have been shared or halved, such as damage from drought, storms, or the like, advances in medical treatment—there are countless things that were warped or stunted without a free mingling of the peoples of Verillium."

"Was the war that bad?" Another student raised her hand. "That the creator of the black zone felt it was necessary?"

"There are no written records remaining to give us insight into that time, or the name of the creator, or what concerned them enough to form the black zone."

"Do you suppose," Rade held up his hand, but hesitated on speaking his theory.

"Yes, Rade?"

118

"Do you think that the creation of the black zone kept the war fresh in everyone's minds, rather than eliminating it? It seems that the moment Cjerl's forces found a way around it, war was foremost on their minds."

"Ah," I smiled at him. "Yes. That barrier is a constant reminder, is it not, of why it was erected in the first place."

"So, you're suggesting that it was a bad decision?" Keela asked.

"I think we're back to the conundrum of the creator, and what his or her purpose was in creating it. We've discussed many negative aspects of the black zone. What if the creator feared something far worse than all those negatives combined?"

"Are we assuming there was only one creator?" Keela went on.

"Points to you," I beamed at her. "Without supporting documents, none of you have any idea who—or how many. Now, let's get down to business, and imagine what the economic advantages and disadvantages were since the creation of the black zone."

Keela

"That was an eye-opener," Rade breathed when class was over. "I feel like we're solving a mystery every day, and that only creates more mysteries to solve."

"That's a good description," Hisan said. "It certainly keeps me interested in the class, and honestly, I've never enjoyed a class before in my life."

"So far, it's my favorite, with the fighting class a close second," I said. I didn't add that I adored the dreams I'd had of Iris' teachings. Those had to remain secret—for now.

What did you want to teach us tonight? Rade asked as we gathered for transport to the keep.

Holding spells. You'll love what you can do with them.

Pauly

At dinner, I watched as Mey walked past the table where Keela, Hisan and Rade were eating. I didn't miss that she surreptitiously dropped a note at Keela's elbow.

Wisely, Keela waited until Mey was long past before opening the note. What she read made her go pale.

What does it say? I sent, immediately concerned.

She's warning me that Yolanna plans to remove me from class tomorrow and send me to the kitchens—in front of everybody. Keela sounded close to tears.

Hold on, we may have a solution for you, I sent. *Nak and I will come for you tonight. Do you mind if Hisan and Rade come, too? They need to hear this.*

What solution?

A good one, I think. Don't worry, we'll work this out.

Then we need to hurry; she can't wait to destroy me.

There are ways to get around time limitations. Just let me talk to Cassie, first.

I don't understand, but I trust you.

Thank you.

∾

Keela

"You need to eat," Hisan coaxed.

"I feel sick," I moaned, clutching my stomach with a hand. My body wanted to vomit what I'd already eaten before the note arrived. "I'm going to my room."

"We'll come with you," Rade stood and held out a hand.

We'll be behind you, Nak sent as the three of us walked away from our table.

I was grateful I had so many witnesses when I reached my room; the door hung off its hinges, and inside, everything I had, which was very little, was broken, torn and strewn about.

No doubt, I was expected to find this on my own, and then try to explain it after I'd gotten advanced news about becoming a servant. Nobody would have believed me when I said I found the room that way.

Now, though, I had witnesses.

"Well?" Pauly turned to Nak.

"I wonder what the one responsible will do if everything is put back as it should be?" Nak mused.

"We know who did this," Pauly nodded at Nak.

"Doesn't take much scrying to see it, either," Nak agreed.

"What are you talking about?" I struggled to swallow the sob in my throat.

"I think you'll be away from here tomorrow," Pauly said. "Cassie?" He spoke to the air.

Cassie appeared—she'd heard Pauly as clearly as I had.

"Well, well, somebody needs watching," Cassie's fists went to her hips. "Nak, put it back together. Zaria and I have a meeting scheduled, but we'll be back to move the three of you to better quarters. Keela," she turned to me. "We're going to take care of this, all right? There's no need to worry."

Cassie disappeared quickly, leaving me agape while Rade and Hisan asked questions at the same time.

Pauly pulled us aside; we watched as Nak employed power to put the room back together. "Pack your things, Keela," Nak said when he finished. "I'll stay with you while Pauly goes with Rade and Hisan to do the same thing. We'll be out of here fast, trust me."

Cassie

"What's the meaning of this?" Yolanna demanded when Zaria, Morrett and I appeared in her study. I watched her eyes and posture—she was terrified.

As she should be.

"Word has reached us that you plan to make a servant of Keela.

Frankly, we didn't bring her all this way to wash dishes," Zaria didn't hide the anger she felt.

"The girl's useless," Yolanna sniped.

"To you, perhaps. She's done very well in the fighting class, though. Therefore, we're taking her to the army, where she'll fit in better."

"Good. It saves me the trouble of forcing her out."

"Rade and Hisan also wish to go to the army," Zaria said, examining her fingernails. Yolanna was about to turn purple with rage; I doubted Zaria liked that shade of the color, so she didn't look.

"Fine. Take the other slow learners, too, if you want. We need those who can be ready quickly, or have you not seen what Cjerl is capable of?"

"Oh, we've seen it," I said. "Far closer than you ever will, Yolanna. Morrett, she's all yours," I turned to him.

"You will not speak of our conversation or recall that we were here. This decision was yours and you will say that when questioned about it."

"Of course." The obsession settled over Yolanna like a cool wrap of calming leaves.

Zaria transported us to Keela's room, where she and Nak waited, their bags packed and ready to go.

"There are a few with talent who stayed behind to train with the army," I explained as Keela and her two companions studied the barracks where we'd landed. "They'll have the choice of joining you here to train, and you'll spend part of your day working with the regular troops."

"One side is for women, the other for men," Pauly pointed left and right. "Bathrooms and showers are at the end of the hall. An invisible barrier will be put up at night to prevent wandering. Commanders Travis and Trent's quarters are nearby, so don't think about circumventing the rules too much."

"I like it better already," Keela declared.

"Regular army doesn't get an individual room like you have here, but you do have a common area to talk, practice, trade ideas and study. You'll still have your history class to go to. Clare and Rajeon will be in the cabin next door. They'll keep order if it's needed. Trust me, you won't want to get on Rajeon's bad side."

"I don't want to be on anyone's bad side," Keela said. "I just want to sit down and let all this sink in."

"I'll show you the common room, then," Pauly motioned for everyone to follow him. Keela, Hisan and Rade followed, while Zaria and I stayed behind.

I think they'll be better off here, Zaria sent. *At least Pauly and Nak can keep an eye on them without ruffling Yolanna's feathers.*

Or sending her into a rage. I wasn't impressed by her attitude earlier, I said.

You going to bed after this?

No—Nefrigar, Zarigar and I are going to visit the catacombs beneath Cjerl's palace. It may be a late night.

You're looking for written histories and journals?

Yes. Want to join me?

I do. I'll see if Valegar would like to come along.

Sounds great. See you there.

∾

Keela

"Here, I think we need this," Nak set a bottle of wine on a table in the corner where Hisan, Rade and I chose to sit. "Pauly and I will join you for one glass, then you're off to bed. Breakfast is at five and a half bells tomorrow morning, after which you'll return here to begin training as a battle mage."

"Please say there's no lifting of rocks," Rade complained.

"You'll only be lifting rocks to hurl them at an enemy," Pauly grinned.

"Now that sounds far more useful than anything we've done so far," Hisan accepted a glass of wine from Nak.

"This is—really good," I breathed after tasting the wine. It was a red, with the barest hint of sweet.

"It came highly recommended," Nak said. "Glad you like it. Drink up—it's late and you all need your sleep. You'll have a full day tomorrow, so be ready. Also, there will be uniforms delivered soon; dress in those when they arrive."

"So we'll blend in," Rade teased, which made me laugh.

Cjerl's Palace, Sorvus
  Cassie

"This room is filled with materials from the time the black zone was created," Zaria said. "Call it a hunch, but I think the prophecy that worries Cjerl so much may have come around the same time period."

Glancing around the room, which Zaria lit with floating globes of light, I felt daunted by the sheer amount of material to go through. Books were stacked haphazardly atop one another; piles of leather-bound journals and sheaves of crumbling paper lay on narrow tables shoved against a wall.

All those materials didn't include the vellum scrolls piled in a corner—I worried that rats, mice or insects may have rendered much of it useless. In addition, a very thick layer of dust covered all, and cobwebs hung between table legs and off three stools that would likely disintegrate should anyone sit there.

"I shall deal with the dust," Valegar offered. I watched in fascination as every speck covering books, papers and scrolls rose above our heads and hung near the ceiling. "It will be returned, as if nothing has disturbed these rooms when we leave," he added.

"You guys are good," I said.

"Watch this, dearest," Zarigar told me as Nefrigar lifted a hand. The top layer of books and such also lifted about a foot off their pile, and then each item separated into covers and individual pages.

"These can all be turned over or moved with power. They will also be left in their original condition when we leave," Nefrigar smiled.

"Not a smudge, fingerprint or anything else will remain," Zaria said. "Come on, let's get to work."

"Gonna be a long night," I sighed and studied the first page of the nearest journal. My thought was that we'd be more likely to find a prophecy that way, rather than digging into textbooks or tax records.

Keela

My eyes felt as if they'd been glued shut when the bugler woke us in the morning. Nearly falling when I dropped off the narrow bed, I pulled myself up and dressed quickly in the clothes I'd worn the night before.

I hoped we'd get uniforms soon; I didn't want regular troops at breakfast noting our differences and making a topic of discussion out of it.

My worry was unfounded; when Rade, Hisan and I found our way to the regular mess, soldiers were far too busy eating quickly and not talking. Of course, an officer nearby made sure there was no talking, so Rade and I made passing remarks in mindspeech while we waited in line for our trays.

We did get curious looks, but nothing more. *I wonder who's going to teach us*, Rade sent.

They didn't say last night, I replied. *If it's somebody from the castle, I hope it's Mey.*

Same here. At least she warned us, and I figure Yolanna has no clue she did that.

It was awful news, but it would have been worse going to class and being hit with it then.

Too bad Hisan can't talk to us like this, Rade complained.

I agree. Maybe he can learn it.

Let's ask Nak and Pauly, first.

Good idea.

Soon enough, breakfast was over and we walked back to our barracks. We found one of our new instructors waiting there for us.

Rade went as still as stone; I'd never seen him look at anyone like this before. He had reason; the man who met us in the common room was perhaps the handsomest I'd ever seen.

"Hello, I'm Bel Erland," he introduced himself to us. "You can call me Instructor Bel from now on. I'll be teaching you three days per week, while someone else will take the other three. You'll have End-day off, and the Commander will let you know how much liberty you have to explore the grounds—or whether you're allowed to leave them."

"Uniforms, Instructor Bel," Pauly and Nak arrived, bearing a large crate filled with folded clothing.

"Good. Let's get these sorted, then you three go change. By that time, the other trainees will be here and we'll get started."

Twelve others waited for us when we returned to the common room, where Instructor Bel waited.

Several of them I recognized; Commander Jek chief among them. A few others from his small company were also there and somehow, that didn't surprise me. Commander Jek had a talent for choosing those with power, unless I missed my guess.

"Shall we get started?" Instructor Bel announced. "First, for those who've just arrived, I will assess each of you to see what you have."

That involved putting his hands on each head; Rade watched in fascination. He appeared disappointed when he wasn't included in the touching.

"This is a good, diverse group," Instructor Bel said after the assessment. "I'll do my best to get you to the limits of your power, and perhaps a bit beyond that. One other thing; trainee Keela is only observing these classes; she will not participate in the exercises. I have heard that she has an excellent memory, however, and can help others who are having trouble completing their spells and such."

Slowly, I released a breath I hadn't realized I'd been holding. Instructor Bel was more than smooth in his instructions, and he had a hard glint in his eyes when he said that bullying or belittling had no place in his classroom. That all power was power—and could be used singly or combined with others to achieve a desired result.

I like that idea, Rade observed when Instructor Bel finished his speech.

"Today, we're going to learn the most important lesson any battle mage can learn," Instructor Bel began. "And that is the art of shielding. Shielding yourself and others is the best way to keep your troops alive and fighting. Once we manage that, we'll learn how to hold a spell in place while we're doing other things. Are there any questions?"

Nobody raised their hand.

"All right, let's begin."

Cassie

We'd already taken one rest break. I'd slept for a few hours before Zaria bent time and took us back to our work in Cjerl's catacombs.

"Another pile of tax records," I sighed, shunting them aside and digging for another journal, employing power to move everything. All around me, books and notes hung in the air; those already examined were put back together and floated just beneath the dust layer near the ceiling.

"Here is information regarding one of the King's seers, but there's nothing in this record regarding a prophecy," Valegar sighed.

"Does it mention whether the black zone exists?" Nefrigar asked his second eldest son.

"It appears that the black zone is in place," Valegar responded.

"Then we need to find records of a seer before that one," Zarigar said.

"Let's keep digging," Zaria shook her head at the mound of materials still left for us to search. "It has to be here somewhere."

~

Bel Erland

"Hisan and Rade already have the basics down, and Keela was able to help two of the others with the shielding lesson," I told Pauly and Nak as we ate our noon meal in Randl's kitchen. "They ate and now they're out drilling with the troops. They'll go back to hand-to-hand lessons tomorrow, plus they'll get weapons training—after Travis decides which company to train them with."

"Jek's," Pauly and Nak said together.

"You two working with the same brain?" I teased.

"That would be a time saver," Nak grinned. "We'll see whether Travis agrees with us."

"Speaking of Travis," I said, "he told me that idiot farmer got caught trying to sneak up the mountain to the keep again, last night. They're putting a shield around his farm, this time—nothing much; just enough that he can't get through it."

"Is he that hard up?" Pauly asked. "Wait, let me rephrase that," he grinned when Nak laughed aloud.

"What kind of farmer is he?" I asked.

"Chickens and pigs, near as I can tell," Nak replied. "Maybe a few vegetables. He and the other farmers are supplying half of the fresh produce and meat for the keep."

"Did he say who he wants to see at the keep?"

"I have the feeling that anything of the female variety will do."

"He'll have to settle for living alone for now," I said. "Travis is pissed."

"First law of self-preservation," Pauly quoted. "Never piss off a dragon."

CHAPTER TEN

Mey Standing at the back of Yolanna's private classroom, I waited for her to look up from her instruction to notice me. Already she was cutting into Bette and Nettle's midday mealtime by snapping at both for not getting the holding spells right.

By now, they should be able to tie off the simple spell they'd cast and turn to other spells. In fact, they should be able to tie off a string of at least three and keep them operative while forming another.

Yolanna was already frustrated; what I was about to ask her would likely make things worse.

I wanted to follow those who'd chosen to go to the army. They were learning battle mage tactics, and I wanted to learn those things, too. I'd never been trained for battle.

And neither had Yolanna.

I worried she was out of her depth, and I wanted to meet the instructors chosen to train the talented troops.

Two other students also wished to join the troops. I could go with them, if Yolanna released us. After all, Clare, Rajeon, Nak and Pauly had already left the keep. They wanted nothing more to do with Yolanna.

When she'd first met Keela, Yolanna firmly believed the girl was the one she'd been waiting for. Now, she pinned her hopes on two others, who weren't any more talented than a dozen others I'd seen through the years. It's as if Yolanna's insight had dimmed in some way, and I didn't understand how that could be.

We're all going to have to fight for Verillium, I told myself. Learning battle mage tactics had to be better than what I already knew.

"That's all for now," Yolanna dismissed her two students. Once they were out of the room, she turned to me. "You can leave the keep. Go ahead. You're useless here anyway."

Yolanna was neither a seer nor a mind reader. With no idea how she'd known why I'd come to see her, I whirled and stepped out the door before she could berate me further.

~

Cassie

"Hmmm," Zaria mumbled as she crooked a finger to read a second and third page of the small journal hovering before her.

"What's that?" I asked.

"A King's daughter wrote this when she was young," Zaria said. "I may borrow this one and go through it carefully. I'd like to read the thoughts of a girl before the existence of controllers on Verillium changed everything."

"That sounds interesting. Can I borrow it when you're done?"

"Sure."

Zaria set the small journal aside before going back to work.

~

Keela

"What the," Hisan didn't finish his sentence. The following morning, Mey and two other students from the keep joined the class. Without asking, I knew Yolanna was so angry she'd have nothing to do with Mey from now on. Mey understood it, too, and it weighed on her.

"We're working on shields, so we'll catch you up today while the others practice making theirs stronger," Instructor Bel said. "Before we're finished, even the weakest in the class should be able to shield against a small explosive. If you combine your shields, you should be able to protect against much more."

Mey's indrawn breath drew my attention. She'd never done this—at least to those standards. I'd been worried that she'd outclass everyone here. I shouldn't have worried—Instructor Bel knew what he was doing.

Besides, I'd had another learning dream with Iris. During that dream, I'd tied off fifteen different spells while performing a sixteenth. My dream instructor had been quite pleased.

Yes, a part of me insisted that the dreams were my way of having my wish—of successfully performing spells and such. Regardless, everything Iris taught me in those dreams had practical use—so far.

"I'm here to help, today," Nak walked in. "For those of you who are performing well, I'll place a shield behind yours while Instructor Bel tosses wizard blasts at you. It's to test how well your shields are holding. Mine will keep you from harm if your shield fails, but you should always build the best shield you can."

I could see many in the class expressing relief at Nak's words—their body language spoke, even if they didn't.

"Keela, Rade, will you help our newest members with shielding?" Instructor Bel asked. "Nak and I will take the others outside for our experiments."

Mey's eyes widened in surprise when Rade and I went to her; I recognized the other two as well. Maxx and Leri smiled self-consciously at Rade and me.

"You'll have uniforms by this afternoon," I told them. "Now, let's get started. Your shield starts in your mind," I said, while Rade nodded. "Here," I touched Leri's forehead and sent an image to her.

Leri gasped as she saw it—then accepted my instruction to transmit the mental shield through her fingertips to build it in reality.

"Here," Rade tossed one of the soft, fuzzy balls against it. Leri laughed as the ball bounced off her shield and landed in a corner opposite her.

"Well, I'll be," Mey whispered in wonder, while Maxx appeared to be stunned.

～

"If I'd known how interesting the history class would be, I'd have come before," Mey said as we walked out of Master Leare's classroom.

"It's our favorite," I told her. "But we like all the others, too."

"Now, you do," Mey said what I hadn't. "Don't worry, I fully understand. I enjoyed everything today, even if I do have to clear the rust off my hand fighting skills."

"Got anything new to show us tonight?" Hisan dropped back to walk beside us.

"How about pushing and pulling?" I said.

"What's that?"

"Pulling something toward you; pushing other things away. I think, if you get good enough at it, you can actually pull things from a great distance, and push things away the same distance."

"Or place them on a shelf hundreds of miles away, or take them off the shelf hundreds of miles away," Nak and Pauly were with us, now.

"You can do that?" Mey asked them.

"Nak can do it without thinking very hard," Pauly replied. "I—have to get help to do it."

"Then teach us pulling and pushing," Hisan grinned. "Sounds like something useful."

"But first, you have to understand that breaking the law is breaking the law—unless it's to save your life or that of others. During wartime it's acceptable, but the enemy will have their things shielded against you," Nak lectured.

"That makes sense," Hisan sighed. "I suppose we'll have our things shielded, too."

"Which is why we need to learn the holding spells," I said. "Those two go hand in hand to protect what's important."

"I heard that as of tomorrow, you'll be in Jek's weapons training class, but Vik will be your close-combat instructor."

"I like Vik," I shrugged. "Sal is good, too, and I know he's teaching the same thing."

"Yes, but Sal can't neutralize your power. Vik can," Pauly grinned.

"Is that true?" Mey asked.

"It's true. This way, no spell caster will have the upper hand over his instructor. Plus, he's an expert with hand-to-hand and weapons combat. You should watch him and Sal spar with blades. It's enlightening," Nak said.

Nak and Pauly came to the common room after dinner, where Rade and Hisan were prepared to learn pushing and pulling. I didn't know whether to be flattered or afraid when most of the others also wished to learn.

"We'll work with the soft, fuzzy balls, first," I said. "That way, nobody should be hurt if things go wrong."

"How do you start?" Maxx was excited to try something new.

"See what you want to move in your mind," I said, and went to stand before him. "See?" I asked as I touched his forehead. The image of a ball on the table appeared in both our minds.

"I see it," he acknowledged.

"Hold out your hand. Tell it to come to you," I said, following his movement as he held out his hand.

"Come," he said.

The ball rolled off the table, but failed to travel any closer.

"Don't let the image leave your mind for even a blink," I said. "Order it to come to you—and mean it."

"All right." Closing his eyes, he nodded. "I have the image."

"You know what to do next," I said softly, moving out of the way when his hand lifted.

"Come," he commanded. The ball snapped into his hand as if it were a part of him.

"Yes," Nak leapt to his feet and clapped. "Exactly like that."

Leare

I'd begun watching Bette and Nettle carefully, while they were in my class. I'd also given several reading assignments, but Bette couldn't answer even the simplest questions regarding the material.

I held her back after class the day before, while Nettle glowered at me from several feet away.

"We can help with the reading problems," I told her.

"I don't have a reading problem," she tossed her hair back while she hissed the lie.

"Then I worry that you're not learning the material as you should," I countered, hoping she'd back off the falsehood and admit her weakness.

"I will tell Yolanna that you tried to assault me," she snapped. "You'll be out of a job by tomorrow."

"You will do nothing of the kind," I breathed softly, employing power to make the compulsion stick. I'd been taught that trick by a friend, but only used it when nothing else would do.

Bette's face paled as she backed away from me quickly. Once she reached Nettle's side, both girls turned and ran.

Pauly

"By the time we sent them to bed, they were pushing and pulling balls to themselves and to the others," Nak informed Bel. "Damn, she has a way with this stuff."

"Many of the rules of spell making and that sort of thing have common roots, so it makes sense that the teachings also have common roots," Bel replied. "I learned that from Uncle Nefrigar. The Larentii have an entire section in the archives devoted to spell casting, wizardry, witchcraft, warlocks and anyone else with power or talent."

"How do you think she comes by this information? Keela, I mean?" I asked.

"Gran says she could be clairvoyant," Bel explained.

"That could account for it, especially if she's a strong one," Nak appeared thoughtful. "Do the archives have a section for that, too?"

"Clairvoyance, telepathy, prophecy and a very special, but very small, section on the Q'elindi of Karathia. I was only allowed to read about Q'elindi from the past—nothing current. Uncle Nefrigar says those histories are still being written."

"Bummer," I said. "I've been to the archives several times, but I haven't seen that section, yet."

"How do we find out if she is clairvoyant—for sure?" Nak asked.

"When something she's said comes to pass, and then a second and third, with no other explanation as to how she'd have that information."

"We'd better start paying attention, then, I guess," I said. "At least we're not prevented from talking to her here."

"You're not part of the army, so there's no favoritism involved. Should have been the same at the keep, but," Bel said.

"Clare says Yolanna didn't seem that way at the beginning. I guess you never know about people."

"We're still working on knowing about people from Verillium," Bel pointed out. "I worry that the students being trained at the keep will be worthless when the time comes and we need them."

"True. I worry that they'll be trying to drop rocks on heads that are shielded, while the rest of us are creating or filling trenches, building metal barbs to keep vehicles from approaching, and blasting missiles from the sky."

"Not to mention one-on-one combat with an enemy wizard," Bel nodded grimly. "My worry is how well-trained and experienced the enemy may be, when ours are fresh out of training."

"We have to build their confidence," Nak said. "We have one major thing going for us, though, and that's Keela. At the keep, they were leaving the students alone to fumble for their power. Keela gets right to it and shows them what to do and how to achieve results. If that's her real power, then it's already useful to us."

"I don't believe for a moment that this is all her power. I can feel it from yards away," I said. "However it is that she's learning these lessons—whether it's clairvoyance or something else, if she were still at the keep she'd be washing dishes rather than teaching others. I've never read of anything like this before. I still want to try to tap her power. The plan we made last time to do it was shunted aside."

"We'll have to find a reasonable way to approach that," Bel became thoughtful. "The last thing I want is to frighten her."

"Same here," I agreed. "Pulling power isn't painful, but you feel it just the same."

"I can verify that," Nak grinned. He'd know; I'd pulled power from him several times when I was learning spellwork from my adoptive father.

"We'd be nowhere with this if my mate hadn't seen this talent in you," Bel grinned at me. He was right; Quin had seen it and told Bel and my adoptive father, Ilya Ironsmith. Dad offered to help train me, and, as powerful as he is, he was still patient and understanding as I slowly made my way through the lessons using borrowed power.

Bel Erland's grandfather, Erland Morphis, also helped teach me. I learned how to create a powerlight cage from him.

I'd also learned from a few others—those who'd be considered unconventional by most wizard or warlock standards. Kaldill Schaff, King of the Elves, had also taught me a few things, after offering me a bit of his power to do so.

I'd gotten much advice from Quin's Larentii mate, Daragar, too. He'd taken me to the Larentii Archives on many occasions. Liron, the Avii King's nephew, had come along on many of those trips. He was a Scholar, no doubt about it, although he'd trained with the Avii guard to learn how to protect himself and others. His wings were multicolored when I first met him. After two moltings, his feathers had regrown in a Scholar's blue, with black tips. Master Scholar Gurnil began calling Liron the Warrior Scholar, and so his title was changed by the King himself.

He'd also asked to have his name changed from Liron, as the name wasn't respected by the Avii as it once had been. King Justis approved the request, and on official records, Liron was now known as L'on.

"You went quiet," Nak nudged me. We'd found our way to the officers' mess, which held a private meeting room in the back. Travis, Trent and several others would meet with us and discuss training status.

"I was thinking about L'on and how his wings changed to indicate his status," I said.

"That's a good idea," Bel lifted an eyebrow at me. "Status. Something to work toward, without being beaten over the head with it. I'm a fifth level warlock; you're a first level wizard. We've worked hard for that. Our trainees have no idea what level they are, or what level they want to achieve."

"I say we leave Keela out of that, until we know for sure," Nak began.

"Or, we create a special status, just for her, so nobody looks down on her."

"I'm on board with that," I said.

"Then let's hammer out a rough status chart, and what has to be achieved before they get to the next level," Bel grinned.

Travis

"What in the name of total fuckedness were they thinking?" I pounded the table when Trent arrived with the news.

"She was found face-down in a pig pen, while the other one stood over her, screaming. The farmer is in a holding cell; we're waiting for Morrett to arrive before we question him," Trent sighed, flopping onto a nearby chair.

"What about the body?" I thought to ask.

"Zaria and Uncle Karzac are coming."

"Thank goodness. Look, the meeting is scheduled in five. Should we cancel?"

"No. The others should know about this, too. If Zaria needs us, she'll let us know."

"What happened?" Bel knew something was wrong the moment he walked into the meeting room. Pauly and Nak were right behind him.

"Sit down," I sighed. "There's been a murder on one of the farms."

～

Pauly

Holy crap—that's—remember when Bette insulted Keela, who snapped and told Bette that she'd die facedown in pig muck? Nak sent to me. *It was all over the keep in less than ten minutes.*

Damn. Put one point in the clairvoyant column, I replied. He and I sat next to Bel as we listened to Travis describe the murder—as much as he knew about it, anyway, with Trent providing additional information here and there.

"We don't have a cause of death, yet, but the other girl—Nettle—was given a sleep draft after she was taken back to the keep. There's another problem, too."

"What's that?"

"Yolanna is accusing Keela of murdering Bette."

"This camp is shielded and a perimeter spell is set," Bel growled. "Nobody got in or out today."

"It happened shortly after the evening meal, and we know Keela was with others the entire time. That evidence has had no effect on Yolanna, who's still screeching that Keela threatened Bette about this very thing," Trent growled.

"Ahem," Nak cleared his throat.

"Nak?" Travis turned swiftly in his direction.

"Bette insulted Keela, Rade and Hisan one night at dinner. Keela, without thinking, told Bette that she'd die face-down in pig muck. Pauly and I think Keela is clairvoyant."

"That could explain things," Trent locked eyes with Travis. I knew they were having a private conversation. "Has she done anything else?" he asked Nak.

138

"She knows the lessons before they're taught or even mentioned—and can transmit the information on how to perform a spell if she touches a student. I've seen this for myself," Bel answered before Nak could.

"We can explain all this to Yolanna, but the damage has been done already," Zanfield said. "Everyone in that keep will either believe Yolanna or have doubts about Keela."

"What can we do to counteract this?" Rajeon asked.

"We were discussing how to rank the students in the battle mage class," Bel replied. "And we came up with the idea of giving Keela her own, special rank. I say we give her a Clairvoyant's status, and let others make of that what they will."

"I want it done by tomorrow," Travis said. "We'll put the records together and certify that nobody went in or out of the training camp today. Bel will sign off on those statements, as he's the one who created the perimeter shield."

"From now on, we should study anyone coming here from the keep. We don't need revenge seekers," Jincus said.

"Good point," Travis nodded at Jincus' suggestion.

Keela

"Look, Hisan, we're both Class M-mages, first level, second step," Rade tapped the list we'd found tacked up in the common room after breakfast.

"Is my name on there?" We'd had to wait our turn while the other students read their status first.

"Yours is at the bottom," Hisan turned to me.

"As expected," I hunched my shoulders. I was last in the class —*again*.

"No, Keela. You have a special designation. You're all by yourself in the Clairvoyant section."

"What?" I crowded in next to Rade, so I could see the paper. There at the bottom, my name was listed.

139

Keela, Class C—Clairvoyant. Level: 3.

"Really?" I breathed, stunned and excited at the same moment. "I finally know what I am."

"We'd like to speak with you about your status, too," Instructor Bel appeared beside me.

"We?" I suddenly felt afraid. "Something happened, didn't it?"

"Something did happen." He wore a grim expression, which heightened my fears. "Commanders Travis and Trent would like a meeting with both of us this morning."

"Oh. All right. Am I presentable?" I asked. I was dressed in my uniform, and it was clean and neat enough when I put it on earlier, but I'd never met the camp commanders before.

"You're fine and you're not in trouble. At least not with us. The commanders have some questions, that's all."

"She called Rade a nebble." I worked to keep tears from my eyes and my voice. "That's a terrible insult. It made me angry, and the next thing I knew, I was snapping back at her with the first thing that came to mind."

"Did anything else come to mind in any of your interactions with Bette?"

"The last time I saw her, she insulted us again, and I snapped at her about her reading skills. I'm not sure how I knew it, but she couldn't read very well."

"I'll check on it," Commander Trent strode out of the room. In moments, he was back. "Yolanna has it written in her assessments," Trent confirmed. "Record dated nearly two weeks ago, in fact. Nobody else was aware, I believe."

I sagged in my chair at the confirmation; Commander Travis saw and offered me tea. I accepted, the cup sloshing as I took it in trembling hands.

"We have everything we need, Keela. Except that you probably deserve a level four clairvoyant status. Most clairvoyants aren't nearly this good."

Blushing, I rose to leave Commander Travis' office.

"Take the tea with you. Instructor Bel can bring the cup back when you're finished. Also, I'd like you to report anything that comes to you in the future, regarding this camp, anyone in this camp, the keep or the farms farther down. A clairvoyant can save lives, Keela. From now on, you will advise Commander Trent and me. Instructor Bel has mindspeech, just as you do. You can contact him if the message is of a delicate nature, and he'll bring the information to us. Otherwise, tell any officer here, and they'll escort you to this office."

"I will. Thank you for the tea, Commander."

Cassie

"This has to be the weirdest thing I've ever seen," Clare mumbled as we watched Zarigar's replay of Bette's murder—which now appeared to be a suicide.

Except Bette wasn't the suicidal type.

"She and Nettle get to the farm, they go straight through the slop in the pig pen rather than skirting around it, and then Bette pulls the knife and stabs herself. This makes less than no sense."

"Was she the one the farmer was trying to get to at the keep?" Clare asked.

"They didn't know one another, so this journey down the mountain is a puzzle, according to Zaria," I nodded. "But I just don't get this part of it. If she was looking for a roll in the hay, why would she bring Nettle with her?"

"Maybe Nettle was supposed to be the lookout," Clare suggested.

"Could be. Damn, this is confusing. Yolanna has all the evidence that Keela had nothing to do with this, but she's still complaining about her. Nettle is the only special student Yolanna has left, and she just slumps around, as if Bette is still cowing her."

"Did Zaria and Karzac find anything in the autopsy?"

"Nothing out of the ordinary," I shrugged. "Bette lost a lot of blood, but that's expected when you stab yourself with a huge kitchen knife."

"I know what pig muck smells like," Clare shuddered. "Not a place I'd choose to off myself."

"If she did off herself—by her own choice."

"Well, there's that. What happens to the farmer?"

"Somebody else is taking over his place."

"Where do we go from here?" Clare asked.

"Watch and wait, I suppose. Zaria and Zarigar have eyes in and out of the keep. If somebody else did this, I hope we find them before something like this happens again."

"I thought everybody passed a test of sorts before they were brought here," Clare frowned.

"They did. Something's happened since then, I think. We just don't know what or how, but we have one death to blame on it."

Yolanna

"I do not accept that this was suicide," I hissed.

"Then we agree on that much, at least," the one called Zaria nodded. "What we disagree on is what or who is responsible."

"You can't convince me that Keela had nothing to do with this."

"First, you want to send her to the kitchens because she has no power, and then you want to blame a murder on her, when she was sixty miles away. You can't have this both ways, you know."

"She told Bette how she'd die, and that's exactly what happened," I shouted.

"Because she's a clairvoyant," the woman snarled at me. "You should have seen this yourself, yet you didn't. I have no more patience for this." She disappeared right in front of me, with no warning.

"Good riddance," I shouted at the empty chair. "Someone find Mey for me."

"Mey is with the army, Yolanna," Waren, the keep's High

Seneschal, bowed as he walked in. "She will not return, per your orders."

I cursed him, Mey, the keep, Bette and myself.

Bitterly.

Ver'Dak

"Have you located any of them yet?" I demanded.

"No, Master."

"Then we depend upon our hidden servants to achieve what we cannot see."

"As it was decided and designed, Master."

"Cjerl still refuses to leave his palace?"

"Yes, Master."

"Unfortunate."

"As you say, Master."

"You're sure that we have no recourse?"

"Not with him, Master. He is protected there."

"As I've ah, noticed. We may be forced to proceed with more deadly measures."

"I fear he may be protected against those, too."

"That cannot be. I will consider this. However, Tekar, if no other inducement may be found, then I will command you to act on my behalf. Other places have been compromised, you know."

"Of course, Master."

Waving a hand casually, I sent him back to his small home outside Cjerl's palace. The fool would do my bidding or die. Nessil had already fallen, as had his palace, but then he'd walked out of the castle to speak with his guards.

The fool.

Leare

Yolanna was slipping. She knew it. Something wasn't right, but she refused to ask for help or speak to anyone else about it.

I worried that she wasn't the only one, but as yet could find no reason for what appeared to be a slow-spreading malady. Bette suffered from the same thing, unless I was badly mistaken.

Everything now pointed toward suicide, while Yolanna still blamed someone who'd had nothing to do with Bette's death. So far, Yolanna didn't connect her difficulty with what may have affected her favorite student.

I intended to listen more carefully from now on; this was a mystery and I wished to solve it before it spread and became worse.

All while protecting my identity—if that were possible.

"Tomorrow is End-day," I reminded myself. I had a trip to make— to Verillium. Several things required my attention, and one of those things was the royal palace in Vorus.

What was left of it, anyway.

CHAPTER ELEVEN

K eela

"I had no idea we'd get treats on End-day," Rade bit into a cookie and sighed in pleasure, leaning back in his common room chair to savor his sweet.

Instructor Bel had brought enough so every student in his class had four each.

"These—I've never had anything this good before," Hisan sounded surprised.

"Me, either, and I was," something—a wisp of memory perhaps, had almost made itself known before I hit a mental wall, destroying the information.

"You were what?" Rade sat up straighter and blinked at me.

"I almost remembered something, I think," I said. "Like it was right there—and then gone."

"Maybe it will all come back with time," Rade said. "Just don't fret about it."

"Right. At least you both know who you are and where you came from. I have nothing. I have to wonder if there were clairvoyants in my family, or, if they were women, a controller sucked all the talent out of them."

"That's a horrific thought," Hisan said, his voice sounding strange. Was it only horrific, or was there a bit of guilt there, too?

"You weren't the one who placed the controller in my neck," I told him.

He stared at me for a moment before rising from his chair. "I'm going for a walk," he muttered. "Need some alone time."

"That was weird," Rade said after a while.

"I was thinking a nap might be nice," I said. "See you at dinner."

"Sure thing. You think we'll get cookies again next End-day?"

"Hope so," I said, walking down the hall that led to the womens' side of the barracks. A nap sounded really good.

"Well, well, an afternoon visit," Iris smiled at me when I found myself inside her classroom. "Tell me, how are things going with you and the others?"

"Fine," I shrugged. "Except I predicted someone's death and now, a few are claiming I had a hand in it."

"Your clairvoyance is making itself known, then. I hoped it would. It can keep you safe."

"But the death is peculiar," I said. "There was no real reason for it."

"Strange things are prophesied, by some who came before you. Don't worry, when the time is right, you will know many things. The enemy grows restless. Soon, he will become impatient. You and your friends must be ready when he strikes. I have much to teach you before then."

"Then show me what I need to know. I want to keep my friends safe."

"A noble endeavor. Shall we begin?"

"Yes. Please."

Hisan

No, I hadn't shot the controller into her neck, but I'd ordered it done and laughed while she begged us not to do it. One moment, there'd been sentience in her eyes. The next, only blankness. I shivered at the cruelty of it all.

If she knew who I was, she'd never speak to me again. For now, she couldn't even recall who she was, and that was a terrible shame.

She deserved better.

I didn't.

"Hurry or we'll miss it," two women soldiers ran past me.

I stopped and blinked—I found myself walking toward the training grounds. More people now ran past me, some brushing my shoulder in their haste.

"What?" I said aloud.

"Come on, man, Instructor Sal and Instructor Vik are having a sparring match. With blades," a soldier slapped my arm before hurrying away.

I'd been trained to wield a sword. With my interest piqued, I began to trot after the others, until we found the proper field.

There, Sal and Vik were doing a limbering exercise, preparing for the match. Real blades wouldn't be used—only dull, practice blades. Still, this was almost as good a treat as the cookies had been.

I expected a bout much like I used to see in the royal courtyard, between two experts—who fought with a single blade.

Gaping as Sal and Vik lifted a practice blade in each hand, I couldn't stop myself from shouting and cheering with the others as two masters showed us the true art of the sword.

Keela

Our second instructor arrived on First-day. "Good morning, students," she greeted us. "I'm Instructor Nissa. I'll be teaching you how to deal with metal, whether it's blades, weapons or vehicles. Some of you may be able to melt the metal gears or wheels on an armored tank from a distance, if Instructor Bel's assessment is correct."

Hisan, Rade and I exchanged glances.

That would be—outstanding, Rade sent.

Absolutely, I replied, turning back to Instructor Nissa. "We'll begin small," she said. "You'll learn to tell the difference between actual metal and something made to look like metal. This way, the enemy won't be able to fool you with false constructions."

"Does that happen?" Mey asked.

"Battles have been won because of clever construction," Nissa responded. "It's our job to ensure that the enemy doesn't gain the upper hand by presenting false weapons or vehicles."

"I never knew battle mages could be so talented," Maxx said. "I always thought they merely lobbed blasts or bombs at the enemy."

"Wait until you begin laying traps for the enemy," Nissa smiled. "Imagine the ground falling beneath the enemy's front line, pitching them into a deep pit. Imagine huge barbs emerging from the ground to halt their vehicles, or the ground rising beneath your own troops to give them a better vantage point. Even if the enemy has mages of their own, it will take time to remove all these obstacles, which, as you know, can mean the difference between winning and losing."

"Thank you for coming to teach us," Mey dipped her head to Instructor Nissa. "You and Instructor Bel, too. I never imagined employing my talent in these ways."

"It is my understanding that Cjerl's forces are better equipped than you have been in the past, both in weapons and troops. We must use everything we have to stand against them. Now," she said as two polished metal balls appeared in her hands. "One of these is metal. One is not. You may not touch or feel either."

The balls were set on a nearby table. "Take a seat on the floor and turn your thoughts to both. In your mind, determine which is heavier."

I sat with the others, but I already knew what Instructor Nissa wanted. The ball on the right was metal, but hollow inside. The other was a wooden shell, painted to look exactly like the other. It was heavier because it was filled with sand.

"Write your answer on the paper I'm handing out. Include your name, please," Nissa walked around the room, handing each student a slip of paper.

I know you know, she sent as I was handed my paper. *Keep it to yourself, please.*

I will, I replied.

"Answers, please," she collected all the papers she'd delivered, and handed each of us a second paper. "Now," she said, "tell me which ball is metal."

A quiet gasp came from one or two students, while others quickly wrote on their second slip of paper. I filled mine out, too.

"Hold your papers up," Nissa instructed. Each one lifted from a hand and floated toward the desk, where they neatly piled atop one another.

"How many of you assumed that the heaviest ball was also the metal ball?" she asked.

Several hands flew up.

"That may seem logical to you—and to most people," Nissa said. "Hands down, please. As expected, our clairvoyant knew what each of those balls was when she focused her attention on them. Several others examined the balls mentally, as requested. Others, once I asked you to determine which was heavier, suspected a trick question, and went with the opposite answer, without focusing on the balls themselves."

"Was it a trick question?" Jek asked.

"In a way. The enemy will attempt to trick you in every way they can. Those who assumed the heavier ball was metal were wrong. In war, never take anything for granted, and thoroughly examine every angle before making a decision. Lives depend on it. There are no shortcuts or easy ways when battling a cunning enemy. You know that, don't you, Commander Jek?"

"Yes. Very well."

"You have something you'd like to add, don't you?"

"A successful army needs to be a cohesive army," Jek told us. "All focused and working toward the same goal. Think about that if you encounter petty politics, jealousies or other obstacles that could create a rift in your forces. I speak from experience when I tell you this."

"An excellent point," Nissa agreed. "Thank you, Commander Jek."

~

"Right now, I can't say which instructor I like better. They have different methods, but their classes are more than useful," Mey said. She, Leri and Maxx had joined us in the common room before we went to dinner.

"I have the feeling they'll divide the topics between them," I said. "Perhaps they've sorted their strengths and made their decisions based on that."

"You'd probably know," Mey nodded to me. "I wish I'd known better about what to look for in you," she said. "I'm sorry I wasn't attentive enough."

"I'm better off here," I told her. "I think you feel the same."

"I do," she smiled. "Come on or those other louts will eat everything."

"Can't have that," Rade teased. "Let's go."

~

Cassie

"Well, that was unproductive," I grumped while watching Nefrigar resettle the room exactly as we'd found it.

"If somebody removed the book in the past and placed it elsewhere," Zarigar mused as the final mote of dust fell upon the lowest stack of books and materials.

"Please don't say we have to look through every one of these rooms," I begged him.

"Perhaps we were wrong to look down here to start with," Zaria sighed. "Let's check Cjerl's private suite the next time he's out of it."

"Now we're talking," I grinned at her. "Has to be more interesting than all this stuff."

"I still have that memoir, but we can put that back anytime. For now, let's get some rest. Four days in this place is enough to discourage anybody," Zaria said.

"Thanks. Let me know when it's time to come back. I'll meet you here."

~

Keela

While on our way back to the barracks after dinner, Hisan described what he'd seen when he'd gone for a walk. "It was so fast at times, the movements were a blur and my eyes couldn't keep up," he explained.

"In your knowledge, Mey, has anyone ever fought with two blades instead of one?" I asked.

"I don't recall anything of the sort, but I didn't visit the soldiers' training grounds or the training of the palace guards. Single blades are what I recall."

"Nothing like that in my memory, and I was an army trainer until recently," Rade reminded me. "We only trained with rifles, and I thought those were ancient enough. Swords? That has to be from centuries ago."

"It could be useful if you run out of bullets," Maxx observed.

"I think spelled blades would be more useful," I said. "That way, no mage could disrupt your fight."

"Sounds reasonable. Let's ask Instructor Nissa if it's possible," Mey said. "Some could have a talent for spelling weapons, but not be suitable for the battlefield. It has to be chaos there, don't you think? There are people who don't react well to those situations."

"You're thinking of Yolanna, aren't you?" I blurted before rethinking the question.

"Yes," Mey said flatly. "She prefers quiet, tranquil teaching spaces. Anyone interrupting her will be subjected to her wrath. It's well-known among the keep's instructors."

"You know, it was either planned or a fortunate coincidence that Master Leare's class on battlefield tactics fit so well with Instructor

Nissa's lecture today," Leri noted. "All those things armies have done in the past to protect a stronghold or such—including the creation of dummy vehicles and empty tents, making the opposition think there was a well-armed force there, when in reality there was nothing."

"And that's why we need to learn how to tell the difference from Instructor Nissa," Hisan said. "Imagine pitting the bulk of your forces against empty ground, leaving your rearguard open to attack."

"We have so much to learn," Maxx sighed. "I think I'll start reading those books Nissa left for us. I'm ashamed of how little I actually know."

I'm ashamed of how little our drones were taught before we sent them to die, Rade confided. *Keela, I'm sorry I was ever a part of that.*

What could you have done? I returned. *If you'd disobeyed, you'd have died with the drones.*

I'm not sorry Nessil's dead, he admitted. *If we can pull this off, I'm hoping for a new day for all of Verillium, where every citizen's life is important and equal to any other.*

That would be my choice as well. It's long past time for us to protect what we have; people, villages, farms—everything. The laws must be changed to reflect those things. As for the controllers, they would be the first thing outlawed, if I were in charge.

I agree with you. Had you been able to advise the King, perhaps he wouldn't have thrown his army away against a mightier foe. Placing controllers is the same as cutting off your own hands, he added.

I doubt I would have advised the King. I may have worked against him, though. I feel he was only interested in himself, rather than protecting his kingdom.

I would have liked to stand with someone like you, if I hadn't been so afraid.

Weren't we all afraid? I asked him. *I can't recall my past, but surely there was fear before I was tapped.*

I'm afraid that if a controller had been in my future, the black zone would have been my means of escape, he replied.

I may have thought the same thing, I admitted. *I just can't remember it.*

"What are you thinking, Keela?" Hisan asked. "You have such a worried look."

"Fear," I blew out a breath. "How all of us were afraid of the King and his tappers. Too afraid to oppose him or the laws that allowed any of that to happen."

"I—understand," Hisan drew a shaky breath. "And I'm sorry the laws were never challenged. Perhaps a day will come when they will change. That is my hope, anyway."

"That's why we have to learn everything we can while we're here," Mey sounded determined. "Even the smallest thing can make a difference."

∼

Yolanna

"Yes, Yolanna."

I wanted to shout at Nettle; she never met my eyes, acted meek around everyone, and, since Bette's death, had no friends at all inside the keep. She'd just performed the spell I was teaching her, but the results were far too weak for someone of her capability. With dark hair hanging like a curtain around her face, she studied her shoes.

"That's all for today," I snapped, louder than intended. "Read the book again and come tomorrow better prepared."

"Yes, Yolanna."

Clenching my fists rather than reaching out to strangle the girl, I watched her shuffle out of my training room.

My temper ran quite short since Bette's death. Too many people said suicide was the culprit, and that included halting testimony from Nettle. *How had she stood there while Bette stabbed herself with a knife?*

Nothing made sense anymore, and I still felt too afraid to say anything to anyone about it. A part of me continued to blame Keela, too. Why hadn't anyone taken her words as a prediction? Why hadn't she come straight to me with that knowledge?

Why had I been so short with Mey? She could have offered advice and a cup of tea while we talked.

Would they allow me to visit the army camp, so I could see her? I knew she would refuse to come back to the keep. If we met on neutral ground, would she accept an apology and speak with me?

"There's only one way to find out," I whispered aloud. Striding out of my classroom, I began my search for a suitable messenger to send on my behalf.

~

Cassie

The small journal landed on my bedside table with a soft plop. Inside was a note from Zaria.

I don't have time for pleasure reading right now, she wrote. *So you can read this first.*

"What is it?" Denevik walked out of the bathroom, freshly showered, his hair still damp.

"Zaria sent a book to read," I held up the journal.

"Any word on when you'll go back to dig through Cjerl's suite?"

"Not yet. Zaria is hunting Ver'Dak again. How can he remain invisible, when his fingerprints are everywhere on Verillium?"

"Evading an enemy means you stay alive longer," Denevik said. "He knows what happened to his brother. Je'Dik was a hands-on sort; that's how he died."

"I hope each one of Liron's half-Krelk children aren't more devious as we go along," I complained. "This is so draining, fighting an invisible enemy."

"You know he has tricks up his sleeve we haven't thought of, yet," Denevik snorted. A curl of smoke drifted from his nostrils, a sure sign of banked anger in any High Demon male. "It's as if he suspected Nessil's forces had some help—I think he sent his army to Nessil's Royal City faster because of it."

"You're right," I admitted, setting the book down with a sigh. "I thought we'd still be harrying his forces. Instead, we're here, working furiously on plan B."

"I hope moving the trainees here to Sirena gives us an advantage," he went on. "That didn't prevent Bette's suicide, though."

"We have one dead and one sent back where he came from. Out of nearly a thousand, that's not so bad."

"Out of that many, how many understand the urgency?" Denevik's dark eyes locked with mine. Worry creased his forehead, and he was right to be concerned.

"Maybe half."

"I'd say that's very optimistic."

"What do you think we ought to do?"

"Season the troops. Perhaps take some of the better trained on night raids. Some of us can go along to keep them out of trouble, but they need to see what they're really up against."

"Then we should talk to Travis and Trent. They'll know the best trainees to send, and when they'll be ready for something like that."

"Perhaps we should also include some of the power wielders. We can't have them freezing on a battlefield because they haven't been exposed to real danger."

"True." My shoulders sagged at his words. Some would prove themselves far more capable than expected, while others could react as Denevik suggested and freeze. "When do you want to talk with Travis and Trent?"

"Maybe we can meet with them over dinner?"

"I'll see if they're available."

"I love you, avilepha. We've worked too hard for this to fail. These people have their part to play to protect their planet. We have to make sure to place ourselves between them and Ver'Dak, so the outcome will be determined by Verillium's own people."

"That means taking down Ver'Dak's wizards," I pointed out. "They don't belong there, either."

"Then why don't we start tracking them? Does Bel believe that any of his students are capable of such?"

I blinked at Denny for several seconds. "I think Keela may be able to do something like that."

"Then let's look into combining some of the best troops with the best power wielders."

"In Jek's case, he'd be in both groups."

"Even better. Come, my love. Let's have breakfast and discuss the future of Verillium."

~

Leare

I needed the Eye, but he was still weary—not only from his last assignment, but of the worlds in general.

Weary and still suffering, I reminded myself. Regardless, I needed his help. What I was hearing from various sources at the keep disturbed me—not so much in words, but in stifled sounds of struggle.

The Eye could see, and I could hear. Together, we might learn something valuable. Otherwise, I worried that those chosen to fight for Verillium could become the planet's downfall.

Besides, I was instructed not to reveal myself. How could I express my concerns without ignoring that command?

You know how, a small, rebellious voice informed me.

I could be destroyed if I chose that route. I'd slyly worked around commands in the past, creating my own solutions to sticky problems. I'd been warned about doing it again. Direct disobedience? That could bring about my demise.

And swiftly.

Eye? I sent.

I—answer reluctantly, he replied.

~

Cyrus

At times, my aliases are so jumbled in my mind that they're difficult to sort, like a wadded, many-knotted, ball of string.

Forced to delve deeper, I arrived at my first given name—Cyrus. I owed Leare favors. He understood my weariness; it was silently conveyed when he called out to me. This wasn't a difficult assignment; I merely had to choose which person to replace to get the job done.

Leare and I would link—he'd see what I saw, while I'd hear what he heard. Gathering my strength, I reached out with my gift of sight for the first time in years. This choice would be important; ever since the Ear conveyed his concerns, I knew it to be true.

Leare and I—we wanted eyes and ears closest to the sources he suspected, but he also wished to remain invisible. There was only one way to do that—and three choices. The Seneschal who served the upper echelon at the keep could be the safest bet; he was a quiet, authoritative sort, who'd served in that capacity for years.

Yes. Waren, High Seneschal to Yolanna and the other power-wielders, would be the best choice. He moved about the upper levels of the keep, unnoticed most of the time. Tonight, while he slept, I'd replace him, leaving him in stasis on a hidden world.

I'll be there tomorrow, standing in for the High Seneschal, I informed the Ear.

Thank you, he replied. *I owe you, my friend.*

Then let's discuss that over a glass of Elven brandy sometime.

I have some. Just say when.

~

Keela

"I don't want to see her," Mey said. Nissa asked Mey and me to stay after class so she could ask a question. The question turned out to be a message from Yolanna, asking to meet with both of us on neutral ground.

"Why does she want to see me?" I frowned at Nissa's message. "Does she want to accuse me to my face of having something to do with Bette's death?"

"She told me I was useless before throwing me out of the keep," Mey muttered angrily. "I'm still upset about that."

"I don't have answers or soothing words to give you," Nissa sighed. "But I do have an invitation from Commander Trent to have lunch with him and a few others to discuss this. Listening to what he says costs us nothing, and we may get a better meal out of it," Nissa smiled at us.

"Then we should go," I nodded to Mey. "I'll be interested in his opinion, I think."

"Great. Come on; I'll transport us to the officers' dining hall."

"Nissa," Commander Trent greeted her warmly when we arrived, with a light kiss on both cheeks. Somehow, they knew one another, like a brother and sister might.

Mey and I'd been transported to a smaller room outside the main dining hall, where Commander Trent and several others waited. Three of them I recognized—Instructors Bel, Sal and Vik.

"Keela, good to see you again," Sal grinned.

"I heard plenty about your sword fight," I grinned back at him.

"It was nothing," Vik waved a hand in dismissal.

"Probably embellished far beyond our capacity," Sal teased.

"Most definitely," Instructor Bel agreed with Sal.

"Don't listen to them," Commander Trent laughed. "Please, sit. Food is on the way."

The food ended up being chicken in a wine and mushroom sauce that was wonderful. I ate every scrap, then devoured the dessert, which Instructor Nissa described as a redberry cheesecake.

"That was delicious," I breathed when the plates were taken away.

"Doing exercises, both with power and physical ability, does require sustenance to make up for the drain on the body's resources," Instructor Bel agreed. "Plus, the food was prepared by a master today."

"Please thank him or her for me," I said.

"I'll let Fes know," he replied. "Wolter asked for help, so Fes came to lend a hand."

"Now, let's discuss Yolanna's request to meet with you and Mey," Commander Trent announced. "She didn't give a specific reason for the meeting, but Travis and I think it may be a good idea to honor the request."

"May I ask why?" Mey began. "This meeting will surely serve to upset Keela and me."

"We know. That's why Vik, Instructor Bel and I will attend this meeting, hidden behind an invisible barrier. She won't know we're there."

"Because you're afraid she'll attempt to harm us," Mey spoke decisively. She was upset—that was more than clear.

"That is a concern, yes," Trent agreed. "What we're more interested in is whether Keela develops any insight on Yolanna and her ah, recent outbursts."

"You'll be safe," Vik assured us. "She won't be able to harm either of you, guaranteed. With us there, you'll have plenty of protection."

"When?" Mey was resigned to a meeting she didn't want.

"Tonight, after dinner."

Keela? Instructor Bel sent. He'd likely noticed that my hands were clasped so tightly the knuckles were white.

"Danger," I hissed. "Take care." Those words came unbidden from my lips.

Trent exchanged glances with Vik and Instructor Bel.

"We'll take care," he promised.

Cassie

"She said there was danger?" I asked Bel.

"She was quite emphatic about it, too."

"Then I'll be there, too. Is there enough room to hide all of us?"

"Yes. More than enough," Bel shrugged.

"You think she included you in the danger warning?"

"It certainly sounded that way."

"Well, I suppose there's only one way to deal with this, and that's to take care, like she said."

~

Keela

"I dislike this," Hisan mumbled as we walked toward the soldiers' mess that evening.

"You dislike it?" Mey huffed. "You don't have to see Yolanna's sour face. Keela and I do."

"We dislike it on your behalf," Rade clarified. "None of us want you exposed to anything that could prove dangerous—or someone with unclear intentions who may become dangerous."

"Before now, I wouldn't have thought Yolanna dangerous—just unpleasant," Leri sighed. "When Mey told me that Keela gave a warning," she didn't finish.

"I still don't know why—it just came out of me," I said. "Maybe I'm wrong."

"Have you been wrong? Since your clairvoyance made itself known?" Hisan asked. He didn't expect an answer—it was a rhetorical question.

"I really don't feel hungry," Mey said.

"Me, either. We ought to eat something, though. It'll be a long night if we don't."

"I suppose you're right." Mey resigned herself to an evening she wanted no part of.

~

We're here, you just can't see us, Instructor Bel sent when Commander Travis ushered us into the same room where we'd met earlier.

"I'll bring Yolanna in shortly; make yourselves comfortable," Travis indicated chairs against an adjacent wall.

I suppose the chairs were arranged so we wouldn't run into Instructor Bel and the others who'd hidden themselves inside the room. Another chair, presumably for Yolanna, was set across from Mey and me. In between, a desk had been placed.

I assumed the ample space behind the desk was enough for Bel and the others. Commander Trent would likely take the desk chair; at least someone in authority would be visible if Yolanna began a tirade of accusations.

Moments later, Yolanna followed Commander Trent into the room. He offered her a chair, but she declined, choosing to stand in front of it, instead. Trent moved behind the desk and sat down.

She looks pale, I sent to Commander Travis. *Like she's uh, sick*, I added.

What? he replied.

I ah, I didn't finish. Couldn't, because I was shrieking aloud.

Before anyone could stop her, Yolanna pulled a short, sharp knife from a robe pocket and slashed her own throat. Blood fountained outward, splashing on the Commander's desk and onto the floor. My screams became words of warning that I couldn't hold back as Yolanna's body crumpled to the floor.

"Blood! Invasion! Danger! Burn it! Burn it!"

"Burn. It!"

CHAPTER TWELVE

*C*assie

"What else was I supposed to do?" I paced inside my suite while Zaria sat on my bed. "Keela was screaming for me to burn her. She was already dead, Zaria, and not a candidate for *Changing What Was*."

"I know. You did the right thing, Cass. It's just that we now have nothing to test regarding a hidden illness or something else to cause the second suicide in as many weeks."

"Nobody at the keep knows she's dead yet," I pointed out. "I worry what will happen if we tell them the truth—that she did this to herself."

"Because they may not believe us, especially after Yolanna said all along that Keela was responsible for Bette's death, and here she was, in the same room with Yolanna when it happens again."

Zaria was frustrated, that was clear enough. I was, too, but I felt guilt eating at me that I'd done as Keela asked rather than questioning the wisdom of burning away all evidence of Yolanna, including her blood.

"So, we're left with the warning Keela gave—*blood, invasion, danger*," Zaria lifted a hand in helpless resignation. "I suppose we can go back and look for evidence."

"Which we may or may not find," I nodded. "Bette's body was examined before it was cremated and we found nothing, but something was definitely going on."

"Yeah. This sucks."

"Unless," I said.

"Unless what?"

"Since nobody at the keep knows about her death, how about we put somebody in Yolanna's place? If we have somebody there who nobody will question, maybe we can get some answers."

"Keela and Mey know," Zaria pointed out. "Where are they?"

"In a healing sleep," I said. "Mey was in shock; Keela couldn't stop saying those three words after I burned what was left of Yolanna."

"Well, then." Zaria squared her shoulders. "Maybe that's not such a bad idea after all."

"Who can we put in Yolanna's place?"

"It'll have to be somebody who can do what Yolanna could," Zaria replied.

"That shouldn't be too difficult, then."

"Somebody who knows discretion."

"True."

"There are two options, and frankly, Perri needs Zanfield with her in stressful situations. That only leaves one other that I can trust with this."

"Who?" I asked.

"Lexsi, Reah's daughter. She can do whatever Yolanna could, and, as a High Demon, I pity anyone who tries to use power against her."

"You think this could be connected to power, somehow?"

"Let's face it—the strongest student, according to Yolanna, anyway, offs herself, and then Yolanna, the strongest at the keep, does the same. How else would that work?"

"That's kinda scary—when you put it like that."

"It is, isn't it? Now, all I have to do is convince Reah and Kory that we need Lexsi for this."

"You think Lexsi will want to?"

"She will. She's bored to tears on Kifirin."

~

Cyrus

Yolanna killed herself—slashed her own throat, Leare sent. *Zaria wants to send in a replacement.*

Who? I asked, while walking through the Seneschal's quarters, cleaning and sanitizing all his clothing and belongings with power. The entire keep could use a good cleaning, in my opinion. Even the walls, higher than most servants could reach, were layered with dust.

Leare hesitated for a moment, which let me know that it could be someone connected in some way. *Lexsi, the Crown Princess of Kifirin,* Leare admitted. *She has enough talent from her grandmother—and others in her family.*

Yes, enough talent, I agreed. *Will they allow her to come without bodyguards?*

I don't know—Zaria is waiting on a firm answer from Reah and Lissa.

Wait—the answer has arrived, Leare added. *They want bodyguards. Randl has offered Ocenosek and Cudworth. Some excuse will be given for Yolanna needing guards, now.*

Then it's just as well that I'm taking over for Waren.

Yes. Things will go smoothly with both you and Lexsi there.

Let us hope that's true. Two suicides in such a short amount of time? That is a mystery we must solve, my friend.

I agree. Whether it is an illness or something else, these acts cannot be a coincidence. They cannot be allowed to become a distraction, either. The training of Verillium's people is the best idea, so they can fight for their own future. This, however—if it happens again, I worry about the cohesion of the effort.

As do I.

~

Keela

"We're allowing your memory of Yolanna's death to remain, but we've suppressed it in Mey. Can we count on you to keep this information to yourself?" I'd been brought to Commander Travis' office before going to breakfast the following morning.

"Can you tell me why?" I asked.

"We know it's a burden for you to bear alone, but the simple fact is this—these two deaths cannot be coincidence. That's why we want to replace Yolanna with someone we know, who can help discover the reason for these unnecessary deaths."

Commander Travis appeared quite grim as he spoke; he'd witnessed the suicide, just as I had.

"Actually, I'm glad Mey won't remember that part. What will we say to the others about the meeting?"

"That's part of why I wanted to see you. Tell everyone that Yolanna offered an apology and nothing else—that is what Mey will recall, too."

"All right." I allowed my shoulders to sag. Commander Travis was correct—this was a difficult burden to bear alone.

"If this troubles you too much, alert me or your instructors. We can help."

"If this isn't a coincidence, then what can it be?" I asked the question that troubled me most.

"We don't know. That's why we're replacing Yolanna with someone who'll investigate. Whatever this is, it needs to stop quickly."

"I agree. Thank you, Commander."

"You're welcome. Go to breakfast, now; your friends are waiting."

I was happy to allow Mey to do the talking when Rade and the others asked questions later. "Can you believe it?" she asked. "Yolanna thought a simple apology would convince me to run right back to the keep. No, thank you. I'm learning more where I am. She wanted to command Keela's clairvoyance, too. We both declined."

"I'm glad," Rade grinned at me. "Training wouldn't be the same without you."

"I'm more than happy where I am," I agreed. "This is where we all belong."

~

Lexsi

Well, well, aren't we structured? I mused as I read through Yolanna's notes. I looked like her, sitting at her uncluttered desk at an early hour, while the kitchens prepared breakfast in the keep's lower levels.

Yolanna was quite rigid in her training schedules; if a student fell behind, it irritated her greatly. She kept notes on her students, as if writing down her frustrations helped her deal with them.

Promising myself to read all of Bette's records later, I turned to Nettle's. I'd be training her after breakfast, and I needed to catch up on what the girl could or couldn't do so far.

I'd already thanked Gran and Zaria for the influx of information and a confirmation that whatever was required I could do as Yolanna's replacement. Zaria and Cassie were also prepared to help quickly, if I needed it.

"Good morning, Yolanna," Seneschal Waren stood inside my open doorway. "Shall I bring breakfast?"

"Yes, please."

"Very well. Do you have instructions for the day?"

"Will you see to it that everything is dusted, please? There's quite the layer on the walls and high places."

"I'll see to it."

He disappeared from the doorway; I heard his footsteps fading down the hall toward the nearest stone steps leading to the lower levels. I hoped his knees were good. He had three levels to go down and back up again, just to bring me food.

The girl has trouble focusing, I read Yolanna's notes on Nettle. I wondered if she had a learning difficulty of some kind. If so, there were ways to teach her that didn't involve Yolanna's routine, stiff-armed approach.

After several minutes of studying Nettles records, Waren was back, bearing a tray which he set carefully on the desk. "It is oatmeal and fried pork," he informed me as I lifted the cover and blinked at my plate of food.

"I see that," I replied, realizing the major flaw in this assignment. I probably wouldn't get good food again until I went home.

"Is there anything else?" he asked me.

"Not now. Thank you, Waren."

Nettle didn't look at me when she shuffled into my study. Dark hair hung about her face, like a veil she employed to separate herself from all others.

How long has she been like this? I sent to Cassie, along with the image of Nettle.

Let me check. I'll get back to you.

Thanks.

Keela

"Make sure you're tossing projectiles at actual enemies, instead of false images." Instructor Bel was back to teach us, taking up where Nissa left off in our training. "Can anyone tell me how they'd go about that? If you're not a clairvoyant?" He gave me a slight grin.

"Uh, do the images have actual weight and mass?" Maxx asked.

"Not unless the one creating them is extremely powerful, and let me tell you, if you're faced with one of those, then something far worse than war is happening."

"Can you tell us about the ones who can do that?"

"Not in this class. Perhaps you can learn of them in your history class."

I hoped Instructor Leare would be ready for a barrage of questions from the talented students in his class. I could tell that Maxx, Hisan, Rade and Mey all wanted the information.

I was content to let them ask; I still had visions of Yolanna's violent suicide in my mind from the night before.

Will you be all right in the combat class after the midday meal? Instructor Bel sent.

I don't know. I can't pull my mind away from last night.

I can make an excuse for you today and tomorrow, if you'd like. You can spend the time reading, instead.

I think I'd like that, I said.

Then it's done. Just come back to the barracks after lunch and stay there until it's time for your history class.

I will.

Leare

I was already aware of the question before they arrived. Bel had mentioned the extremely powerful, and then deflected all questions to me. He doubted I'd be able to answer those questions truthfully.

Should I?

Should I tell them that if Ver'Dak arrived to fight alongside his wizards and Cjerl's troops, they ought to flee by any means possible and let others take up the battle?

Others who were among those extremely powerful beings that Bel not only referred to, but was related to on several fronts?

There were a few students in my classroom who deserved the truth —but not yet. That time had not arrived. For now, it would be enough to vaguely refer to a few battles fought between the powerful and their equally talented enemies, leaving the finer points for later, to be shared with the handful who ought to know those things.

"I have a question," Rade held up his hand before I could begin my lecture.

My dance around the truth had already begun.

~

Keela

"Do you really think those battles were fought by gods, like some people say?" Hisan asked as we walked toward the barracks after history class.

"Master Leare was rather vague about it all," Mey observed. "As if he has trouble believing what has been written about all of it."

I silently agreed that Master Leare was being vague, but I didn't think it was because he didn't believe what he'd taught us.

No. I felt he knew far more than he was saying, and perhaps we weren't ready for all of it, yet. Most of his students still struggled with the notion that there were other worlds beside ours, who'd fought their own wars and demons.

"If there are gods, then where are they? Don't we need them as much as anyone?" Maxx complained.

"How do you know they aren't here?" I blurted before thinking. "Instructor Bel and Instructor Nissa are teaching us. So are the officers and the camp commanders. Did any of us, besides Mey, know of the keep and what they could teach us?"

"I didn't," Leri hunched her shoulders. "I didn't know that anybody alive on Verillium had any talent at all."

Mey hadn't spoken, and I felt it was deliberate. She knew something the rest of us didn't. I intended to find out what that was. Likely, Yolanna had known it, too.

What were they hiding?

"Do you have anything new to teach us tonight?" Rade asked, changing the subject.

"I do, but it's something to use only in the gravest emergency, and with the other person's permission."

"What's that?" Mey blinked at me in concern.

"Pulling power away from another," I sighed. "You can kill someone else if they're fighting their own battle and you steal power from them. It works better the closer you are to someone who's lending their power to you willingly."

"Yes—I can see how you could kill someone else if you pull their power away," Hisan breathed.

"And, if you don't have their permission, they will fight you, distracting both of you from the enemy. This can end in two deaths, rather than one. I was cautioned to teach this maneuver carefully."

"And that's why we shouldn't use it unless there's no other choice," Leri nodded.

"Exactly. That's why I only want to teach it to you and not to the others. All right?"

"Because we can trust each other," Rade sighed. "I understand."

Iris had come during my nap earlier, when I was allowed to skip combat training. She'd laid warning after warning while instructing me how to perform this spell.

"After dinner, then, let's meet somewhere private," Mey said.

"Where might that be? We're not allowed on each other's side of the barracks, and the common room is open to everybody."

"Maybe Pauly and Nak will help," I said, hoping they'd understand why I wanted a separate space for this particular lesson.

We'll find a place, Pauly replied to my mindspeech quickly. *I have some experience with this type of activity*, he added. I felt the smile in his words.

Good. You can help me, then.

Will you mind if I pull from you?

I'd be happy to allow it. Remember, you'll barely be able to move water.

Huh. We'll see about that. I'll let you know when we're coming to get you later.

Thank you.

"All we had to do is ask," Nak grinned after he transported us to a meeting room inside the officers' offices. It was empty for the evening, so Nak led us to the room he wanted, which held a rather large table and chairs.

"Let's get these out of the way, first," Nak said, lifting his hand and causing the table to disappear.

"We'd like to learn how to do that, too," Maxx begged.

"Bel will get you there," Nak replied. "Just give it time."

"All right, Keela, time to do your magic, and let the others see how it's done," Pauly said.

I did, going to Mey first.

"That's—interesting," Mey breathed. "I wish I'd known about this before."

"Who will you pull from?" I asked.

"Leri?" Mey turned to her. "Do you mind?"

"No—especially if you'll let me pull from you later."

"Sounds great," Mey said.

"First, let me give Leri the same information," I said, touching her next.

"Will I feel tired?" Leri asked.

"Some—like you've been using your power, which is true, but you'll be giving it all at once instead of in a steady sequence of acts."

"All right, I'm ready," Leri gave Mey a determined nod.

Mey only got a little power on her first try, because she disengaged too fast. "Take more time—make sure you have what you need," Pauly helped me instruct the older woman. "Think of it as a vehicle battery that needs charging. You shouldn't disconnect from the power source before you're charged up."

"That makes sense," Mey agreed and sent a questing tendril of power toward Leri, who held her breath, hoping it wouldn't hurt.

"Ah," Leri drooped after Mey disconnected. "Yes, I feel drained—like I've been working all evening."

"What about you, Mey? Do you feel charged up?" There was a glint in Pauly's eyes.

"Yes. I feel—almost too full. What can I do?" Mey had no outlet for the release of the extra power.

"That's what the stump is for," Nak said.

"Stump?"

"That stump." He pointed a finger at the opposite end of the room, where a hefty stump, roots included, appeared. "I have the area around it shielded, and I'll let Bel know that we did some target practice," he chuckled. "Keela, do you know how to toss a blast, yet?"

"I haven't tried it," I began.

"Come here," he motioned for me to approach him. "Put your hands on my face. I'll do my best to transmit the information."

A shiver went through me as I placed hands on either side of his face—we'd never had direct contact before. *See?* He sent as the images and instructions were melded together into what it felt like to release a blast.

"Give that to Mey, and we'll see if this works," he breathed when I took my hands away.

With my heart thumping and feeling breathless for a moment, I turned away from Nak slowly, trying to pull myself together before approaching Mey.

"Oh," Mey whispered as I gave her what Nak had given me.

"All right," Nak came closer. "I have the surrounding area shielded. Mey, teach that stump a lesson. Lift your arms and aim fists at our wooden enemy."

Mey released a blast, leveled at the stump. It wasn't hit dead center, but the wood splintered in a fiery explosion anyway. Pauly shouted his approval; Mey hugged Leri.

"Perfect example of combining power to defeat an enemy," Nak complimented Mey. "Your power was almost doubled, and you employed it very well."

"This—could be more than useful," Rade said. "Can Hisan and I try it next?"

"Of course. Who wants to give, first?" Nak asked.

That's how our evening was spent; the others all took turns giving power to one another. Nak and Pauly left me out every time.

"I'll take the others back to the barracks," Nak offered when the others were too tired to continue. "Now it's Keela's turn—to see if she does have enough power to lend someone to move water."

"I'll be back," Nak gave Pauly a curt nod before he and the others disappeared.

"Will we learn how to do that—the transporting?" I asked Pauly.

"Not everyone has the talent for it," Pauly said. "We'll find out if you'll be one of the lucky ones."

"I'm back," Nak announced. "Pauly, do your thing."

"This won't hurt," he told me, before taking my hand.

I almost jerked away when his eyes widened and his body went rigid, as if he were in pain.

"Pauly?" Nak breathed softly.

"I," Pauly wheezed. Jerking my hand away, I took a step backward. Pauly looked as if he were ready to explode.

"We'll be back." Nak grabbed Pauley's arm and both disappeared.

Pauly

"Release it," Nak shouted, after transporting me to an empty planet. I did.

A forest of dead trees flattened before us, as if a hurricane hit them. The ground quaked beneath our feet from the force of the power.

"That wasn't any wizard's or warlock's power—not that I'm aware of," I doubled over and coughed, then, as if my lungs had been emptied of air with only a few words.

"Maybe we shouldn't try that again—I thought you were about to explode," Nak took my elbow and helped me straighten my spine. Still, I struggled to breath normally.

"I wasn't able to direct it," I panted. "At all."

"Then we probably shouldn't let anyone else draw power from her," Nak shook his head, his expression grim. "You're the model of control with someone else's power."

"I'd say that's good advice. I need a drink."

"I'll haul you to Randl's, then go back for Keela."

"Thanks."

～

Keela

"Your power is—different," Nak informed me when he came back alone. "Pauly needed a drink, so I left him with a friend."

"Is he hurt?" I was suddenly concerned.

"No," Nak waved off my concern. "Just surprised, I think. However, I'll warn you and your instructors—in the future, don't let anyone pull power from you. It may be from your clairvoyance, I think, but it's different enough that they may not be able to use it successfully."

"That sounds bad."

"Tell me, do you feel tired, now? Did you feel anything after Pauly pulled from you?"

"Not really. I thought I'd be debilitated. Are you sure he got anything at all?"

"He got something. As I said, it was different. Come on, you need to go back to the barracks and get some sleep. You have an early morning, remember?"

～

"Well, they found something, but they couldn't use any of it," I grumbled to Hisan and Rade the following morning. "Nak says it's clairvoyant power, whatever that means, and won't be useful to any of you."

"That's too bad," Rade said. "I was hoping to have some of your talent—temporarily, of course."

"That would be more than helpful, if it worked," Hisan agreed. "I'm sorry it won't work for us that way."

"I'm sorry it won't work for you, either," I sighed. "It would be nice if you could see what I see, sometimes."

174

"You'll have to keep us informed," Rade grinned. "Look, the others are coming. Let's wait for them and walk to breakfast together."

∼

Pauly

"It felt foreign—it didn't belong," I explained to Cassie, Zaria and Randl. "It's like eating something that immediately made you sick— you have to get it out of your body."

"Was it malevolent?" Cassie asked.

"No. It—just wasn't for me, that's all I know."

"Can you handle pulling from one of the other trainees?" Zaria enquired. "To see if it's similar?"

"I can, but I won't pull much, just in case."

"What do you think?" Zaria turned toward Randl.

"We need to know. Pick one of the others, and we'll set this up."

"How about Hisan or Rade?" Cassie suggested.

"Either one is fine," I said. "Can we do it tomorrow? I need time to prepare myself, in case it happens again."

"Understood. Tomorrow, we'll bring in both of them," Cassie said. "Get some rest before then."

"I will. Damn, that was awkward—and weird."

∼

Lexsi

"Now, link the spells—like I showed you."

Nettle couldn't string more than three spells together, and that was turning into a problem. Why had Yolanna believed this one could be part of Verillium's salvation? The trainees who'd gone to the army were doing far better than this one.

At first, I worried that she had a learning disability, but after contacting Karzac, he'd said no. Her reading skills were better than average, and her initial performance was the same.

Why had she been paired with Bette as the best in the new crop of trainees?

Bette was dead; only Yolanna's notes remained of that one, and her reading disability was noted in Yolanna's records.

Nettle shrunk into herself after attempting to link four spells as I'd asked her to do, and failed at it. With black, straight hair almost obscuring her pale face, she gathered her power to try again.

"No, that's enough for today," I held up a hand. "It is time for the midday meal. Go eat. I'll see you tomorrow."

"Thank you, Yolanna," her voice was next to inaudible as she rose to her feet and walked out of my study.

Yolanna hadn't kept tabs on Nettle's handfighting class, or anything else the girl was doing. I was about to do both those things.

"Do you want your meal served here?" Waren poked his head in the doorway.

"Thank you, no, Waren. I think I'll go downstairs. Might you know where Master Neek may be found? I wish to speak with him."

"He will make his way to the common dining area for his meal," Waren replied. "He meets with other instructors at a round table near the kitchen."

"I'll find him. I'd like to compare notes on trainees," I said, rising from my desk.

"Will there be anything else, then?"

"No, Waren. Get food for yourself and enjoy your meal."

"Thank you." He dipped his head to me and walked away.

"May I join you?" I asked, after arriving at the round table Waren described. He was correct—it was near the kitchen, and too far away from the closest students to be overheard.

Four instructors blinked at me in surprise, before Neek jumped to his feet and pulled out a chair for me.

Yolanna didn't mingle, I admonished myself while taking the offered chair. Maybe this wasn't such a good idea after all.

"We are grieved by your student's death," Neek sighed. "That has not happened here in a very long time."

"Yes," I nodded, ducking my head and studying my hands. "It shouldn't have happened. That's why I'm here, actually. I'd like to compare notes on Bette's behavior with all of you, along with that of the other students. If something has gone wrong, we must do something about it."

"Agreed," Neek nodded.

"Here you are," a castle servant arrived with a tray of food; another came behind with a pitcher and glasses.

"I can turn my notes over to you, as long as I get them back," another instructor, Mistress Laina, offered.

"We can do the same," Neek indicated himself and the others.

"I'll have them back to you quickly," I promised. "I merely want to look for patterns or such."

"Yes, these things often happen in multiples," Laina replied. "We must stop a pattern from emerging."

Laina had no idea how correct she was; already there were two suicides and I wanted to stop a third from happening, if there were any indications of it in instructors' notes.

I wished, too, that the pig farmer hadn't already been taken away; I wanted to question him myself.

Zaria had dumped him on Verillium after Morrett's questioning under obsession revealed nothing. Uncles Travis and Trent had directed the questioning, though. Maybe I could get information from them. Bel had witnessed Yolanna's death with them, too, so I'd ask for details on it, as grisly as they were likely to be.

"Shall I send Waren to collect notes later?" I asked as a plate of food was set in front of me.

"I can have mine ready at the dinner hour," Neek said.

"As can I," Laina nodded.

The others also agreed to have records available for Waren to collect, so we agreed that he'd pick them up at the dinner hour.

"More snow coming in," Neek observed as we began to eat.

"Perhaps knee deep?" I asked.

"Hmmph," Neek chuckled. "Hip deep, maybe. If we're lucky."

Bel Erland

"I'm not willing to stop a snowstorm, but I can clear snow off training fields after it stops," I told my class. "That's why you'll have the afternoon field training time off, but you're expected to study your battle strategy notes in the barracks instead. You'll be walking in heavy snow to reach Master Leare's class afterward. If you don't have heavy outer gear issued, let me know and I'll have it delivered."

"Maxx, Leri and I don't have any," Mey lifted her hand.

"I'll get some over here right away," I said. Moments later, labeled bags of gear plopped onto a classroom table.

"All right," I lifted the first bag. "Maxx," I floated it toward him. "Leri," I pulled up the second bag and sent it toward her, "Mey," I conveyed the last bag to her. "Is there anything else that anyone needs to deal with heavy snow?"

"Heavy socks?" Keela raised her hand.

"On it," I grinned. In seconds, enough socks in the proper sizes were sent for everyone to have three changes.

"Nice," Jek ran a hand over the soft wool.

I didn't tell him that these socks were made from falaca wool. The Larentii kept herds of the animals on their homeworld, and wore clothing made from the same type of wool in all its natural colors.

"Anything else? Last call—does everyone have gloves?"

A blank stare was my response.

"Gloves," I called out. This time, gloves dropped in front of each student, who tried them on immediately.

Scarves and wooly hats dropped down without my asking. Somebody on the other end was thinking, and it was probably Zaria. That's why the socks, scarves and hats were made of falaca wool.

"Now that everybody is equipped for a snowball fight, it's time for the midday meal. Don't be late," I teased and dismissed the class.

Keela

I felt like a round, well-fed bear as I dressed to walk to the mess hall.

"It's snowing really hard," Hisan said as I joined him and the others in the common room. "I looked out the door to see."

He'd been forced to look out the door; all the windows were frosted over from the cold and moisture in the air.

"Let's get going," Mey wrapped her new scarf around her neck. "I don't want to be cold longer than I have to."

We trudged into the snow, grateful for the warm clothing; a fierce wind blew snow into our faces as we rearranged scarves to cover noses and mouths. What would normally be a short trek to the mess hall turned into a bout with nature as we huddled farther into our coats and made our way to the midday meal.

At least the wind will be at our backs when we leave, Rade sent.

Small comfort, I retorted while my teeth chattered.

True enough.

Cyrus

Lexsi is here, posing as Yolanna, I informed Leare. *Two High Demon guards remain in the shadows while she works.*

That makes a certain kind of sense, I suppose. She'll be immune to anything those students or instructors throw at her.

Plus, she can take the entire keep down if she wants, I replied dryly. *I'm not sure they're prepared for an angry, silver Thifilatha if they think to try anything.*

True. How are things going so far?

I believe Lexsi's wondering why Nettle was chosen by Yolanna in the first place. The girl has a social awkwardness that ought to be addressed—if they plan to use her in the fight against Cjerl's army, anyway.

Is Lexsi searching for a correlation between the suicides?

First thing, right after her lesson with Nettle. She joined the other instructors for lunch to ask for their observations and copies of their notes.

Smart woman.

Takes after her mother—and her father's mother.

And her great-grandfather, perhaps? Leare teased.

I'd like to think so, but I won't be so bold as to claim it.

Has she asked for anything unusual?

She wanted the dust and cobwebs gone. I took care of it already. Sent the dust back to Verillium, where it belongs. Disinfected it, too, in case it picked up anything from this planet. Don't need cross-contamination at this point, especially if there's a connection in two suicides.

Caution is always a good idea, he agreed. *There's something else happening here that you should know about*, he added. *Pauly drew from Keela's power, and almost couldn't handle it. He was forced to discharge it immediately.*

What does this mean? I asked.

They're going to have him pull from one of the others tomorrow, to see if the results are similar. They won't be.

What do you know about this, Leare?

Something I can't discuss, and you can probably guess why.

Ah. Will you at least keep me apprised?

Of course.

Lexsi

Every instructor had remarked on Nettle's shyness and apparent anxiety. She held power, that was plain enough, but I couldn't see much difference between her and several others in the regular classes.

Perhaps it was time to delve into her past—before making a decision on her position as a private student, or whether to send her back with the others. The ones Yolanna should have been teaching were all with the army now, including her former assistant.

Yolanna didn't know how to prepare them for battle, I reminded myself. They're better off getting lessons with Nissa and Bel, combined with the history course taught by the man Gran chose.

I hadn't met Leare. Perhaps I should speak with him, too, about Nettle's attention and learning level in his class. Her history class was the one immediately after the midday meal, whereas Keela and the others with the army were in the last history class of the day.

As for Nettle's performance in the hand fighting class—she was failing it. Her instructors only kept trying with her because Yolanna demanded it.

That was about to change. Not everyone was cut out for close combat, and Nettle was among those. I doubted warfare would be something in which she'd ever become functional, if all indications remained true.

"Go see Leare," I spoke aloud, tearing myself away from my thoughts. "Get his opinion. Perhaps speaking with those students who'd shared beginning classes with her could reveal something."

Had the girl ever smiled or laughed?

I was beginning to wonder.

"Nettle always followed in Bette's footsteps, and seldom spoke."

I'd found Master Leare having lunch in the keep and took a seat at his table to ask questions. "I keep assignments to a minimum, since their days are filled enough already," he went on. "Bette was the one who wanted to argue or question everything. Bette also had a marked reading problem. I offered help, but she refused it."

"Have there been significant changes since Bette died?"

"No, and I find that strange. Nettle was allowed to skip classes for three days to mourn her friend but showed up anyway."

"Does she talk with any of the others?"

"No. She lets her hair obscure her face and hides behind it. The others flow around her like water around a stone."

"So far, the only emotion I've heard come from her is the screaming when Bette—did what she did."

"I heard that, too, but as I wasn't there," Leare shrugged.

"Thank you for answering my questions," I stood and nodded at him.

"Any time, Yolanna."

Something about the way he said my assumed name almost made me turn and study him intently. That would be a mistake, so I walked away as if nothing had perturbed me. My next stop would be with Travis and Trent; I needed information from Keela and the others, and she didn't need to see me, even when she'd know I wasn't Yolanna.

"Nak and Pauly are the best ones to ask those questions," Travis said. I sat in a chair in his office, sipping Falchani black with him while we talked. "Let me see if they're busy."

His eyes unfocused for a moment while he sent mindspeech. Less than a minute later, Nak and Pauly arrived.

"How's the new gig going?" Nak grinned at me. He and I were cousins, after all.

"It's complicated, that's how it's going. I'm trying to discern why Nettle was included in Yolanna's private class with Bette—the girl doesn't have that much going for her. Rade, Keela and the others are better suited for that sort of thing."

"She always slumped along behind Bette," Pauly said. "Everybody noticed it at the keep. Did Yolanna put anything in her notes about why she chose her?"

"Nothing, other than writing that Bette and Nettle were the two best students in the common classes."

"Hmmph. I disagreed with her from the beginning—I could feel their power, when Yolanna didn't have a clue other than performances on the idiotic exercises they assigned," Pauly huffed. "Now that Keela is showing the others how to do more advanced spell work, they're far ahead of anything they're doing at the keep."

"What are you thinking, Lexsi?" Travis wisely noted my silent concentration.

"I'm thinking about asking Cassie or Zaria to bend time. I want to go back and see what was happening in Nettle's past. If they allow it, I also want to see Bette's suicide."

"Not a pretty thing to watch, by any stretch," Nak whispered.

He'd witnessed Yolanna's suicide, so he understood how things would be. "Would you be willing to replay Yolanna's death?" I asked him.

"I can do that for you," Travis offered. "Nak doesn't have to."

"I'd prefer that," Nak looked queasy.

"When are you going to pull from one of the others?" I asked Pauly.

"Tomorrow," he said. "I see word gets around."

"Cassie sent me the information. I'd like to be kept in the loop."

"We can do that," Nak agreed.

"Anything else?" Pauly asked.

"That's all for now. Just send information if you can get it regarding their thoughts and memories of Nettle."

"Will do." Nak folded Pauly and himself away.

"You really want to see this?" Travis asked as he pushed his chair away from his desk.

"Yes. I know it isn't pretty."

"All right." Travis lifted his hands, preparing to render a two-dimensional image of what he'd seen the night Yolanna committed suicide in front of him and several others.

He was right—it wasn't pretty.

What I eventually focused on, however, was Keela's terrified voice as she screamed about blood, invasion and burning.

Cassie

"She's focusing on Nettle," I told Zaria, regarding Lexsi's first days at the keep. Zaria and I sat in the galley of BlackWing XII, having tea while we talked.

"I never read Nettle," Zaria sighed. "Her hair was always covering most of her face. One of the others brought her in. They wouldn't have done that if they hadn't detected power in her."

"That's what I remember, too. I think Lexsi's concerned because Nettle isn't showing the aptitude that Yolanna thought she had. She told me that the girl would be better suited to the regular classes—in her opinion."

"Probably a sound opinion," Zaria nodded. "I have no trouble sending her back to the classroom with the others. Have any more students expressed interest in the army training?"

"They haven't, but it could be because they're afraid of trying something new at this point."

"Or they're still afraid of the old Yolanna."

"That's—entirely possible."

"I'm thinking that perhaps Nefrigar would be willing to take Lexsi back to Bette's death," Zaria tapped her teacup absently with a fingernail—regular taps, like a clock ticking.

Only this would be time ticking backward.

"Nefrigar will know not to intervene," I said.

"Yes."

"What do you think Lexsi is hoping to find?"

"A connection." Zaria stopped tapping and lifted the cup to drink. "There has to be one, don't you think?"

"Yes, but what could it possibly be?"

"Perhaps Lexsi and Nefrigar will figure that out."

CHAPTER THIRTEEN

*L*exsi
    Uncle Nefrigar sent mindspeech after Zaria contacted him. He told me he'd come tonight and together we'd revisit Bette's suicide and Nettle's reaction.

I couldn't shake the feeling that there was something in all this that we were missing, but I had no idea how to begin the search. Therefore, I'd start with Nettle and work my way backward.

Kory sent mindspeech, too, asking if I wanted him to come with Nefrigar.

It would be nice if you were there, I told him. *Travis let me see Yolanna's death, and that was hard to watch.*

Then we'll be there at bedtime, he replied. *I don't have to tell you how much I love you, do I?*

You don't, but it's nice to hear anyway.

        ~

Eliagar
    "What is wrong," I asked, setting breakfast in front of Zak. His

eyes were clouded with confusion and he moved awkwardly, as if he'd forgotten how to use his limbs properly.

"I—had a dream," he blinked at me. "It was," he didn't finish; instead, he wrapped arms about himself.

"A nightmare, then," I sighed. "They can be terrifying," I added.

"I—felt so confused," he admitted. "And afraid. I watched strange events, and I think something terrible was happening, but I didn't know where I was or why those in my dream would be doing such things. I felt so tired, too, and I don't understand why."

"Don't let it trouble you," I soothed. "Sit down and eat your breakfast; I kept it warm for you."

Pulling out his chair, Zak settled himself and lifted his fork. "Thank you for taking care of me," he sighed. "I don't know how I deserve it."

"I do it because you are dear to me. Never forget that."

"Like a father and child?"

"Yes," I beamed at him. "While I can never be your biological father, I can certainly be your chosen one."

"Thank you for choosing me, then." Zak began to eat his eggs, nodding that they were cooked to his liking.

❧

Cassie

Do you mind if I come with you, tonight? I sent to Lexsi.

Of course not. Kory and Nefrigar will also be there.

Good. Where can I meet you?

Come to my suite at bedtime. That's where we're gathering.

I'll be there.

I could hear the curiosity in Lexsi's mindspeech; she wondered why I wanted to see Bette's demise with her.

I'd been considering the same thing all afternoon. Travis liked the idea of letting his best troops do patrols on Verillium in tandem with the power wielders, to give them field experience. Before I allowed it, I wanted to be sure that the suicides were unrelated. If not, we could be carrying trouble back with us and that wouldn't be a good thing.

I hear Lexsi's going back to witness Bette's death, Vik sent. *I want to go with my daughter.*

Well, here was another one. *All right*, I conceded. *But you're the last one.*

Who else is going?

Nefrigar, Kory and I, I replied.

That should be enough, then, his chuckle came through with his words.

Wait, I want to come, Denevik informed me.

Right. That's the final tally, I said. *No more, and I mean it.*

Except Nefrigar asked me to come, too, Zarigar said. *There. That's your final number.*

Nobody listens to what I say, I complained.

They hear you, they just ignore it, Lexsi joined my complaint. *It's the general superior attitude of the common male.*

Dearest, I beg to differ, Kory noted. *None of us are common males.*

In Lexsi's and my case, that is certainly true, I snipped. *I have things to do. I'll see all of you later.*

Keela

It was my first day back at combat training, and I felt the two days I'd taken off. Nak and Pauly arranged to meet us in the common room after dinner to talk and play a game they'd suggested. Any of the students in our barracks were welcome, but it was our small group, consisting of Rade, Hisan, Maxx, Leri, Mey and I, who agreed.

"Block the first blows with your arms," Sal instructed as a regular army student and I squared off in class. "Follow with a takedown move, if you can," he shouted as my classmate and I went after one another.

What followed was a flurry of moves as we attempted to best the other, until I was able to shove my shoulder into his chest, then step in quickly to place a leg behind his and hook his arm with mine to drop him to the floor.

"Good. Very good," Sal said. "Get up and try again," he told my opponent. At least he wasn't angry that I'd knocked him off his feet— he rose, nodded to Sal and took up his combat stance.

I was the one to hit the floor this time.

"Good. Both of you. Maxx, Hisan, you're up."

"You're tough to beat," my opponent grinned as we walked toward the edge of the room, where a container of water waited.

"Who was it again who knocked me down that last time," I told him. He laughed. "Chuk," he introduced himself.

"Keela," I took his offered hand.

"I heard we may be sent out on field exercises," Chuk said as he filled a cup with water and handed it to me before pouring one for himself.

"I heard that too, this morning in class," I nodded and drank.

"My instructor says they will only take the best students, to give them experience," Chuk went on. "I do and don't want to be a part of it."

"It sounds daunting, doesn't it?"

"Yes—good description," he agreed. "I know you're in the power-wielders' class. Do you think you'll all go or just some?"

"I don't know," I shrugged. "Our instructors will make those choices, not us."

"True enough. If I'm chosen, then I hope to see you there, too."

I didn't tell him that I'd probably be chosen to go out; I was the only clairvoyant available. As for others, Jek, Mey, Hisan and Rade would be my choices, along with one or two other students, perhaps, for the first outing.

We'll know tomorrow whether the field exercises are a go, Sal sent to me. He'd heard us, somehow, from across the room.

Thank you for letting me know, I replied. *I think it's a good idea to let us see what we may face.*

As do we.

~

188

"I've never played this game. It's fun," Rade said as he rattled the five numbered cubes in the cup and slid them onto the table. He quickly gathered the same top numbers and moved them to the side before shaking the rest in the cup again.

"It gives everyone an equal chance, unless somebody cheats and employs power," Nak said.

"It's not my night, then," I said, checking my score sheet. After three games, Mey, Rade and Maxx had all won.

"We have some questions, too, about some of your former classmates—except in Mey's position, when they were her students," Nak said.

"Who's that?" Mey lifted eyes from her score sheet and frowned at Nak.

"Well, it's about Nettle, actually," Pauly said, taking the cup and dice from Rade. "She's not performing as well as she should and was already falling behind when Bette died."

"She was always withdrawn," Mey said. "But if Bette did something, Nettle was able to do it, too."

"Always followed Bette around like a lost puppy," Hisan noted. "Never spoke around me but appeared to support Bette whenever that one said anything to anybody."

I knew Yolanna was dead, as did Nak and Pauly. Someone was surely taking that position and was now questioning Yolanna's choices with Bette and Nettle.

"Did you get any feelings about Nettle?" Pauly asked me casually as Nak tossed the dice.

"Just—emptiness, I guess," I said. "Like she depended on Bette for everything, including her personality. I never did hear where she was from, either, while Bette wasn't quiet about the fact that she came from Sorvus."

"Can you explain the emptiness a little better?" Nak asked.

"I don't know what to tell you," I moved uncomfortably on my chair. "There was nothing I could get from her—like a void, or something."

Nak and Pauly exchanged a swift glance before turning back to the game. I knew they were conversing silently, but I wasn't included, and it was my turn to throw the dice.

Pauly

"One more thing before we go," I said as the group rose to go to their beds.

"What's that?" Mey asked.

"I'd like to pull from either Hisan or Rade—to compare power signatures. I have it from Keela; now we need one from a talented male."

"I'll do it," Rade volunteered.

"All right." I approached Rade and placed my hands on his shoulders. I felt his power—it was quite strong, but nothing compared to Keela's.

Also, I felt the same as if I were pulling power away from Nak or anyone else with the gift.

"Ah," I dropped my hands while Rade allowed his shoulders to droop. "You have strong talent, Rade. You'll be ranked much higher, one day. Go to bed and rest, now. Tomorrow will come early enough for all of us."

What do you mean, the power is like night and day? Cassie demanded when Nak and I reported our findings to her.

Rade's power was no different from most others, I replied. *The anomaly is in Keela. As for questions about Nettle, there's a consensus that she's withdrawn. Keela, however—she says that the feeling she got from the girl is emptiness—like a void. That she copied Bette in everything, and depended on her for her personality, even.*

That's—well, weird. Fucked up, too. I'll talk to Zaria about it. She told me earlier she'd never read the girl. Maybe it's time to rectify that.

This is beginning to look really off, Nak joined the conversation.

Something isn't right. Lexsi is correct that we need to get to the bottom of all this.

We're bending time to go back to Bette's death tonight, Cassie said. *Maybe we'll get some clues while we're there.*

I hope so, I said. *Will you let us know if you find anything?*

Sure.

~

Cassie

Lexsi is as good as her mother at sleuthing, Zaria informed me after I passed along the information Nak and Pauly provided. *Reah has so many awards from the ASD for catching criminals that they fill a small closet. Probably would have gotten more if her cover hadn't been blown by idiots.*

Denevik told me about that. He's her great-grandfather.

We do have convoluted connections, don't we?

Oh, yeah. By the way, who brought Nettle in? It wasn't either of us. Why would Randl bring her in?

Give me a few. I'll find out.

~

Zaria

"Wasn't me," Randl said when I showed him Nettle's image.

"Shall we take a look at her together, then? Keela says she just feels a void when she looks at the girl."

"Lead the way, then," Randl tossed out a hand.

"That's her, at that table by herself across the room," I told Randl when we arrived in the keep's dining hall. I'd had to bend time to get to her while she was upright and conscious, and I'd shielded us from sight and sound.

"Her hair is obscuring her face," Randl complained. "I'd remember that one for sure, and I don't."

"Shall we lend a hand at uncovering it?" I asked before sending a slight breeze toward the girl.

We only got a few seconds to see her full face. Randl drew in a breath and held it while I cursed.

Keela was right.

Nettle *was* a void.

In every possible way.

"I think we'll be going with Cassie and the others tonight," I said. "Fuck. Where did she come from?"

"Damn," Randl shook his head and cursed. "When we get back from our trek into the past, I'm opening that rare bottle of Scotch I've been hoarding. I really need a drink."

Cassie

Nefrigar did the honors, as originally planned, taking us back to a pig farmer's holding. Zaria held us behind a shield so neither Bette nor Nettle would notice us. As for the pig farmer, he sat on a rough, wooden bench inside a shed, not far from the pig pen where Bette died.

They're coming, Zarigar noted as both girls topped a small ridge, heading down the mountain to reach the farm.

As if they were on a plotted course.

Did they know the way already? I asked.

As far as I know, they never left the keep before, Zaria noted.

The pig farmer stood; he'd spotted Bette and Nettle, too.

Look, Bette's heading straight for the farmer, and walking right into that muck rather than skirting the fence, Randl said.

She'd climbed between fence railings to do it, too. So far, nothing made much sense. If she were intent on visiting a lover, she'd have kept herself as clean as possible.

Once Bette reached the middle of the pig pen, she stopped and turned to face Nettle. The pig farmer had moved to the fence closest to him, leaning his arms on it as if waiting for what was about to happen.

Bette pulled the large, kitchen knife from inside her cloak, while Nettle stood still, watching without a word.

I jerked when Bette stabbed herself in the heart; Nettle remained silent until two things happened.

First, Bette crumpled face-down in the muck, then Travis and Jek appeared from nowhere to see who'd breached their perimeter.

It was only as Travis stepped forward that Nettle began to scream. *Loudly.*

At that point, I heard Keela's shout in my head, whether real or imagined, I couldn't say. *Burn it, burn it, burn it,* repeated in my mind; so much so that Zarigar was forced to grab me before I could leave Zaria's shield and do exactly that.

"Nettle and the farmer were expecting what happened, that much is clear," Zaria wasn't happy as Randl poured a small measure of Scotch for all of us—except the Larentii, of course.

"Nettle's wailing was enough to wake the dead," Denevik tossed back his drink.

"Like she wanted somebody to come—after the fact."

"After Travis and Jek arrived, for sure," Lexsi pointed out. "I wonder what would have happened, or what Nettle and the farmer expected to happen, if Travis hadn't folded in."

"I still wish to know how Nettle came to the keep," Vik rumbled.

"She was there when classes began; I've already checked," Lexsi told him.

"When were rooms assigned to the students? Bette and Nettle roomed together, didn't they?"

"Yes, but it wasn't a requirement to choose a roommate. Keela didn't have one," Lexsi replied.

"Who wants to take another trip back in time?" Zaria lifted a hand.

"I do," Lexsi and I chorused.

"I think we all want to get to the bottom of this," Randl agreed. "Lexsi, when was Bette assigned quarters?"

"Forty-one days ago."

"Shall we?" Nefrigar nodded to all of us and bent time.

There's Bette, Zaria sent as students waited in a line for Mey, who sat at a desk in the dining hall, to parcel out room assignments. Bette was third in line; already she was demanding an important place in the scheme of things.

Look who's missing in the line, Lexsi said.

We stood behind another of Zaria's shields while we watched student registration, and Lexsi was correct. Nettle wasn't standing in that line.

Where is she, then? I asked.

I can't find her by Looking, Zarigar breathed.

Not a good sign, Kory said.

Could Nettle have bone dust? Randl mused as Bette stepped to the table and gave her name to Mey.

That could explain her invisibility, but how would she acquire it? Zarigar posed his own question.

Bette's heading for the stairs. We will follow, Nefrigar moved us to the next level, where we parked while watching Bette climb the steps.

We moved a second time as the girl made her way to the third level, where her room was located.

Like invisible ghosts, our feet never touching the floor, we floated along behind her until she arrived at her assigned quarters. Opening the door, she walked inside. We followed. Two beds were in the room; Nettle sat on one of them.

"Her name doesn't appear on any record of the keep's regular residents," Lexsi handed a book to Nefrigar, who asked to see it. "She was never assigned to that room, either, but her name appears in the student lists shortly after."

We stood inside Yolanna's study, where Lexsi now searched the records for information. This continuing mystery of Nettle's appearance in the keep would keep us up all night, I had no doubt. "This record of the residents was made before they all slept in stasis," Nefrigar observed.

"The keep was spelled against invaders," Denevik said. "It was fully intact when they woke."

"The outside wall wasn't," Zaria said. "They had to repair it."

"True enough, but that doesn't explain how Nettle arrived in the keep. Or when." Kory spoke for the first time; until then, he'd been watching and listening carefully to everyone else.

"What if Nettle," Lexsi began, "was in stasis, too, only as a part of the wall or something else?"

"What if someone placed her there to watch for the keep's waking?" Zarigar looked thoughtful as he nodded at Lexsi.

"Someone with less than good intentions?" Kory asked.

"This is beginning to sound scary," I mumbled.

"Why the suicides, though? What would those achieve?" Denevik wondered.

"This is a riddle we may not be able to solve tonight," Nefrigar sighed. "All of you are weary, as am I. Shall we rest and afterward study this conundrum with fresh minds?"

"I think we have to, or I'll be worthless tomorrow," Lexsi confessed.

"Then it's up to you to watch Nettle carefully," Zaria said. "Keep all of us informed if anything looks out of the ordinary."

"I will. Count on it."

∾

Keela

I'd expected another dream with Iris, learning new things I could teach the others. Instead, I'd had a nightmare—as if I'd witnessed Bette's death, and just as I'd done when Yolanna killed herself, I shouted *burn it.*

Many times.

I couldn't help myself.

It was only when Pauly's and Nak's arms went around me that I discovered I'd been sitting rigidly upright in bed, shouting in my sleep.

I hadn't slept the rest of the night; Nak and Pauly left after I calmed myself and told them I was all right.

Nothing was further from the truth, but I didn't want any of us to get in trouble if we were discovered.

Not that I minded their presence—I was grateful they'd wakened me from that awful dream. In halting mindspeech, too, I described it to them in detail.

In the pale light of an illumination ball that Nak floated inside my quarters, I shuddered after finishing the tale.

We can bring a physician, Nak offered.

No—I'll be all right, I told him.

He and Pauly exchanged a glance. *You need to leave*, I told them. *We can't be found like this.*

Pauly's shoulders sagged in defeat. He and Nak understood that, too.

All right, but send mindspeech if you need anything, Pauly told me.

I will. I'm sorry I woke you.

It is no trouble, Nak insisted. *Try to get some rest.* I watched as they disappeared, taking the illumination ball with them and leaving me in the dark. I won't say I didn't see movement in every shadow of my room afterward—because I did.

Pauly

"She described the scene exactly, then," Cassie sighed. Nak and I sent mindspeech the following morning, to report Keela's nightmare and her description of it to Cassie. "You say she was shouting burn it?" she asked.

"Several times—Pauly and I woke the minute it started—we could feel her distress," Nak replied.

"Thanks for getting to her so quickly," Cassie sighed. "We were up most of the night and we still don't have Nettle's mystery solved. We do know this, though. She wasn't part of the keep's regular residents, and none of the rest of us brought her in. It's like she appeared from nothing."

"While we were still on Verillium?" I asked.

"Yes. Zaria didn't move the keep until days later."

"This is really fucked up, then," Nak shook his head.

"You said it," Cassie agreed. "What I can't figure out is how I got Keela's message, when she was here and I was in the past. I heard her screaming *burn it* in my mind after Bette offed herself."

"Creepy—definitely," I sighed.

"For sure," Nak confirmed. "Tell me this, though. When Zaria left a replica of the keep on Verillium, did she also leave replacements for the residents?"

"Sleeping," Cassie said. "Like they all decided to place themselves in stasis again."

"What about a replica of Nettle?"

"No idea," Cassie began before stopping and drawing a breath. "I need to talk to Zaria," she said, and just like that, she was gone.

"At least we have coffee," I lifted my mug to Nak as we remained inside Randl's massive kitchen.

"To coffee," Nak clinked his mug with mine. "After last night, we need plenty of coffee."

~

Cyrus

Nettle.

How many would overlook her? How many of us had overlooked her until now? I'd been watching and listening carefully to the conversation Lexsi and the others had the night before in Yolanna's study.

Leare was now informed, too, and likely wondered the same thing. Where in all the hells had she come from, and why? I couldn't shake the feeling of doom that had settled over the keep while he and I mulled this new mystery.

Zaria had gone looking for the pig farmer after waking; I imagined her efforts would meet with no results. The moment he was taken back to his home world, he'd disappeared.

Want to take a trip backward with me? I asked Leare.

Where and when?

To a pig farm, when it first landed on Sirena, I responded.

I'm ready whenever you are, he said.

"This one seems innocuous enough," Leare said as he and I observed the farmer tending his herd of swine.

"I feel the same," I said. Together, with shields for sight and sound up, we leaned on the pole fence around the herd, where the animals were busy eating their swill.

"Let's take a look at him just before Bette's death, then," Leare suggested.

He moved us, this time. We found the farmer sitting on a wooden bench inside a small, open shed made of rock and mortar, not far from the pig pen. *This isn't—it's not the same person,* I sent.

I'm not sure he's even, Leare's mindspeech was cut off as the man rose from his seat and walked toward the enclosure, an eager expression on his face. *Where are the pigs?* Leare snapped. *Has he moved them?*

He was right—Bette was walking through muck as if she'd been ordered to do so, and around her there was an empty pig pen.

We need to leave, Leare said, flinging us farther into the past.

Cassie

"I can't find anything here that wouldn't belong," Zaria sounded frustrated as we studied the replacement keep. "As for someone watching from a distance, that would be easy enough to do if they had Sirenali or bone dust to hide themselves."

"When did you say the keep was destroyed—likely by Ver'Dak?"

"Fifteen years after our arrival," Zaria hugged herself. "None of this makes any sense," she added. "Fifteen years from the here and now is still several years before Cjerl's attack on Nessil's city."

"And we have no idea what precipitated that attack?"

"None."

At least we were shielded against prying eyes as we searched the outer wall of the keep; it was the only original structure still standing. The keep itself was currently on Sirena, hidden behind so many shields and the bones of millions of buried Sirenali that only those allowed to find it could ever do so.

Including, I drew in an audible breath.

"Ver'Dak is involved in this," I breathed. "Somehow."

"You think he has a link with certain people from Verillium, don't you?" Zaria stared at me, wide-eyed. She was thinking the same thing, now.

"Yeah."

"He'd be cut off from his spies, if that's what they are," Zaria's mind was now considering all angles of this new development.

"What if they're programmed to act autonomously should that occur?"

"Programmed—that's a terrifying thought. Perhaps it's time to follow a pig herder we dropped off on Verillium. I hesitate to remove Nettle for the moment—that could cause a stir."

"The pig farmer saw Travis and Jek for sure," I said.

"And he saw me. Fuck," Zaria cursed.

"If he's back in Ver'Dak's hands," I began.

"Then he knows the powerful are on Verillium."

Leare

Cyrus and I hopped from day to day, looking for the moment when a normal pig farmer was replaced by—something else. After three weeks of wearily following him while he fed pigs and sent a few up the mountain to be butchered, the moment came.

We had to rewind when the replacement arrived to kill the farmer, just to discover where he'd come from.

Shielded, we stood and watched as the replacement made his way out of the thick, rock walls which supported the roof of the farmer's house.

Like a chick hatching from an egg, Cyrus's mindspeech observed.

That portion of the wall was built to be weak, with false materials, I pointed out.

Yes. How did this one know when to break out?

No idea, but something had to trigger it, don't you think?

Undoubtedly.

Shall we go looking for the place in the keep where Nettle was hatched?

Yes. Not only that, but look for other places, too, in case there are more.

What a disheartening thought.

While we're searching, we must determine what their purpose is— and what, exactly, they are.

Agreed.

Do you think Zaria will remove Nettle?

Assuredly. Perhaps we should consider who might replace her, since an abrupt disappearance could unsettle the others at the keep.

Good idea.

Shall we?

After you.

CHAPTER FOURTEEN

$\mathcal{K}$*eela* "Nothing new to teach, tonight," I told Rade when he asked. We walked along, wrapped in our coats and scarves, toward the mess hall. While the snow had stopped after dumping an amount that almost reached my knees, it gave us a frigid, sunny respite, blinding anyone walking through its crystalline fineness.

Pulling my woolly hat down farther and my scarf upward to cut the glare, I squinted in the painful brightness as we walked the now-familiar path.

I didn't explain my nightmare to any of my companions; that was something they didn't need to hear. The dream had frightened me terribly, and I didn't want anyone else to feel even a little of that fear.

"At least Instructor Bel cleared the training fields for us, like he promised. I'd hate to attempt hand-to-hand in this snow," Mey said.

"He left it on the fields where they're doing target practice," Rade said. "Yesterday, they promised to have dark-lensed goggles for us today, if the day was sunny."

"It's to ensure that you can hit a target no matter the conditions," Nak and Pauly appeared beside us. Both wore darkened spectacles.

"I want some," I begged when Pauly fell in beside me.

"Take mine; I can shield my vision with power," Nak handed his to me.

"Will you teach us how to do that?" I asked, taking the spectacles and slipping them over my eyes. Blessed relief ensued; the light was causing physical pain for me.

"I'll ask Instructor Nissa to teach you tomorrow," Nak grinned. "It's something you'll definitely need, along with spells to improve night vision, or seeing through a heavy rain or snowfall."

"That would certainly help," Rade acknowledged. "I've attempted to train in heavy snow before—it didn't go well."

"And the trainees were sent out far too soon, with little to protect them against the enemy," Hisan sounded upset.

"So many deaths," Rade nodded. "What were they thinking, there in the Royal City?"

"They thought themselves safe, and believed the lies when they came," Hisan's shoulders drooped as we walked up the steps to the mess hall. "There was no desire to learn the truth, either. What fools we all were."

"I hate that I was an inconsequential part of that deception," Rade said, patting Hisan's back. "Stop beating yourself up about it. We're here, now, and I hope we can do something to rectify our mistakes in the future."

"Are you having a meal with us?" Maxx asked Pauly.

"Yes. And we've been given permission to talk during the meal. Actually, Cassie and Travis gave everyone permission, and an extended meal period."

"That sounds nice," I said.

"Some of the other instructors are coming, too," Nak informed us as we removed hats and coats after entering the building. An entire wall was equipped with hooks for storing our gear, so we could eat unhampered.

Something is going on, isn't it? I sent to Pauly.

Yes. You're already in, so you won't be tested. This is the final assessment before a team is chosen to go out in the field. Here, we'll determine the best candidates and whether they get along with one another. We have assigned seating for this meal, to ferret out any who might not fit in well enough.

Do you know which instructors will go with us?

Yes, but I can't tell you that.

I may have it figured out before the meal is over.

I know that about you, he grinned.

How many will be chosen?

Not more than twenty, he replied. *Small enough to remain hidden, large enough to be effective. If this is a successful exercise, then another team may go out.*

Then we have to be successful. We need to know how to defeat Cjerl's forces in reality, not just in practice.

Exactly. Here's our table, he led me to a table near the center of the mess hall.

Nak led Mey and Hisan in another direction. Other instructors had come to lead the rest of our party to separate tables; we were being split up and paired with other, regular troops for a reason.

A tall, sturdy woman was led to our table; she sat across from Pauly and me. Before her training began with the troops, she'd been working in the fields with her family. Brown hair, bleached lighter by the sun, curled about her head, as if it had a mind of its own.

"Brenna, welcome," Pauly told her as she took her seat. "This is Keela, one of our power wielders."

"I'm pleased to meet you, Brenna," I nodded to her.

"Power wielder? What sort of power is your specialty?"

Cook's helpers were now carrying trays through the mess hall, setting plates of food in front of trainees and instructors. I waited until our plates were set down before answering Brenna's question.

"They say I'm a clairvoyant," I shrugged. "I hear you're at the top of your hand fighting class."

"I do well enough," Brenna lifted her fork to eat.

She's not comfortable, I sent to Pauly.

Do you know of anything to change that?

"Brenna, the fools who call you those names? They're full of shit," I told her. "Pauly, I can point out to you three who are bullying Brenna.

She doesn't want to make trouble, but then she's not the one reporting them, is she?"

Brenna, who'd stopped chewing in a determined fashion, now stared at me wide-eyed from across the table.

"Tell me who," Pauly said. "I'll let their instructors know later. Brenna, don't worry," he reassured her. "Eat your food. If someone is a bully, then it's likely that they bully others, too. Your name won't come up once when they're caught in the act in the next few days."

Brenna's eyes dropped to her plate while she nodded at Pauly's words. "Thank you," she whispered.

"No need to thank us; I wish we'd learned of it sooner," Pauly said.

"Here are Chuk and Skipp," two more regular soldiers were introduced to our table by Vik, who grinned at me.

"I have hand fighting class with Chuk, and history class with Skipp," I nodded to both as they sat beside Brenna. Neither were Brenna's tormentors, and I breathed a relieved sigh.

"Keela's specialty is clairvoyance," Brenna said. "She's among the power wielders." I blinked; Brenna knew these two as well, probably from arms training or some such. She wasn't uncomfortable around them, either.

"Brenna can beat both of us together in target practice," Skipp said. "I hope I get to serve next to her, sometime. I'd feel safer, I think."

Plates of food were set in front of Chuk and Skipp, who began to eat right away. They'd had physical exercise already and were quite hungry. Brenna had history class first thing, so she wasn't quite as voracious as they.

"So, you have afternoon history class with Skipp?" Brenna asked, cutting into the pork chop she'd been served.

"Yes," I said. "He started out sitting in the back. Now, he sits near the front."

"I've never had teaching like that before. Never knew how much I'd enjoy it," Skipp responded.

"I feel the same," I told him. "There's so much I don't know. Learning some of those things only gave me more questions."

"Have you thought about our assignment?" Skipp asked me.

"What assignment?" Brenna looked from Skipp back to me. "We didn't get an assignment."

"We have to think about the black zone—and write down our thoughts on what it is and how it was created," Skipp shrugged. "Nothing much. Did Instructor Leare not ask your class to do it?"

"Not yet," Brenna frowned. "I only considered the black zone as a barrier before—unless you wanted to do away with yourself. I know a few from nearby villages who've disappeared over the years. Everybody always says they were tired of living and went to the black zone to die."

"Sounds convenient if you want to murder somebody—or sell them," Chuk shuddered.

"I hope that wasn't the case," Brenna shook her head. "Those disappearances never affected my family, so we considered them an infrequent oddity."

"Such things don't generally cause a stir with anyone, unless it hits close to home," Pauly sighed.

Once again, I considered that something terrible was in his past, and it troubled him at times. *Don't let your past destroy your future*, I sent to him. *I don't know what happened, but I beg you not to make yourself suffer further. I just*—I hesitated for a moment. *I just don't like to see you in pain*, I said.

Pauly blinked at me for several moments before ducking his head. *Maybe we'll talk about that sometime*, he said. *Not now. We have a war to fight.*

I know. My shoulders drooped at the thought of it.

~

Leare

Cyrus and I stood in a cellar beneath the keep's kitchen, staring at three holes in the wall, surrounded by debris left behind when the hatchlings emerged.

One of those holes had likely contained Nettle.

Where were the other two?

"This debris—I believe these holes were constructed before Yolanna and the others woke. Someone managed to hide the keep's spies before then," Cyrus shook his head.

"Someone was monitoring the situation even then." I grimaced at the thought.

"Well, we know the who, then. We only need his motive—and the other two from these holes."

"Is it time to send this information to Zaria?"

"Are you prepared for the consequences?"

"There's that," I agreed. "Perhaps there is another way."

"What way?"

"Don't worry, I have a plan," I said.

"Somebody needs a plan," Cyrus huffed. "I'm placing a shield around these holes, so nobody can destroy them until they're found. With two others running amok, we have more to do, my friend."

Cassie

Zaria left me in Randl's kitchen while she went to speak with Nefrigar and several other Larentii. While she was gone, I had some time on my own. I needed a distraction, because my mind kept coming back to Nettle, and how she'd managed to turn two others to suicide.

There was no doubt in my mind that she'd arranged it, somehow. Neither Bette nor Yolanna were the type, in my opinion.

I have a book to read, I reminded myself. I did. The young girl's diary still lay on my bedside table; I only had to open it and discover her life in her own words.

My name is Ajania and this is my book, was written on the first page. *I am eleven years old and my mother gifted it to me for my birthing day remembrance. I don't remember my birth, and I often wonder why that*

occasion is named such. No one I've ever met remembers that
particular event in their lives, so it is a confusing title to me.

"Ajania," I mumbled, "I think I like you."

～

Zaria

"We can place her in stasis and cover her in shields, here in the
Archives," Nefrigar suggested. We were discussing Nettle and her
existence, in addition to how and why she'd managed to influence two
suicides.

"We don't know much about her. I dislike that idea," Kalenegar
argued.

"But we need to study her," I said. "Every inch, particle and
membrane. Is she a construct? You know that's happened before," I
snorted.

"Yes, we are aware," Kalenegar frowned at me. "This one is
dangerous, in my mind. I do not wish for her presence anywhere on the
Larentii homeworld."

"Perhaps Lissa will allow you to take her to Le-Ath Veronis,"
Zarigar turned to me. "We can place Nettle in stasis, then cover her
with heavy shields. That should allow us to scan her carefully to
determine her makeup, or her construction."

"Fine. I'll ask Lissa, then," I snapped, glaring at Kalenegar before
folding to Le-Ath Veronis.

～

"Zaria, you don't have to take her away from Sirena," Randl said. He'd
found me in Lissa's study, presenting my case of Nettle's mysterious
existence to her. "We'll construct a lab, where she can be placed in
stasis and examined. If she's sentient and in league with Ver'Dak, then
she's a criminal and should be eliminated. If she's a construct, we have
several who can research how she's wired or programmed."

"Cassie said that same word—programmed," I flopped onto the sofa across from Lissa's desk.

"You already said she was planted at the keep somehow," Lissa noted. "Have you looked for any others?"

"Not yet, but the idea did occur to me."

"If there are more, they could be running independently, unless they're programmed to contact one another only at a certain point," Randl offered.

"Or if a certain event occurs," Lissa nodded. "This is Ver'Dak we're dealing with. The guy who sends somebody else to do his dirty work so he doesn't have to. If constructs will serve the purpose," she lifted her shoulders in a shrug.

"That's why there are rogue wizards all over Verillium right now," Randl agreed. "All of them are doing his dirty work."

"The farmer you mentioned?" Lissa asked.

"Yeah. That's another problem. He could be in Ver'Dak's hands by now," I observed.

"He probably is," Randl agreed.

"That mistake is totally on me." I felt defeated by my own foolishness. "I didn't bother to really look at him. I was pissed and dumped him on Verillium without a backward glance."

"Zaria, my daughter, that pig farmer you identified in the beginning is not the pig farmer you returned to Verillium. You had faulty information there at the last. This isn't a mistake to flagellate yourself with."

Wisdom, AKA dear old Dad, had come for a visit.

"Charles?" Lissa narrowed her eyes at my father.

"I looked into the matter," he replied indifferently. "If you go to the farmer's cottage which is still on Sirena, you'll find the hole in a back wall where the substitute farmer dug his way out. Also, in the cellar beneath the keep's kitchen, you'll find similar holes where three others dug their way out. Nettle was likely one of those three. I do not have information on the other two as yet."

"Are they constructs?" Lissa demanded.

"Yes and no," my father shrugged. "Do as Randl suggests and

examine them in a shielded laboratory. I fear we may not be prepared for what is found."

Wisdom disappeared, leaving the rest of us stunned.

"There are two more loose," I moaned.

"We'll find them," Randl took my arm. "Come back to Sirena with me. We have work to do."

Leare

"I have to say, calling subtle attention to his role as a father certainly got the job done," Cyrus told me.

"Everything I told him was true," I said. "I need to bend time to teach my afternoon class. Let me know how things go from here."

"Not to worry. I'll be looking for the other two, as will Zaria, Cassie and the others," Cy chuckled. "I feel we'll have some answers very soon."

"I hope the answers are ones we can survive," I said, and bent time.

Cassie

"I was hoping there were enough scents for you to tell who they are," I told Salidar as he followed Zaria and me through the cellar.

"That's—sick," Sal stared at the three holes in the cellar wall. "You say there's another just like it in the pig farmer's house?"

"Yep."

"Definitely scents here," Sal agreed. "That one's Nettle," he pointed to the one on the far right. "These two," he shook his head at the others. "I haven't come in contact with them, yet."

"You think they may be servants? Those tend to be invisible enough," I said.

"The only way to tell is to get close to all of them," Sal told me.

"Maybe we can put one of our own in the work force," Zaria mused.

"It'll have to be somebody who doesn't mind working as a domestic."

"Susan," Sal and Zaria said at the same time.

Susan—the hen shapeshifter who knew cooking, cleaning, handfighting and how to use almost any weapon.

"I'll go see Randl now," Zaria said and disappeared.

"I need to get back to the army," Sal said.

"I have a book to finish."

"Keep me posted." Sal waved and folded space. With a sigh, I followed suit.

~

Keela

"I have the names of those selected from this class to go out in the first field operations group," Instructor Bel held up an envelope as we gathered for our morning lesson. "There are other field operations planned, so if you're not selected now, there's a good chance you'll go with another group."

"If we're not selected this time, will we still have classes?" Leri raised her hand.

"Yes. You'll continue your training, while the first group is monitored by the experienced instructors and adjuncts chosen to mentor them in the field. Instructor Nissa will be working with you here, as I'll be going into the field with the following."

He opened the envelope to read names aloud. "Jek," he announced. "Mey. Rade, Hisan and Keela. You five should go to the mess hall now, to meet with the others chosen for this mission."

"I'll stay here," Nissa smiled as she appeared beside Instructor Bel. "The five chosen, put on your coats and follow Bel to the mess hall, please."

~

"Thank the skies," Chuk breathed as I sat at a table near his. He, Brenna and Skipp, along with two others, occupied his table. Performing a swift count, I discovered nineteen trainees chosen for this exercise.

In addition to Instructor Bel, Instructors Vik and Sal were coming, along with Cassie and Denevik.

Nobody from the keep has been chosen to come, Rade whispered in my mind. *Yolanna will be angry.*

Of all the trainees gathered in the mess hall, only I knew Yolanna was dead; I'd watched her die. Mey's memory had been suppressed— she couldn't recall it. Someone else was acting in Yolanna's stead and asking questions about Nettle. *Don't worry about it, Rade*, I replied. *I don't think they'd fit in with the rest of us, and our instructors know that.*

Probably true, Rade agreed.

"Congratulations on being selected to go on the first field exercise," Cassie announced. "Today, you will be learning from Sal and Vik, who will show you how to pack supplies and gear for this assignment. You'll travel light, vehicles will be provided and we will track smaller patrol groups from the enemy army, both to gather information and eliminate those troops if necessary. This is a dangerous mission. If there is anyone here who doesn't feel up to these tasks, let one of us know after this meeting is over, and you'll be sent back to your training with no recrimination."

They all want to go, I sent to Rade. *I don't see hesitation on any face here.*

I want to go, Rade's right hand opened and closed in a tight fist. *We know so much more, now.*

Clearly, he regretted his substandard military education, slapped together before he became a trainer for the King's army. *We should have been so much better*, he added.

It's different when there are no controllers, isn't it?

Night and day, he replied. *I regret my resistance to their removal. And my ignorance regarding the abilities of females in general. You and Brenna would make a formidable team, all on your own.*

She's certainly a force to be reckoned with, I ducked my head to hide a smile.

"Trainees, stand and follow Vik and Sal from the building. Once outside, form marching ranks and follow their commands," Denevik barked at us.

As one, we rose from our seats and began to walk in silence toward the door, where Sal and Vik waited for us.

Our field exercise had begun.

Cassie

Susan, Zanfield and Perri waited in Randl's study for my arrival. Zanfield would serve as a liaison of sorts between the kitchen servants and Lexsi, so he could be near Perri.

Perri was about to take Nettle's place, so we could remove the mysterious trainee from the keep and place her in stasis. With Zarigar's help, a new lab had been constructed outside Randl's palace, and already it was firmly shielded and protected.

Pauly had been informed of his sister's new assignment and applauded our inventiveness. Perri was a fourth level witch, with formidable skills. Her specialty was power sniffing. Pauly had a similar gift, without having power of his own to use.

"Zanfield, you look almost like a commoner," I teased him. Dressed in brown clothing and boots, he'd asked Perri to match his hair color to the same shade. If anyone could now blend into the background, Zanfield could do so easily.

"I'll take that as a compliment," he grinned.

"You should," I replied. Rather than standing out, as he normally did, he'd gone in the opposite direction to fit this new role.

"Perri, you'll have to tone down your abilities," Randl told her. "You can be yourself when having lessons with Lexsi—frankly, we don't mind if you go shoe shopping during that time, just don't let anyone else know. Otherwise, you'll be attending a handfighting class and a history class with other students. We've shown you how Nettle hides behind her hair and doesn't speak with the others. You can mindspeak with Zan, Cassie, Lexsi or anyone else we have inside the keep. If there's an emergency, contact me."

"I will, Commander." Perri, already disguised as Nettle, let dark hair fall in front of her face as she dipped her head to Randl.

"Susan," Randl turned to the hen shapeshifter. "Your assignment may be the trickiest, trying to find the other two that were hidden in the cellar. Alert me if any of them act suspiciously. I can look through your eyes and make a determination."

"I'll do my best, Commander," Susan said.

"Cassie?" Randl leveled his white-eyed gaze on me.

"Ready?" I asked our newest spies.

"Ready," Perri nodded.

I folded them to the keep and turned them loose, then captured Nettle and hauled her to the newly-constructed laboratory, where Zarigar and several others waited. She neither struggled nor spoke during her capture or subsequent journey.

Keela

We were issued new uniforms, designed to blend into a winter landscape in Vorus, west of the black zone. Boots in a dark gray were also provided, plus warm socks and thick jackets made in the same camouflage patterns. Helmets and hats rounded out our gear, most of which was packed into a single duffle.

A separate uniform we'd dress in when we went out was set aside; we'd put those on when we gathered for deployment.

"We'll go in tonight; Instructor Bel will transport us to the waiting vehicles. There will be four in this convoy, and all of you are expected to follow the orders of your superiors. If you do not, you'll get a fast trip back to your barracks, and punishment will be considered. Is that clear?" Sal snapped.

"Yes, sir," we snapped back.

"Good. You'll have dinner here at the compound. Be ready to go after that."

"Yes, sir."

"You're dismissed."

∾

"What do you think we're in for tonight?" Hisan asked as we carried our new uniforms and boots toward our barracks.

"Probably an all-nighter," Jek answered. "Unless I'm very wrong, we'll camp and sleep during the day; nights are better for hitting enemy encampments."

"You'd know better than anyone," I nodded at him. He'd once been in charge of Cjerl's army. According to Nak and Pauly, he'd been too ethical in his command; therefore, he'd been dismissed and then targeted by his own troops. He and a handful of his followers had been saved by Pauly, Nak and Cassie.

All of them were now among those being trained in a combined army. Three of them would be joining us in the field exercises. Chuk was one of them. The other two, Gil and Lunn, had experience as transport drivers.

Jek would be placed over us, unless I missed my guess, but he would still answer to Cassie and the others. *What was it like—in Cjerl's army?* I sent to him. An audible breath was the only indication he'd heard me. I followed my first question with another. *Did you know you were bombing barely-trained women?*

At the last, yes. I sent a secret envoy to Vorus' Generals, asking them to approach us for a temporary cease-fire. They did so, because they knew as I did that Vorus was killing itself. I sent their message to Cjerl, who betrayed me and everyone else when he ordered an increase in the attacks and the deaths of those who'd carried the messages.

Is he that cruel?

He is cruel, but Tekar, his Advisor, is crueler still. I have no doubt that those decisions were suggested and pushed through by Tekar.

I'm glad we can speak this way, he added. *I didn't know you had the gift. Travis discovered I had it not long ago.*

Rade has it, too, in case it's needed.

Good to know.

Our uniforms had been handed to us already folded; we'd stuffed two in our duffels and kept the third out to wear on our expedition. I shook the outer jacket first, to get any wrinkles out of it, then, laying it across my bunk, I pulled the outer shirt up next, to do the same.

A sealed envelope dropped out.

Keela was written on the outside. Tearing the message open, I unfolded the paper inside to read.

Keela, you and several others are receiving a temporary promotion for the duration of the field exercise. If you perform at or above expectations, the promotion will become permanent. Your uniform will reflect that you have achieved a Lieutenant's status, in the Power Corps division of the Combined Army. Those who outrank you, among the troops selected for the field exercises are as follows: Sub-commander Jek.

That was it—his was the only name.

Who did I outrank? There had to be others elevated temporarily.

Keela? Rade's mental voice sounded hesitant.

Rade? I replied.

I'm a temporary corporal in the Power Corps Division. His excitement bled through his sending.

Good for you! I knew you were going to do well. Pauly said you would, too.

That's right—he did. Did you get a letter?

Yes, I dragged out my reply.

You outrank me, don't you? It's deserved, Keela. Very much so.

Your letter didn't give you a list of who outranked you?

No. Did yours?

Yes. Only Sub-commander Jek is higher than I am. What will the others think?

If they don't see your worth, they should be forced to stay behind.

Thank you for being a good friend, I told him.

How far we've come, he responded. *I know you barely remember me when you arrived for training, but I should have seen the light in you far sooner than I did.*

That part of our lives is over. We have a tough road ahead. We'll face it together.

Hisan is here—he says it's time to go to dinner. See you there, Lieutenant Keela.

See you there, Corporal Rade.

CHAPTER FIFTEEN

*K*eela   We spent most of the night traveling in four transports, two of which were driven by Gil and Lunn. Dave and Morrett, whom I hadn't seen since I'd been rescued from the battlefield, drove the other two.

We had rough going most of the time, as there were no roads to our destination. The transports were designed to deal with uneven terrain, but the passengers were often tossed about, even buckled in as we were.

Yan, another I hadn't seen since my rescue, had also joined us, and rode in the first vehicle with Sub-commander Jek.

Instructors were spread out among the vehicles; I rode in the second with Vik, Chuk, Brenna and three others, plus Dave, our driver. Rade, Hisan and Mey were in the first, third and fourth vehicles.

We were getting a look at how transports and troops should be protected by the Power Corps, and the concept of keeping them separated so all wouldn't die if one vehicle or company were destroyed.

An hour before dawn, we stopped. I was glad to crawl out of the swaying, shuddering transport and stand on solid ground.

"Keela, I'm going to set a shield against sight and sound over the camp, so we won't be seen or heard," Instructor Bel appeared at my elbow. "I want you to put your hands on me while I do it—I'm hoping you'll see how it's done and be able to show the others."

"Of course."

I was tired, but so was he. This needed to be done before we rested.

With my hands on his arm, he closed his eyes and created the shield around us, effectively hiding us and the vehicles.

When he was done, he turned to me. I nodded; I had the way of it now and could show the others, but he and I knew that it would take a great deal of power to construct it successfully.

That meant it could take more than two trainees to get the job done. We'd already practiced such, but I had the idea that next time, Instructor Bel expected us to try doing it for ourselves.

After we rested, I needed to show the others.

With supervision, we put up tents and hauled out bedrolls before we could lie down, then small meal packs were distributed; it was our normal breakfast time.

So many things to be done before we could sleep. I was glad I wasn't on the first latrine-digging duty, but I figured I'd get that assignment eventually.

"I'm glad that's over," Brenna settled on her bedroll inside the tent she, Mey and I shared.

"Absolutely," I agreed. Brenna wore a corporal's insignia on her uniform; she'd gotten a promotion, too. We were going to learn quickly what it meant to be an officer in the field, I think.

Leare

Susan, Zanfield and Perri are watching for the missing two from the cellar, Cy informed me. *I believe they've already formed a short list, and some of those they've noted are also on my radar.*

Any word on Nettle's examination?

Nothing yet. Several are involved, including two Larentii. At the moment, no invasive procedures are planned.

As expected. Larentii should be able to find anything out of the ordinary within the body.

Let us hope that remains true.

You're concerned.

This is Ver'Dak we're dealing with. We shouldn't take anything at face value.

True enough. I sighed; if the Eye had a feeling about something, then it was wise to pay attention. *Any ideas on what devious traps he's set for us?*

Cassie almost had him last time, but he managed to get away. I think that's why he's gun shy and unwilling to personally get involved this time.

No doubt, I agreed. *What I've seen so far has been unnerving, and we still know very little.*

~

Keela

"We've detected movement roughly fifteen miles away," Cassie showed us a map of our surrounding area. I could see outlying, deserted villages, a circle where Cjerl's small band was supposed to be, and where we currently were located.

On the eastern edge of the map, however, the black zone was clearly marked. We could draw a triangle from us to the black zone to Cjerl's marauders.

"Where is the main army?" Rade asked.

"Far to the west," Cassie said. "Far enough that we shouldn't have to worry about them. This small band is looking for us and others like us; they figure there are some of us who've eluded them so far, only to strike now and then, destroying entire units." She tapped their position on the map.

"It's good to hear that some are still fighting against this madness," Jek growled. "And it is madness—make no mistake."

Cassie's head jerked upward from studying the map to stare at Jek.

"You're right," she nodded after several seconds passed. "Thank you for pointing that out."

It came to me, then—she was thinking about Bette and Yolanna.

And madness.

Forced madness.

Nettle figured into this somehow, and Cassie knew it. Could madness be passed from one to another, intentionally?

How?

I see you've discovered a part of our problem," Cassie informed me as she studied the map again. *We're working on it, too, but we don't have any answers, yet. Keep this to yourself; I don't want to frighten the others.*

I don't want to frighten them, either, and this is terrifying. What will be done with Nettle?

She's been pulled away from her studies at the keep. Someone else is taking her place temporarily while we quarantine her. If she has some way of forcing others to kill themselves or commit terrible acts, we have to know.

I understand.

Good. We'll be going out tonight to take down this small company. Prepare yourself—it may be bloody and brutal.

I'll do my best, I replied.

Mey, Rade and I combined shields as we approached the enemy camp. Instructor Bel nodded at us; we'd done a good job keeping our small company hidden while muting the sound of our cautious approach.

They have a wizard among them, Cassie informed me.

I sense him, I replied. *There's a vibration I can feel about him, and I can see a light in my mind.*

Good. Very good. Ask Rade to level a stunning blast at him; he isn't suspecting our arrival and only has a perimeter shield up. Level the blast just before we cross the perimeter.

I relayed the message to Rade, along with a vision of the place inside the camp to target, and the perimeter we were about to cross.

I have it, he responded.

Go, I said, two steps before we reached the perimeter shield. Rade formed the stunning blast and leveled it at the wizard's tent.

The tent collapsed with a loud, whooshing sound, alerting the rest of the camp. Perimeter guards began firing weapons in our direction; our shields held. Other troops, who'd barely gotten into a deep sleep, were forced to wake in an instant and grab their weapons.

Yan, Sal and Vik flanked Jek and his troops as they returned fire, lighting the night with brief flashes as the conflict escalated.

None of our instructors participated; they were there as backup in case we failed. So far, we hadn't failed.

More coming from the back of the camp, I shouted at Jek and Sal. *Bigger weapons*, I shrieked as I sensed three setting up a rocket launcher. In my mind, I could see the entire enemy camp, with live soldiers represented as bright spots of light.

The wizard's light had gone dull; I assumed he was unconscious from Rade's blast. A few lights had winked out—Jek's troops had found targets and taken them down.

Suddenly and unexpectedly, the enemy camp was swarmed with new lights—more troops arrived from nowhere to help.

Trouble, I shouted to anyone who could hear me.

They're surrounding us! Came from Rade.

He was right—what appeared to be an entire brigade had arrived, with numerous points of lights all about us, clouding my inner vision.

Had Cjerl's entire army come to attack our small company?

Hisan's wounded, Rade sent. *Three soldiers are down.*

A roar so loud it shook the ground startled all of us; a giant serpent lifted its head into the night sky, followed by a second one, and then a third and fourth.

Go to Yan and Bel, Cassie shouted at me. *These Ra'Ak will kill all of you if you don't get away. Vik, Denevik and I must deal with these.*

Mey screamed when the bombs began to fall around us, deafening our company and tossing dirt, debris and bodies high into the air. Our shields wouldn't last long against that kind of firepower—we didn't have the combined strength to do it.

Frantically, I searched for Bel or Yan, turning in a circle while another bomb dropped.

Right on top of us.

Jessil, a voice screamed in my head. *Come. Come now. Bring the others with you if you can.*

My mind reacted while my body wished to freeze in place. Someone knew my real name—and now, so did I.

Gathering as many of the lights within our broken shield as I could, I obeyed the command without a second thought.

Cassie

I felt the stir of power when Keela and the others disappeared. Ver'Dak and Cjerl had ambushed us—*as if they were expecting our arrival.*

A fifth Ra'Ak joined the other four. Rising to my full, fiery Thifilatha, I strode forward and forced my fire down his roaring throat.

Nearby, Denevik's Thifilathi downed his opponent, as did Vik. *Two more to go*, I thought grimly and stepped toward them.

Around us, Bel held a shield against the brigade that surrounded us, while Travis' dragon flew overhead after downing the aircraft dropping bombs.

Get out. Get out now, Zaria shouted at all of us. *Keela and the others are beyond Cjerl's reach. Leave now.*

Downing another Ra'Ak without thinking, I joined the others, folding back to Sirena where Randl and Zaria waited for us at Randl's palace.

"Are you all right?" Denevik stepped to my side as I bent over, breathless from exertion and a swift move away from Verillium.

"I'm all right," I told him, panting. "No bites or scratches."

"We're all good," Travis sighed, taking a seat inside Randl's study. "Where the hell are Keela and the others?"

"They're all inside the black zone," Zaria frowned. "And we still don't know what the hell it is or how to get inside it."

～

Leare

"Ver'Dak laid a trap and they fell into it," Cyrus handed a small glass of Elvish brandy to me. "When you asked for my help all those years ago, I had no idea you were as far-sighted as I."

"Not far-sighted. Not me. Someone else had those visions. I merely listened to them."

"You're good about that," Cyrus sipped his own glass of brandy.

"We've had to push our talents and abilities to the limit, my friend," I clinked my glass against his.

"Damn straight," he agreed and sipped again.

"Your grandfather teach you that phrase?"

"Yes. He enjoys his languages. He thinks I'm dead." Cy shook his head with a sigh.

"As do many others," I nodded my understanding. "None of which has been right or fair for you."

"Or for you, brother."

"Hmmph." I rolled my shoulders uncomfortably. So many memories I'd blocked or muted, just to keep myself from going mad. *Focus on the task at hand*, I scolded myself.

"Shall we take a trip to the recent battleground?" Cyrus asked.

"Why not? We're halfway inebriated, and that is the best state to be in while we examine the dead."

～

"The fool was bombing his own people, trying to hit ours," Cy muttered as we surveyed the battlefield. "I suppose he didn't expect a dragon to appear overhead to take out his bomber."

"Who would?" I hiccupped. "It's not," I hesitated, searching for lost words for a moment, "an everyday occurrence. Pilot to copilot, dragon at ten o'clock," I teased.

Cy ignored my attempt at humor. "Those aren't his people who died, either. They're his tools. Come on." Cy slapped a hand on my back and folded us to the center of the battlefield on Verillium.

~

Conner

"Why wouldn't I know about it?" I stood, hands on hips, as Leare and Cyrus, drunk on Elvish brandy, held each other up and blinked stupidly at me. They'd landed at the center of the recently deserted battlefield, roughly fifteen miles from the black zone on Verillium. Once there, they found me searching for souls who hadn't discovered they were dead just yet.

They'd asked me how I'd known what happened. I always know when a multitude of souls leave bodies behind after dying in a surprise attack. In this case, the attack had come from their own people, trying to hit their enemy and taking everyone down around the enemy's shields in the process.

Among the Shining Ones, I was the Voice; they were the Ear and Eye. We could have lost some of ours in this surprise attack, and I was determined to search through the rubble for clues as to how Ver'Dak had known where they were.

"Their shields should have hidden them from sight and sound, and Morrett's presence should have eliminated anyone from searching with power to find them," I mused aloud.

"So, we need to find out what happened, and why," Cyrus wandered toward me. He was using power to sober himself; Leare was still thinking about it. He had his reasons and I wasn't about to call him to task over it.

"Should we take a body or two—for further investigation?" I asked.

"Probably." Leare decided that being sober was the wise thing to do in this case.

"Connegar and I can do some searching," I offered.

"Do you need our help?" Cy asked.

"If I do, I'll let you know. For now, it's better if you stay where you are."

"Agreed," Leare nodded, staring at a severed arm on bloody ground at his feet. It still held a weapon.

"I'll take a look at this," he employed power to lift the weapon, before wrapping it in a piece of cloth and stuffing it in his jacket.

He was the military historian and strategist among us; that was the reason he'd been chosen to teach a history class to the students from Verillium on Serena.

How did I know that?

Breanne. The Mighty Heart didn't interfere with anything Wisdom did, but she kept tabs on those things anyway. He probably suspected as much, but hadn't said anything to the rest of us.

"These troops came from Cjerl's main army, three hundred miles east of here," Cy remarked, stepping between mangled bodies. "I suppose the ones who survived this were sent back there by Cjerl's wizards."

"Four hundred died out of sixteen hundred troops," Cyrus' eyes lost focus for a moment as he searched for information.

"Willingly killing a quarter of your troops tells me how much Ver'Dak wanted ours killed or captured."

"He wants things he shouldn't have," Leare snorted. "Last time he tried brute force. This time, he's playing chess."

"What move was this, then?" Cy turned toward Leare.

"Queen takes pawn," Leare shrugged.

Cassie had certainly taken out two or more of Ver'Dak's Ra'Ak; nobody knew where he'd found them or how long they'd been under his thumb, waiting to be used. Cassie was poised to burn the rest of the army, too, until Zaria called her and the others away.

By that time Jessil, whom they'd called Keela, had already pulled the small group of trainees to the black zone.

We knew little of that anomaly; I hoped she and the others survived it.

Lexsi

"The only ones I haven't seen so far are the butchers," Susan and Perri sat on chairs in Yolanna's study, having tea with me during Nettle's lesson time. Susan was the one who spoke; she'd carefully vetted all the kitchen help in a short time. Only three were on her suspect list, and they were being watched by the rest of us.

Zanfield had his eye on two servants who shirked their duties for the most part, and sometimes disappeared from sight altogether. They could be sleeping or cooking up trouble; we merely had to catch them at it.

"Where are the butchers?"

"Picking out a steer or two to supply the keep with beef for next week," Susan told me.

"Good, I was getting tired of pork," I sighed. "I want some fish, too, and there isn't any to be had."

"They do have a limited menu," Susan nodded.

"What about you, Perri? Has anyone tried to talk to you?"

"They've been avoiding Nettle like the plague," Perri reported. "I must be doing a great acting job; they don't talk to or around me, either."

"I hope you don't find that upsetting," Susan reached out to pat Perri's arm.

"I don't. It keeps awkward questions from popping up that I don't know how to answer," she grinned.

"How are you doing in the hand fighting class?"

"Zanfield tells me jokes in mindspeech to keep me from doing too well," Perri snickered. "Nettle was a total washout in that class, so I'm keeping up appearances."

"Tell me one of his jokes," I begged.

"Okay. How many Nakilis did it take to solve an equation?"

"I don't know. How many?"

"None. Nakilis never solved anything."

Nakil was a dead world, with written evidence that time after time, they repeatedly made the wrong decisions until the planet died beneath them. Their historic incompetence left them much surprised—and dying from their own foolishness.

Susan smothered a laugh. I ducked my head to hide a grin.

"He says he'll be here all week," Perri added. I guffawed.

Keela

"I think I want to keep the name Keela," I told Iris. The black zone I'd entered with the others contained a city, I discovered, where Iris, my dream-invading instructor, waited for us. "Jessil—I don't like the memories attached to that name."

"Do you wish to leave Hisan's name alone?" She frowned at me. I sat on an embroidery-covered chair in her sitting room, talking while we drank tea.

"I think that's up to him." His disguise had been wiped away upon entering the black zone; he was being treated for his wounds in an infirmary nearby. When I first saw him as he was, I was furious.

Then visions came to me, of how he'd been forced to suffer—at his own hand—and how he'd asked to be given scars afterward, as a penance. Several of Iris' healers had met us when she did, and Hisan begged my forgiveness as he was carried away on a stretcher.

I wouldn't forgive Verlin.

I'd already forgiven Hisan.

"There's something else you should know, Granddaughter," Iris set her teacup down carefully.

I blinked as she called me Granddaughter, but didn't comment. "What is that?" I asked.

"There was something small infecting all of you before you passed the boundary of the black zone. It has been eliminated by your successful entry."

"Successful entry?"

"Not all who enter will live."

"So those tales are true."

"Yes. Many we call to us, but those who enter of their own accord rarely survive."

"Who called out to me?" I asked. "It was a male voice."

"I cannot say at this time. My voice would have followed his quickly, had it been needed."

"You heard it, too?"

"I heard it, too. Now, on to other things. I wish to teach you and the others while you are here," she told me. "This way, you will be better prepared for battle when you leave the black zone."

"We were trapped on our first night out," I hung my head.

"We know this. The true enemy is quite cunning, dear girl. He has many traps planned for you and the others. We must prepare you for this and many other things."

"Cjerl?"

"Hmmph," Iris sniffed delicately. "Cjerl is merely a tool for the true enemy. Tell me, have your instructors ever mentioned one called Ver'Dak?"

"I haven't heard that name," I shook my head.

"They wish to spare you, but in this case, it is a mistake. Ver'Dak is very powerful and not of this world. He was born on a world far from here and given terrible talents with which to take whatever he wants. He wants Verillium and its mineral wealth. He has no real knowledge of what, exactly, it is that he desires."

"Thank you for this information. Will you teach me as much as you know about this—Ver'Dak?"

"Of course. This knowledge will be necessary to eliminate his hold on what is left of Verillium. He has no right to any part of it."

"Are the instructors who were with us dead?" I thought to ask.

"No. They are also from elsewhere, and powerful in their own right. They stayed behind to combat the giant serpents sent against you and the others. They also seek Ver'Dak, to kill him. In this, they should have united with you and your team and informed you of their mission."

"Why didn't they?"

"Ver'Dak is not the only one of his kind, and they have done this before. It is commendable that they risk their lives for worlds that have no knowledge of their existence or continued vigilance to keep them safe. It is only in this instance that they should have been more forthcoming."

"I don't want to fault them; they have taught us much," I said.

"And you are correct. They are friends, not enemies," Iris smiled at me. "Go and rest, child. Tomorrow, your lessons will begin."

Cassie

"I finished the diary," I told Zaria over coffee the following morning. "It—just ends abruptly, the day before Ajania's twelfth birthday."

"Any idea why?"

"None. She mentioned her birthday plans, and a party which she was excited about—but then nothing."

"An accident? Early death?" Zaria frowned at me.

"She didn't mention any health issues, and she put everything else into that diary," I said, *Pulling* it into my hand and giving it to Zaria. "Including the punishments from her father for being too headstrong. A third of the pages are blank after her last entry. Still a good read. I think you'll like her," I added.

"If we had time, I'd say let's bend time, but we don't. Have time, that is. A part of me says that Keela and the others are alive, but the evidence says otherwise."

"Those were our best troops and power wielders, too," I grimaced.

"Travis says we need to bring the others up to that level, and I worry that time is growing short. For all of us. We should have seen that trap from two miles away, and we didn't."

"We've gotten so complacent over Ver'Dak's non-interference," I said. "We were expecting maybe a wizard or two to show up. We got Ra'Ak and an army brigade with wizards instead."

"I hear they lost at least a quarter of their troops and some of their wizards when they started bombing. If they're willing to bomb their own, they won't stop at anything."

"Here's my question; why are they willing to bomb their own?"

"Obsession?"

"Or a controller, maybe?"

"You know, you just scared me." Zaria rose from her seat, grabbed Ajania's journal plus her coffee cup and folded away.

I'll be back, she sent.

Okay, I replied.

"Damn," Randl swore after folding into the breakfast nook. "I missed her, didn't I?"

"She just left," I nodded. "Took her coffee, though. What's up?"

"Susan says the butchers just returned from the farms with two butchered steers. She asked Lexsi to take a look at both those men, because she thought it was strange to butcher steers and then haul heavy, dead meat up the mountain, when the steers could have walked themselves up and then given their all. Everything they need to accomplish the task is at the keep. I thought Zaria and I ought to look into those men, too."

"That doesn't make sense to me, either," I frowned at Randl. "Tell Lexsi we're on the way."

"Already done," he said. I let Randl move us to the keep; two men waited for our perusal.

Our questions were met with absolute silence. Like Nettle, these men appeared to be just as much a void as she. We stood inside the keep's dim, outside meat storage room, where sides of raw beef now hung from thick, overhead beams.

Our prisoners stood inside a shield Randl built around them so they couldn't escape or attack us. *We're making room in the lab for them*, Zarigar replied to my mindspeech. *Turtle and Flyer have agreed to assume their identities, since they're experienced in dressing out animals for food.*

Thank goodness, I told him.

"I'll take them back with me," Randl offered, nodding at our prisoners. Turtle and Flyer folded in right after Randl left with the butchers.

"Haven't seen conditions this rough in a while," Flyer said while he eyed the small room. He and Turtle, their long, black braids hidden beneath their coats, studied their new workspace with a critical eye.

"Do you need anything?" I asked.

"We'll get better knives and cleavers *Pulled* in; Dori said she'd send whatever we needed to get the job done."

Falchani were always particular about the sharp metal blades and utensils they employed; they knew how to take care of them, too. The butchers we'd just sent to the lab hadn't cared for their tools at all, and after looking at the dull, bloody things piled on a stained work surface, I wondered why the entire keep hadn't gotten sick.

"We'll clean this mess up first," Flyer shook his head at the conditions inside the room. "Then we'll make a list of what we need to send to Dori."

"Let me know if you need my help with anything," I said.

"Under normal circumstances, I'd ask you to destroy the entire space and begin anew," Turtle muttered. "As it is, we'll do what we can to make it presentable."

"Thank you," I told them. "Really. If you need my help, send mindspeech."

"We've got this," Flyer nodded, pulling leather gloves from a coat pocket and putting them on before touching a bloody cleaver. "We'll get rid of this mess, first thing."

Randl

"All our scans reveal nothing out of the ordinary," Karzac accepted the Refizani beer I offered. "Something is amiss, however, and I am currently considering how to go about finding it."

"This is from Nettle only, or have you started on the butchers, yet?"

"Nettle, so far," he shrugged. "The butchers are in stasis. Zarigar, Nefrigar and two other Larentii are doing their own sort of scans on those two before I get started."

"When I look at them, I don't see anything and that's unusual. Zaria says the same thing—that they're a total blank. I wanted to talk to her this morning before she got away, but missed her by seconds. Cassie said she sounded worried when she left."

"What set her off? Do you know?"

"I can ask Cassie."

"Please. I feel an urgency about this and cannot explain why that is."

Cassie? I sent.

What do you need? She replied promptly.

Karzac is asking what set Zaria off this morning.

"Well, we were talking about whether the troops firing on their own people had an obsession, or maybe controllers," Cassie appeared next to me.

"Controllers? Shall we go back and lift a body or two to find out?" Karzac's left eyebrow was lifted in speculation.

"How about we go into split-time and take one of the soldiers inside an aircraft?" I suggested. "They're the ones firing on their fellow troops."

"Shall we?" Karzac was on his feet in a blink.

"Need me to come along?" Cassie asked.

"I think we have this covered," I said. "Thanks for the info."

CHAPTER SIXTEEN

*C*assie

"He's in stasis right now; we pulled him out just before his aircraft was destroyed," Randl told me. He and I stood outside the lab's observation window as the soldier floated in midair inside. The Larentii suspended their subjects like this so they could view the bodies from every angle.

Each of our suspended subjects was in a separate, sealed room, so there could be no cross-contamination. Each room was temperature and humidity regulated, so there'd be no variants to skew our studies.

"Karzac and the Larentii are having a meeting; they're discussing a new testing procedure," Randl went on. "So far, they've been noninvasive. This test—if they go ahead with it—will employ the microscopic cameras the Larentii sometimes use for observational purposes. They're so small they shouldn't disrupt anything, but you know how the Larentii are about non-interference."

"How would this be different from injecting dye for tests or giving medicine or vaccines?" I asked.

"Well, that's a good question, I suppose."

"We're going ahead with the procedure," Karzac and Zarigar appeared. Zarigar rubbed my back gently and smiled down at me.

You are very tense, dear one, he informed me.

Yeah. Last night, I may as well have slept on bricks, I replied. *I was stiff and sore when I woke up.*

This situation is indeed troubling, he agreed. *Continual worry will not solve anything, however, and will only sap your energy when you may need it most.*

Yeah.

His hands went to my shoulders and began to knead, while he fed me a sense of calm and gentleness. Clever, blue fingers worked out muscle kinks as I began to feel boneless.

"I will take her," Denevik whispered as I was lifted off my feet. A finger touched my forehead and sleep descended. If I'd been conscious, I would have expressed my deepest gratitude.

Eliagar

"Zak, wake now—you are having a bad dream," I said gently, while placing a calming hand on the boy's shoulder. Until then, he'd been mumbling in his sleep and jerking about, as if he were attempting to escape something terrible.

He woke with a deep, indrawn gasp, his eyes wide and frightened. "Save me," he burrowed into my arms and wept.

"Of course I will save you," I held him close and rocked his body. "What has frightened you so?" I begged.

"Holes. In walls." He shuddered against me. "They were shutting people up inside them."

"People? Inside walls?" I asked gently.

"After they," he gulped out a sob. "After they gave them bugs."

"Bugs?"

"In their blood. Bugs in the blood. They wanted me, too," he sobbed again and couldn't finish.

Zarigar, I sent, *there may be terrible trouble coming your way.*

In what manner?

The boy keeps having nightmares. He is dreaming of people being locked inside walls, after they've been given bugs in their blood. That is his explanation.

We are about to attempt an unusual procedure to test for something similar, and we indeed have three who escaped from holes in walls, he responded. *Thank you for the information—we will proceed with haste and employ every precaution.*

~

Keela

"I never want to hear that name again," Hisan paled. "I know I wear that face—that is a terrible punishment in itself. How stupid and cruel and puffed-up I was," he shuddered.

"At least you're well enough now to sit here beneath the trees with us," Rade said. He was right; Hisan had only been well enough to come to lessons for two days out of the twelve we'd already spent inside the black zone.

Rade, Hisan and I sat beneath a trailing tree, its slender, small-leaved branches hanging low and swaying about us in a light breeze.

"When you were hit, I didn't think you'd live. Others didn't," Rade told Hisan.

"I would have deserved my death."

"Stop talking like that," I scolded. "That is in the past—like other things are in the past. Regardless of what happens going forward, Verillium will never be the same as it was."

"I am grateful some of those things are in the past." Hisan swallowed with difficulty.

"As am I. Let anyone try to place a controller now," I huffed.

"Ah, here you are," Iris bent low and walked beneath our trailing tree. She smiled at us as she straightened. "Ready for your afternoon lessons?"

"Of course," I rose from the ground and dusted off my trousers. "I still can't figure out why my power works inside the black zone, when it didn't outside."

"Hmmph," Iris sniffed. "Perhaps we'll study that conundrum soon. Come, now, midday meal break is over."

Dutifully, we followed her outside our sanctuary until we reached the stone path that led to her classroom. Mey and Jek would join us, and we'd begin our intensive training once more.

The regular troops were doing their training with others Iris handpicked to carry on with their handfighting and weapons courses. Brenna, Chuk and Skipp were enjoying themselves.

Iris had a particular date in mind for our training to end; I had the feeling that she knew better than anyone when we'd be needed to combat the enemy. Therefore, I paid close attention whenever she showed us something new; it could save our lives or prevent our capture at the very least.

~

Cassie

Somehow, Zaria and Zarigar had arrived at the same conclusion, while worlds apart. Randl and I were called in to discuss the findings.

"So far, we haven't determined their makeup, only that they exist and depend upon the blood pumping through the body to get about," Zarigar presented an enlarged image of such microscopic proportions I had no idea how they'd been created in the beginning.

"What is their purpose? Do we know?" Randl asked as he studied the image. "It looks like a tiny oval. Do you suppose it's a nanobot?"

"Also something we don't know," Zaria sighed. "So far, we've counted roughly a thousand of those things in Nettle's blood stream."

"Maybe this is why Keela was screaming about blood and an invasion—and yelling at me to burn Yolanna's body."

"I believe that is exactly what she meant," Zarigar said. "You were wise to follow her instructions."

"I still don't know why I did that," I confessed. "She was so insistent that I did it without thinking."

"And now we don't have her to ask more questions," Zaria sighed.

"My fault," I admitted. "I should have known they'd set a trap for us, and I fell right into it."

"None of us expected that," Zaria argued. "Therefore, if you're at fault, then so are we."

"Placing blame isn't going to help us solve this riddle," Randl pointed out. "If these things are nanobots, then what activates them?"

"I've asked for technical assistance from two of yours," Zarigar smiled at Randl. "Barry and George are on their way. If these are nanobots, then perhaps those two can communicate with them and learn their purpose. It could save us a great deal of time."

"Let me link with Barry and George while they're studying these things," I suggested later, when both arrived at the lab, smiling widely at me.

It was only a matter of time before my younger sister, Destiny, was done with her extensive studies and they'd ask for her hand, I just knew it. Destiny loved both of them; they were together whenever she was on break and they didn't have an assignment.

"Thank you," George hugged me. "Barry's ancestry provides some protection against evil, but I do not have such."

"Then we'll do this together," I hugged him back.

"Is it possible to put my hands on her?" Barry asked, referring to Nettle.

"In most cases, I'd say no, but if Cassie is connected with you," Zarigar shrugged. "I will connect with her if it becomes necessary," he added.

What he wasn't saying was this; if those nanobots were able to breach my defenses, then he'd offer the vast resources of the Larentii to help extricate us.

"Let's do this," I sighed. Zarigar opened the door to Nettle's quarantine room. The four of us walked inside while Randl and a few others watched through the window.

~

Randl

"Can you take them into split-time if it's necessary—to remove those things if they gain access to any one of them?" Zaria asked.

"I can do that, although I've never taken a Larentii with me," I told her. "Why do you ask?"

"Something about all this troubles me. How can one, minuscule nanobot cause so much destruction on its own? It has to be communicating with the others, right?"

"That would be my guess."

"But an individual nanobot shouldn't have enough power to cause the problems these have caused. I can only assume that Bette and Yolanna were somehow infected with those parasites."

"Were they concentrated in one area in Nettle's bloodstream?" I asked.

"No. Zariagar says they were found throughout her body."

"That makes no sense, then."

"Exactly."

We watched as Zarigar lifted the sheet away from Nettle's body with half a thought. Cassie, standing between George and Barry, held onto one of their hands while they reached out to touch Nettle's arm.

I drew in a breath as I saw Zarigar settle his hands on Cassie's shoulder.

The visions he sent to Zaria and me made us gasp.

Stop it, stop it, stop it, Zaria shouted into all our minds, before Nettle's body broke out of its stasis and she twisted in midair, much like a cat, before she landed on her feet in a defensive pose.

And exploded.

~

Keela

"Other types of power or magic will not work in the black zone," Iris explained. Hisan asked the question—whether the enemy's wizards could invade and destroy us. "The barrier acts as a filter—those abilities will be left behind when any of them enter here. Only when we allow them to leave—*if* we allow it—will they regain what they lost."

She didn't dwell on the fact that anyone unsuitable entering the black zone was deprived of their life. I was afraid to ask how they were killed, since I didn't want to hear tales of painful deaths. I'd witnessed too much pain during my life already.

"It isn't painful," Iris turned toward me. "The filter knows which ones to allow through. The death is painless, if it is deserved."

"Thank you," I mumbled, ducking my head in embarrassment.

"Granddaughter, never be ashamed of wishing to withhold pain. It is a gift and a credit to you."

Hisan reached out to squeeze my hand; with my head still down, I nodded without looking at him.

I'm relieved, too, Rade's voice whispered in my mind. *If I'd gone through with my plan all those years ago, do you think they'd let me in?*

Yes, Iris' voice joined his. *You would have been welcome here. Many in your circumstances came. Many are still among us. Do not regret your decision, Rade. You have helped many and did not know it.*

Thank you for being my friend, I told him. *Until you, I never had one.*

"Shall we continue with our lesson?" Iris spoke aloud. I looked up at Rade, who gave me a crooked smile.

Cassie

"They thought they were being attacked, and were programmed to combine and retaliate," Barry sighed. We sat in Randl's bar inside his palace, having a drink while we considered our close call with Nettle's self-destruction.

"I saw them gathering in the brain," Zaria nodded at him. "I have a feeling that if we do this with the butchers, we'll get the same results."

"Did you get any idea of their construction?" Randl asked.

Barry exchanged a swift glance with George.

"We heard—communication," George dipped his head in a slight nod. "There is something there that we have not come in contact with before."

"Besides the wizard's power infused in each of them?" Zarigar settled his hand over mine, his blue fingers covering my entire hand and wrist.

"I've never seen a wizard's power be so effective in something so small," Randl pointed out.

"There must be something else—a component or such, that is aiding those spells," Barry suggested. "I couldn't get a feel for it, though. When the spell activated, forcing the nanobots to combine, I lost the trail."

"What about Nettle herself?" I asked. "Was she humanoid or a construct? Could you get a feel for that?"

"She was quite elegantly constructed," George said. "If my kind hadn't been outlawed, it's what we may have advanced toward. So human, there is no good way to tell the difference without microscopic examination."

"So Ver'Dak has gone into the serve-bot business?" Randl shook his head.

"Call her a construct," Zaria responded. "I thought only the Mighty and those slightly less powerful could accomplish this. I suppose Liron's children now have the ability, too."

"She had no soul—that's why she appeared to you as a void," Barry said. "George has a soul. We all know that. How that happened we don't know, but I am more than grateful. He is a brother to me."

"At least Ver'Dak doesn't have power over souls," I released a heavy sigh. "Not sure what that one weakness will do for us, but it's something we know."

"I'm more worried now about the one who got away," Randl said.

"It's my fault; I shouldn't have reacted so blindly," Zaria countered.

"Mother, look at it this way," Zarigar told her. "We saw earlier what each of these constructs is capable of doing. Dumping him away from the others may have been the prudent thing to do."

"Now that you put it that way," I nodded at Zarigar. "He didn't come in contact with any others that he could infect or destroy—not on Sirena, anyway."

"That concerns me," George said. "How many other constructs wander Verillium? How many more may still be waiting within their cocoon of bricks and stones? Ver'Dak has planted a terrible crop, has he not?"

"Do you think that's why Cjerl won't leave his palace? That Ver'Dak can't invade it, for some reason? That somewhere along the timeline, that's what the prophecy was?"

"But how could it be protected? Who would do that?" Zaria frowned. "Nobody that I know did it, that's for sure. There are no power signatures."

"None that we can detect, anyway," Zarigar agreed.

"So we know only slightly more than we did," Randl grimaced. "I need a drink. Anyone else?"

All except Zarigar raised their hands.

Leare

The ones who'd asked the right questions were missing from my classes. They'd been shoved into the black zone; I knew it in my heart and soul.

Where they were, they couldn't be pulled away. They'd have to leave on their own or choose to stay. The newest information I had, from listening to those who'd attended the latest experiments on the constructs, let me know that the end of all this was nearer than might be expected.

For now, there was a sense of loss among the trainees, when Keela and the others failed to return. Travis and Trent met with all of them, explaining that the enemy had laid a trap and we'd lost those on the mission.

Everything they'd said was true—up to a point. The trainees believed those sent into the field were dead, including the instructors, who'd also not returned. Cassie and Zaria believed that was the best way to handle it—that all could be considered lost, although it hadn't specifically been communicated.

My students now wore grim expressions when they attended class; they'd developed a determination of sorts, to avenge deaths. If any students had lacked a will before, that lack had now gained intense focus.

As for Keela and those of her company who'd been pulled to the black zone, I hoped they'd be released one day, although I had no reason to feed that hope and keep it alive.

Things will turn out as they will, I reminded myself and strode into the afternoon class. Several empty seats reminded me of the final, fundamentally painful, cost of every war ever fought.

Cassie

"It took a great deal of careful maneuvering," Karzac tapped his comp-vid. He and several Larentii had managed to pull away a single nanobot from the pilot he and Randl had captured before the aircraft on Verillium was destroyed. "We had to replace it with a similar construct while all were dormant," he added.

"Because Ver'Dak's nanobots can count?" I blinked in confusion.

"Something like that, I suppose. We've isolated this one, so it can't communicate with its fellows while we examine it."

"Are there spells on it?"

"Yes. We're doing everything we can to determine the best way to work around that."

"Get Denevik to be there with you. If a wizard or anyone else has laid a spell, I hope a High Demon's presence can neutralize it."

"I hope that remains true," Karzac agreed. "If so, then we need a High Demon present whenever one of the others is examined. Perhaps that will prevent the nanobots from combining and creating an explosion."

"Or combining and becoming a controller," Zaria appeared. "I've been doing some experiments with Kal and the Wise Ones. In theory, those nanobots can do either."

"So we're facing an army who can turn itself into a massive bomb and take down their enemy?" I asked. "Their enemy being our troops," I added.

"I'm afraid that may be true," Zaria sighed. "Ver'Dak has plotted this carefully. Je'Dik wasn't nearly this smart."

"Wow. We've been fucked from the get-go," I covered my face with both hands.

"This is my concern," Karzac said, his voice flat, his tone fatalistic. I dropped my hands to stare at him. When the ultimate healer had concerns, then everybody should have those same concerns.

"Tell us," Zaria said.

"We must examine your troops, both at the camp and in the keep," Karzac told us. "If they have the same nanobot invasion in their blood, then Nettle and her cohorts have managed to infect all, and not just Cjerl's forces."

Zaria cursed in the Larentii language.

"How fucked up is this?" Travis demanded. I sat in his office at the training camp, with Trent occupying another chair next to his brother's desk.

"We need a few from here, and a few from the keep to examine," I relayed Karzac's request. "Call it special training or whatever you want; we can ask Morrett to lay an obsession to reflect that afterward."

"But what if the same thing happens to them that happened with Nettle?" Trent was clearly concerned.

"You want it to happen under controlled circumstances, or out on the battlefield, while handing everything to Ver'Dak?" I asked.

"Good point," Travis and Trent spoke simultaneously.

"This was his way of hedging his bets, in case we showed up, isn't it?" Travis' brow furrowed as he gazed at me. "He's hoping to take some of us out when he unleashes his little sideshow."

"No doubt," I agreed. "Zaria thinks the same. That's why he sent Ra'Ak, I believe—to see how they were taken down. Now, he likely knows we have High Demons in our company."

"And a dragon, too," Travis snorted.

"Yep."

"This means he can plan his attacks better, doesn't it? Specifically designed to take each of our kind down." Trent blew out a frustrated sigh.

"That's what it looks like."

"So much for trying to hide what we are and keeping him unaware that we were on Verillium in the first place," Travis grumbled. "Looks like we were doomed to fail from the start."

"Choose subjects for us from the troops," I said. "We can pick them up after they're asleep and return them afterward, unless we can't stop the nanobots from destroying their host."

"We don't know that they have them, yet," Trent argued.

"I think we were outmaneuvered on this long ago," I replied. "I'm going to see Lexsi—she can choose the ones from the keep."

"We'll have six names for you in an hour."

"Thanks."

"How do you suppose Nettle and the others transferred those things—if they have been transferred?" Lexsi asked.

I sat inside her borrowed study with Perri, Zanfield and Susan, discussing which keep residents to choose for examination.

"We don't have an answer," I confessed. "Not yet, anyway. Zarigar and Nefrigar are hoping Barry and George can get information through the one we extracted from the pilot, before the others notice and combine to take action."

"Which translates to blowing the hell up?" Lexsi lifted a delicate eyebrow.

"Pretty much."

"Then let's choose those less important," Zanfield said. "We'll get better at this, surely, so those less important won't impact our efforts."

"I agree with that suggestion," Lexsi nodded.

"Good. I have two who sneak away every chance they get to sleep or filch food and hide while they should be working," Zanfield offered.

"Those two, for sure," Lexsi said. "What about students and others?"

"I think we can put a list together," Susan sounded confident. "When will you take them?"

"Tonight, while they sleep," I replied. "Zaria and Karzac will do the honors."

"Good enough. Is there anything else I can do for you?"

"Not right now."

"Good. I've been reading up on the history of the keep. Apparently the first Mistress of the Keep kept a diary. I'm reading it, and it's really good," Lexsi said.

"I might be interested in reading it, too, then," I said. "Just to see what her life was like."

"I'll let you borrow it when I'm done," she smiled at me. "We'll have names for you in an hour."

"Thanks—I'll pass them along to Zaria."

"Clare and Rajeon are doing a good job replacing Sal and Vik," Travis told me, handing a comp-vid over. "The names we've chosen are on that list."

"Thanks. We'll let you know what we find—if we find anything."

"Frankly, I think I'd like to be there when the testing's done. Trent said he'd cover for me tomorrow if the wait is too long."

"That's fine," I said. "Several others have asked to come. Your mother is one of them."

"Because she's figured out that this may not be an isolated incident, hasn't she?"

"Got it in one," I said. "We need to know whether Ver'Dak has hit other worlds with this little trick of his, or whether this is his first foray, using Verillium as his Petri dish."

"Cassie, what if we've been infected? Is that possible?" Travis allowed his real concern to surface.

"You just scared me more than I was already."

"We need to know. I'll volunteer, if Karzac and the Larentii need one of us to check."

"Damn, this is way too fucked up," I rubbed my forehead. "Look, I have to go, but feel free to show up at the lab anytime—I'll let them know you're coming."

~

Leare

Cy, they're going to pull several away to test for those nanobots, I informed the Eye. *I'm concerned that they are infected and some could be lost if the bots react as they did in Nettle.*

That's a concern, Cy responded quickly. *What do you want to do about it?*

When is the last time you went Looking *for something that small?*

Probably the last time you were listening for something that small.

Are you thinking what I'm thinking?

I am now.

Who, then?

Let's take one of those lazy louts who only pretend to work in the keep and constantly claim an illness, Cy suggested.

When?

How about now?

My classes were over for the day, and I needed something to do to quash the growing concerns invading my mind. *Sure,* I replied. *Where?*

Meet me in the Seneschal's quarters. I'll bring the malingerer in— he's currently asleep in a corner of the pantry.

I'll be there shortly.

~

"I placed a healing sleep," Cy shrugged when I asked. The servant, Meki, floated in midair inside the Seneschal's quarters, where Cy had taken up residence. "As long as we don't physically touch him, I think we'll be all right."

"Keep a shield up anyway," I cautioned.

"Already done. Shall we?"

Closing my eyes, I filtered everything else out, attuning my ears to hear the sounds inside Meki's body. Cy began the process of *Looking* into every minute nook and cranny of the man's blood vessels.

I see one, Cy reported. *Now, a second one.*

Are they congregating?

Not that I can tell—they're allowing the blood flow to carry them throughout the body, like an ever-present patrol.

Wait, I responded. *I think I can hear their communication. Hold on.*

Can you interpret it?

They know he was moved, my eyes flew open as I stared across the floating body at the Eye.

Time appeared to slow as Cy attempted a warning; it had taken a matter of only a few moments for the nanobots to combine into a deadly explosive.

The body blew outward in a furious blast of light, until it stopped just short of reaching Cy and me.

And it stayed that way while I blinked in confusion at the one who'd joined us.

"Breanne?" Cyrus breathed her name like an almost-sob.

"This is a real mess, huh?" the Mighty Heart shook her head at Meki's suspended, exploding form. "Come on, let's get him back to his hidey-hole before I *Change What Was*."

CHAPTER SEVENTEEN

*C*assie

"They're learning—the nanobots. You won't be successful if you pull the subjects away from their beds tonight," Breanne informed us. She'd sent mindspeech an hour before our scheduled testing of troops and keep residents. All of them would have died if we'd taken them for examination.

"How did you find this out?" Lissa asked. She'd come anyway, as had many others, to hear what Breanne knew about Ver'Dak's tiniest spies.

"I had a conversation with the Ear and the Eye, and they confirmed it," Breanne explained. "The Ear heard their communication; the Eye confirmed that all from Verillium are infected."

"How? Were they passed along, like a virus?" I asked. Zaria sat next to me in Randl's study as we discussed this new development.

"The Ear, the Eye and I went in search of that very thing, and you won't like what we found," Breanne stated baldly. "It's in the food— specifically the animal protein. Those things were fed to every animal produced on the farms pulled away from Verillium. It was designed to infect the population on Verillium, but then these were brought here, and we've imported the infection with them."

"What about us?" Travis spoke up. "Are we infected, too?"

"Whatever you've consumed has been destroyed—like any other virus that might invade your system. Your immortality assures that this happens."

"So we're not in danger, but all the others are. That's how they forced Bette and Yolanna to commit suicide—an attempt to hide their contamination from the rest of us, I suppose," Randl surmised.

"It wasn't until Bette crossed Travis' perimeter shield that she killed herself, and Yolanna was surrounded by shielded people when she did the same," I pointed out.

"We're still left with the question as to why Bette and Nettle went down the mountain to begin with," Travis said.

"Well, it's a safe bet that none of those nanobots will be answering that question—her blood was spilled into pig slop," Lissa grumped.

"No wonder Keela was shouting in my mind to burn it," I said.

"The next, necessary question is this—what can we do about it?" Randl asked. "All the people we've been training are infected. We take them back to Verillium, they're subject to Ver'Dak's control, which leaves us worse off than we were—nobody on the planet can stand against Cjerl's troops if they're all forced to serve the same side."

"I can try to mist those things out," Lissa offered.

"The bots may become suspicious and we could have a mass suicide attempt," Breanne replied.

"That's no good, then," I shivered.

"What's that phrase from Earth?" Barry asked. "Beverly says it, sometimes—fighting fire with fire?"

"What are you saying?" Randl turned swiftly in Barry's direction.

"We can design nanobots, too," he shrugged. "We know where these congregate to either control or destroy their hosts. We can design ours and place them there in the beginning—to destroy the invading force. We can leave ours inside, in case the hosts are re-infected on Verillium."

"We will be forced to proceed with caution, as we know there are spells attached to these devices," Zarigar pointed out.

"We have spell-casters, too," I said, my brain working rapidly to understand Barry's suggestion.

"How should we proceed, then?" Lissa asked.

"First, we must replicate the invading nanobots," Zarigar said. "To determine whether our opposing bots will be successful if introduced inside a host body."

"How long will this take?" I asked.

"Months, at the very least," Barry said. "I'm hoping Zarigar will take us backward in time to accomplish this. I fear time is growing short for Verillium's survival."

"The Ear said as much," Breanne confirmed.

"We'll need a specialist in spellwork or such, to gauge the strength and type of spells used in the originals," Randl said.

"Erland may be able to help," Lissa began.

"Pauly," Bel spoke up. "He knows exactly how much power anyone has, and what type it is. And, if we can convince Kaldill Schaff to work with him, I believe you'll have your answers very soon."

"I'll talk to Kaldill," Lissa said before folding away.

"I'll talk to Pauly," Bel nodded and disappeared.

"Barry, George, I am at your disposal," Zarigar dipped his head to them. "I will give you as much time as needed to develop a reply to Ver'Dak's invasion."

"Let's hope it works, then," Breanne shook her head. "I'll have another talk with the Ear and Eye; perhaps they can supply more specific information for your trials."

"Thank you, Grandmother," Zarigar told her.

"Honey, you are more than welcome."

Keela

Jek took over our handfighting lessons, with help from two of Iris' associates. We now had those lessons after the midday meal, with spells and casting lessons before and after.

It was during one of those morning lessons on spell crafting that Iris asked me to reveal the stone I wore about my neck.

I hadn't told anyone about it or shown it to anyone else. Nevertheless, she knew. "That is known as a focus stone," Iris explained as I held up the stone for the others to see. "It is made of a particular quartzite found here on Verillium. Focus stones were carried for centuries, until the knowledge and habit of keeping one was hidden away. There was a reason," she noted as the murmurs began. "Tuck it back in," Iris nodded to me. I was relieved to do so.

"Today, we will issue a focus stone to the rest of you and show you how to charge it. It can serve as a backup for extra power—and will also carry information you wish to store inside it. This includes information on difficult spells, or a recipe for mutton stew."

Mey snickered behind me; I recognized her mirth.

"What if this information falls into enemy hands?" Rade asked.

"Unless you have instilled in the stone your wish for them to use it, it will only answer to you. It is easiest to give your stone to a blood relative, in fact, and only if you designate it to be so."

"The chains have been spelled against breaking," Greer, one of Iris' trusted assistants, arrived, bearing stones and necklaces to give to the others. "Keela, the one you have is yours."

I blinked at him before turning toward Iris, who nodded slightly at me. Wherever Pauly and Nak had gotten the one I wore, it was truly mine to work with.

"The first thing to do with your stone, is to lock it to your power," Iris began after each of us held an amber-colored stone in our hands. "Close your eyes and find the center of your power, as I've shown you before."

~

Cjerl's Palace
Tekar
My hands were slick with sweat as I concealed the dagger beneath

my mattress; *he'd* given it to me with specific instructions. One blow was all I had time for, before the palace guards would descend.

This was my death as well as the King's. Shaking, as if I had a chill, I stumbled toward the door of my suite. Surely a servant would be near enough to order a bottle of wine from the cellar.

Either get him out of the palace so I can reach him, or you kill him with the dagger, Ver'Dak ordered. I could not disobey; I discovered that the moment he laid the command. How and why had I fallen in with this one?

The promise of money and a high office? Those desires tasted of ashes on my tongue. "Fetch wine," I croaked at a passing manservant. "Quickly."

He trotted for the stairs. "Faster," I shouted after him. I heard his running steps on the treads.

Cassie

There's something going on—I can feel it, Lexsi sent to Zaria and me. *Like there's a heaviness in the air inside the keep.*

We'll be right there, Zaria replied. She and I were in different places, but she hauled me to the keep, regardless, where we landed in Lexsi's borrowed office.

Girls, Breanne sent to all of us, *the Ear says he can hear communication between the nanobots, and it's spreading from person to person. I doubt the trainees and servants are aware of the source of their unsettled feelings, but they're experiencing them anyway.*

What happened to the tainted meat? Lexsi asked after a moment's thought.

We destroyed it—wait. Do you suppose the bots were programmed to look for a cessation of the nanobot invasions? Breanne appeared beside us before the last of her mindspeech infiltrated our heads.

"I think that's very likely," Zaria breathed.

Outside Lexsi's office, someone shrieked, followed by another cry.

As if in tandem, Zaria and Breanne reacted at the same moment, the urgency of their mission clearly revealed in their frightened but determined expressions.

～

"This one isn't worth saving," Breanne shook her head at the frozen suicide before us. One of Zanfield's shirking servants had nearly sliced his head off with a fatally sharp kitchen knife.

His friend and fellow shirker who'd stopped, mid-shriek, stood nearby, horrified at what his friend had done. Raising her hand, Breanne released the suicide's particles, including the blood spray that hung ominously in midair.

All the keep, plus the training camp and the farms farther down the mountain had been placed in simultaneous stasis by Zaria and Breanne. It was the wise thing to do—we'd already heard a report from Travis, letting us know that seven others on the training grounds were stopped in the midst of their own attempt at self-destruction.

"Shall we take a look at Travis' troubles?" Zaria squared her shoulders.

"I'll transport," Breanne sighed.

～

Four out of the seven received the benefit of *Changing What Was*—two each by Zaria and Breanne. The other three had particles released while I stood by with Travis and Trent, hugging myself at this painful turn of events.

"I believe the nanobots were programmed to notice when the influx of new bots ceased," Randl folded in next to Travis. "I suppose they stepped up their communications from one body to the next, and a mass suicide was triggered."

"At least those two stopped it before it went any further," Trent nodded toward Bree and Zaria, who walked toward us after stabilizing the ones they'd saved.

"What if we've saved them for now, only to have them turn against their own world?" Travis snapped. "There's no doubt in my mind that once we take them back to Verillium, they'll fall under Ver'Dak's control and all this will be for nothing." He swept out a hand to illustrate his frustration.

"They're not dead, yet," I muttered, a wave of fierce protectiveness washing through me. "Now, it's up to us to find a way to help them."

"I worry that Barry and George won't be successful, and these things will find a way to circumvent our stasis," Zaria appeared pale as she and Breanne arrived to join our conversation.

"I've got a shield over everything," Bree said. "Let's leave them for now—there's nothing else we can do at the moment."

"Here," Lexsi skipped in, handing the journal she'd been reading to me. "I finished it last night. There's a kicker at the end, too—a few words written by the brother when the keep's First Mistress died."

"Thanks," I held the book to me, as if it would provide protection against my fears and worries. "I'll need the distraction, I think."

"Come on, then," Randl pulled me away. "Dori tells me dinner is almost ready. We can kick ideas around while we eat."

"Yeah." I let him transport me; I felt as if a cosmic rug had been pulled from beneath my feet, leaving me disoriented and tumbling in a vertiginous freefall.

Keela

"Nak and Pauly brought it to me—to see if it would help me with my training at the keep," I told Rade when he asked about my focus stone. "It helped, but only a little. Here in the black zone, I can do anything I want—nothing is holding me back. Iris says she'll explain that soon. I hope so, because I'm really curious about it."

"It's more than twice the size of the others," Hisan observed as I held my stone in a hand, looking at the intricate carving it bore.

"Maybe those two had no idea what a normal size would be. They knew about focus stones but may not have known much else."

"Well, you're the one who has to wear it," Rade teased.

"Greer says this is really hard stone and takes a special spell to carve and shape it," Hisan said.

"Nak doesn't lack for talent, as far as I've seen," I shrugged. "I wish he'd told me how he did this, though. The carving is so—delicate." Blowing out a breath, I slipped the stone beneath my tunic and patted it. At least I'd learned earlier how to tune it to my power. Tomorrow, Iris would show us how to place spells and power inside it, for use on another day.

$\sim$

Leare

"You don't have to answer if you don't want to, but can your hearing penetrate the black zone?" Cy asked. "I can't see through it."

"I don't want to even consider trying," I shifted uncomfortably. We kicked our heels inside a dimly-lit bar on Le-Ath Veronis after the keep and training grounds on Sirena were placed in stasis by the Mighty Heart.

"Sorry I asked, then."

"No worries." I held up my empty glass. The attentive bartender poured another double for me and set it on the bar.

"I hope all the missing ones are all right, then."

"Who knows?" I emptied this glass as quickly as the one before it. "Stop digging for information, all right?"

"I'm concerned," he sighed and turned away to stare at the wall of alcohol bottles lined up on shelves behind the bar. He signaled for the bartender this time. "You've worried about my ass in the past—too many times. I've gone looking for you several of those times, to pour my troubles into a sympathetic ear. No pun intended," he shoved a fresh glass of terribly expensive bourbon toward my waiting hand.

"Fancy finding you two here," the Voice joined us, taking a stool beside Cyrus'. "I'll have a glass of oxberry wine, please," she ordered.

"Leare is suffering, and he won't let me help," Cyrus complained. "To repay all those times he helped me."

"Honey," her voice fell into the southern smoothness she'd

mastered over many years as she spoke to me, "Don't you need to talk about it?"

"No," I shivered and shoved my stool away from the bar. "No, thank you." Before they could attempt to stop me, I folded away. My suffering was my own to deal with, and I didn't feel the need to share that pain.

With anyone.

~

Cjerl's Palace, Sorvus
Tekar

The plot was too simple—*why hadn't I thought of it before?*

"You're drinking, Tekar?" Cjerl found me in the library, working on my second bottle of wine.

"Yes. It's a fine vintage, my King. Want to join me?"

"Of course," Cjerl took a seat and waited expectantly while I rose to fetch a glass. The idea hit me while I'd had my second glass of wine inside my chambers; therefore I'd ordered a third bottle, puttered about my suite for a few moments, then carried my bottles to the library, just outside Cjerl's royal suite.

"This smells wonderful," Cjerl sniffed the delicate aroma before drinking.

"I asked for the best your sommelier could find, when I realized we hadn't celebrated your victory over Vorus."

"And so we haven't," Cjerl grinned and sipped more wine. "Why have I not had this vintage before?" he muttered. "It's divine." He emptied his glass and held it out for me to pour again.

I obliged him quickly and kept pouring until he'd emptied the entire bottle and fell asleep on the comfortable sofa.

"Don't disturb the King; he's sleeping," I warned a servant as I left the library and strode toward my own chamber. Soon enough, the poison would do its work and I intended to be far away when the body was discovered.

～

Cassie

Iris was the keep's Warden far in the past, and she'd written the journal I held in my hand. I'd drawn in a breath as she described the first controllers employed in both kingdoms, although Sorvus wasn't as draconian as Vorus became.

Most of that was due to Sorvus' King at the time of the device's introduction; he refused to allow them to be used at all during his reign.

Iris never explained why King Nele refused the use of the blasted things; he outlawed them during his reign. He'd faced a great deal of pressure over it, too, and never wavered in his stance.

It gave me a new respect for Sorvus that I hadn't had before; Cjerl had prejudiced me against his country because he'd fallen right in line with anything Ver'Dak wanted, including the complete destruction of Vorus.

Nele has done the right thing, and I managed to get a message to him, Iris wrote in a passage. *He replied through the same messenger, and it was a blessing to read his words. He sounded much as he did in the past, and it soothed my heart.*

I gasped—she knew King Nele!

How had she known him? Her familiarity made me think they'd perhaps grown up together, although I couldn't say why I had that idea. I found myself wishing I could read the messages they'd sent to one another, but that was an impossibility.

Or—was it?

I disliked bending time—and always let someone else do it for me if possible. This—did I want to do this on my own? Could I presume to enlist help?

Randl? I sent before I lost my nerve.

Cassie?

I ah, have a question, I told him.

～

Randl humored me, mostly to provide a distraction, I think.

Until we found ourselves in split time as Keep Mistress Iris read the message she'd received from King Nele.

That's when Randl grabbed my wrist and drew in an audible breath.

Come, he sent the command to me, and hauled me into another split time scenario. In this one, Prince Nele glared at his father, King Ralen, whose arms were crossed in anger as he sat behind a desk in his private study.

Randl didn't release his grip on my wrist as the scene played out before us.

"It's decided, and that's that," Ralen snapped at Nele.

"This is your daughter—my sister, you're consigning to slavery," Nele didn't hold his anger in check.

"She's been too headstrong all her life," Ralen pounded a fist on his desk. "She has to marry well, and I'm betrothing her to Lord Brell's oldest son—I don't give a sun-mote about what she, you or your mother think," Ralen ground out.

"She's eleven," Nele tried a different tack.

"She'll be twelve tomorrow," Ralen thundered. "Leave me now, or I'll choose another heir."

Randl still held onto me as we followed Nele from Ralen's study. It was a good thing; I'd forgotten to breathe after Ralen's last statement.

Ajania's journal had ended abruptly the day before her twelfth birthday. My first breath was painful, followed by another as Randl hauled us into the Queen's chambers, right behind Nele.

"He intends to go forward with his plan, mother," Nele sounded breathless after shutting the door behind him.

"Then we have to get her out of here," Queen Lael whispered. "Come on, help me. I have someone waiting at the gate to take her if we can gather a few things together, first."

"I'll do anything to stop this madness," Nele replied resolutely. "He may as well kill her as do this."

"I agree," Lael turned toward her eldest son. "There is something you must know, my son. Without Ajania, whole and free, Verillium—all of it—will perish. I know this."

"I feel it, too, Mother."

"You, Ajania and I—we have this gift from your grandmother. We will not scoff at what has been given us, child. It will be passed on through both of you, I swear it."

While she spoke, Lael shoved folded clothing into a rough, cloth bag, but hesitated to pull the strings to close it.

"One last thing," she sighed, and from beneath her dress she pulled what appeared to be an amber necklace on a fine chain. "I have already passed my blessing for Ajania into this," she shoved the necklace into the bag and tied it up. "It is up to her to use it wisely."

"When I am King," Nele's hands curled into tight fists.

"You must stay alive to become King," Lael warned him. "Go, now. You must not know the how of what comes next. Your father can smell a lie, my son."

"Mother," Nele begged.

"Go. Perhaps when you are King, you will be able to find her again. Until then," Lael leaned forward and kissed her son's cheek. "Be well and live justly, my Prince."

Oh, no. I realized then that Lael was forfeiting her life at her own husband's hands to save her daughter. *Please*, I begged, *let Ajania survive.*

We must go back, now, Randl's sending interrupted my silent prayer.

But, I argued.

He pulled me away without a backward glance.

CHAPTER EIGHTEEN

*C*assie

"Is the name Ajania mentioned anywhere in Iris' journal?" I asked Lexsi. She'd read it all, and I was too afraid to read farther than I had already.

"That name isn't anywhere in the journal," Lexsi shook her head. I'd found her in Randl's kitchen with Susan and Fes Desh, where they were calming themselves by cooking.

"This is awful," I muttered. No wonder Randl hauled me back and dumped me in my room before going off on his own. He knew what I was already suspecting—that Lael and Ajania were both killed by Nele's father, King Ralen.

Either that, or he'd placed a controller on both, and they'd lived the rest of the lives as slaves.

"Damn," I muttered, angry at the injustices visited on Verillium by Ver'Dak and his ilk. "Fucking, twisted asshat."

"Huh?" Lexsi looked up from the batter she was mixing.

"Calling Ver'Dak names," I shrugged.

"I've done that," Susan formed round, unbaked rolls in her hands and set them on a pan for baking.

"I think we've all done that," Fes agreed. "Want to taste this salad dressing? I used oxberry wine to make it."

"That sounds great, Uncle Fes," Lexsi grinned at him.

"Look, I'm out of sorts right now," I admitted. "What can I do here to help besides tasting salad dressing?"

"Ooh, you can mix the butter and herb spread for the rib roast," Lexsi said.

"And then we'll let you get your hands messy spreading it all over the meat," Susan added.

"Sounds like fun," I said and went to find an apron.

~

Randl's Study
Zaria

"I think King Nele was the prophet who warned against leaving the palace in Sorvus," Randl said.

"What makes you say that? We couldn't find anything in any of the writings of the time—either about that or the black zone," I told him.

"I may have gone into split time," he confessed.

"Nothing wrong with that—where and when?"

"Back when Nele was still a Prince. It's hard to explain, but while I watched him during a rather—emotional moment, let's say, the idea came to him and I felt the echo. A short time after that, I went into another split time—when he was King."

"And?"

"I don't know why I felt it when nobody else could—especially the powerful. It's there, though. The walls themselves warn anyone descended from Nele not to leave the palace."

"Huh?" I sat up straighter and gaped at Randl.

"I think I can link with you if we go back there now," Randl said. "So you can feel it for yourself."

"Yeah. Let's go," I rose quickly from my chair in Randl's study.

~

I suppose we landed in Cjerl's library because Sorvis' King didn't read and wouldn't be there.

Except he was.

Worse than that—he'd been poisoned. He sat on a sofa, his head lolling to one side while his breaths came slower and fewer. In minutes, he'd be dead.

Gulsit, Randl named the poison coursing through Cjerl's body as he knelt beside the King. *Slow acting,* he added what I already knew. *This is bad, I think. If there's not a ruling heir on either throne,* he didn't finish.

What are you talking about?

Here. He held out a hand for me to take.

Was it because of his original ancestry, perhaps?

For whatever reason, he could sense the echo, where I hadn't been aware of it at all.

Designed that way, my instincts told me.

Visions flashed through my mind as Randl connected me to the spell soaking the walls of Cjerl's palace.

A warning, that should the royal heir die or leave the palace, it would become vulnerable.

I drew in a breath when Ver'Dak's image accompanied that warning.

How?

How had Nele known what Ver'Dak looked like?

I believe he had help, Randl responded to my unasked question.

From whom?

No idea.

Do you think the same warning was given to the royals in Vorus?

One way to find out.

What about Cjerl?

Can we delay the death?

I can, I hedged.

Then do it. We'll go to Vorus in the past. I think I know just when to go.

When would that be?

When Keela—Jessil—was still there.

Fucking hells, I sighed and allowed Randl to split time.

I hadn't seen Nessil before. If Lissa had been here, she'd have know right away that he wasn't Jessil's full brother. The mother, who'd been controlled, had borne both children. The father? Nessil wasn't the King's son.

Who knew what Lord or hanger-on had raped a controlled Queen? I had no desire to delve that far into Nessil's ancestry.

Jessil was the King's daughter, no doubt about that, however.

The King has just died and Nessil is taking over before the corpse is cold, Randl pointed out. Jessil faded from the King's chamber as Nessil and Verlin swept in. Randl gripped my hand.

I felt it as he felt it—the command emanating from the walls— adamantly insisting that the royal heir shouldn't leave the palace under any circumstances.

No wonder Jessil hid in the palace kitchen until Verlin caught up with her. She'd heeded the message. Nessil never got it in the first place.

Fucking hells, I repeated. *Can you tell what will happen if Cjerl dies? What's the curse, or whatever it is?*

It conveniently doesn't say, Randl replied.

So, then, what do we do? Do we let asshole Cjerl die and see what happens, or hold onto his life and try to figure this out? I asked.

Ajania's mother said the girl was the key to saving Verillium, and she probably died when her mother did.

You don't know for sure?

I never saw the girl. I only saw her mother, and her death was a sure thing. Randl was disturbed by that, I could tell. *Cassie was really upset about it, so I hauled her away from Sorvus before we saw the assassinations with our own eyes.*

Cassie was with you? Before?

She wanted to go and asked if I could take her.

Fucking hells. Let's go—I've seen enough here.

~

Cassie

"I know you don't want to go back there, but we need information," Zaria and Randl appeared in the kitchen while I was rubbing a butter-herb mixture all over a large rib roast. Two more waited for the same treatment; we expected quite a crowd for dinner.

"Go back where?" I began before I caught the guilty look on Randl's face. "Let me clean my hands," I said, turning toward the sink.

"No time," Zaria said, and cleaned my hands with power. "We'll be back," she told Lexsi and the others before hauling me to Verillium's bloody past.

~

I wasn't wrong about the bloody part; Queen Lael was already dead, her bleeding body lying on rough, cobbled stones in a narrow alley outside Sorvus' palace. The King and one of his guards were now threatening a swordsman, who held a frightened girl behind him with one hand while fending off the guard's attack with his own blade in the other.

"Stand back, or I'll kill you both," the swordsman snarled, while Ajania wept behind him.

"You're kidnapping the princess," the guard growled.

"I'm taking her to safety after you killed her mother. Do you think the King won't order you to do the unthinkable to the girl, too?"

Something about the swordsman felt familiar. Perhaps Zaria felt it, too, as she gripped my arm tightly and Randl kept us shielded from sight.

"Don't listen to him," King Ralen hissed. "The girl must stay here. She is mine to do with as I please. Now, kill this bastard. I have better things to do with my time."

"Try," the swordsman sharpened his stance, waiting for the guard's attack.

"Just as your lady wife's life was yours as well?" The guard stepped aside and glared at the King. "My father came to the castle as her guard, from her father's estate. I will not commit another murder for you, Ralen."

"At least someone has some sense," the swordsman muttered.

"Take the girl, I'll deal with this," the guard nodded to the swordsman. "Leave now." He placed the tip of his blade against the throat of the protesting King. "Nele will make a good King, methinks," he said, while the swordsman lifted Ajania in his arms and flung her onto a waiting horse, followed by the bag of clothing and such the Queen had packed for her.

Then, leaping astride the horse and holding Ajania before him, he kicked the horse into a gallop. The moment he was away, the guard stabbed Ralen in the heart, then placed the blade beside Ralen's hand. Pulling a dagger from his boot, he set it in Lael's bloody, outstretched hand.

Then, after composing himself, he shouted out the news and other guards came running.

"So. Ajania survived. But where was she taken?" Zaria now paced inside Randl's kitchen while I slathered herbed butter on two more rib roasts. "We have to decide about Cjerl's fate and fast—we can't leave him in limbo forever."

"Are you thinking that with Ajania's escape, there may be a royal heir somewhere?" Randl asked.

"No idea," Zaria grumbled. "But if something terrible will happen if Cjerl dies, then we need to know, don't you think? He's not worth saving, and we all know that."

"Here," Fes held a glass of wine out to Zaria, before pouring two more for Randl and me.

"Does it matter that we know where Vorus' heir is? If we can get Keela out of the black zone?" I asked.

"But that still leaves Sorvus," Randl observed. "Both warn against the heir leaving, or something terrible will happen. Jessil—Keela—was forced to leave, and now there's no palace to return to. What if Cjerl's life is all that's holding Verillium together at this point?"

"This sucks, no matter how you look at it," Zaria set her wineglass down and went back to pacing.

"Daughter, you can't keep Cjerl alive," Wisdom arrived to offer Zaria advice. "Perhaps this is for the best—if the planet dies, Ver'Dak loses what he's trying to gain. This is a setback, yes, but you can continue the hunt elsewhere. He doesn't have the ability to *Change What Was*, dear one. Only you and your mother—and your sister, it appears—have that talent."

He turned to look at me briefly before focusing on Zaria again.

"It's hard to swallow, but his point is made," Randl sighed. "All those here on Sirena—they're infected with those fucking nanobots. Everybody on Verillium is infected, too. Even if Barry and George find a way to save those here, the ones on Verillium will still be just as affected and willing to follow Ver'Dak's slightest whim. Perhaps this is what the curse was designed to do—destroy everything before it could be taken and used for a terrible purpose. After all, we saw Ver'Dak's image as clear as day in Cjerl's palace spell."

"We did," Zaria's shoulders drooped. "This—this is worse than I ever imagined it could be."

"Then let it go, Daughter," Wisdom stepped forward and gripped Zaria's hands in his. "Ver'Dak loses, no matter how you look at this, if Verillium truly is set to self-destruct."

"And if it isn't?" I snapped before I could stop myself.

"Then the war continues, does it not?"

"I feel the uncertainty in all this," Randl said. "That if Cjerl dies, then nothing about Verillium will ever be the same."

"I get that feeling, too," Zaria hung her head.

What about Ajania's heirs? The thought rang through my mind like a bell. I'd gotten so involved with her—and with others in the past. Iris

266

was also someone I'd come to like—through her writings. Surely, there were still people on Verillium who were worth saving. "What about those in the black zone?" I whispered.

"They are beyond our help, I think," Wisdom answered. "If any still live."

"And so, with a wave of our hand, we dismiss an entire world," I quavered, folding away before the tears fell.

Nil'Dek Third-born

"Yes, you have done well," Ver'Dak Second-born gloated. "I can feel the slowing of Cjerl's heartbeat. In a moment or two, I will have complete control." His features reassembled themselves into a grotesque grin. He only did this to frighten those he spoke with, and Tekar was certainly frightened.

"But," Tekar ventured to argue.

"You worry about your elevated place on Verillium?" Ver'Dak laughed. "You were never intended to have one. Have you not paid attention? I care not about anyone on your forsaken planet. Verillium's cache of precious copelis is what I'm after. Your life and that of your fellows means nothing to me."

Tekar's humanoid mouth hung open; his sludge-like brain struggled to process Second-born's words.

Third-born? Ver'Dak sent as his head dipped in Tekar's direction.

Without hesitation, I pulled my ranos pistol from its holster and disintegrated Cjerl's treasonous Prime Minister.

"Just in time, too," Ver'Dak noted. "Cjerl is dead. Shall we?"

"I will call for Fourth and Eighth-born immediately," I bowed to Ver'Dak. "The day is yours, Second-born."

Cassie

I sniffed while staring down the mountain from the keep's highest tower. Would everyone inside it, plus those in stasis at the training camp be allowed to die—as Verillium was about to die?

Cassie? A tentative sending.

From far, far away.

Huh? I couldn't marshal my thoughts fast enough to supply a better response.

Ver'Dak's feet just landed on Verillium. Iris says we could use your help—if you're willing to come.

My breath caught as visions entered my head. Ver'Dak and three others of his kind stood roughly one hundred yards from the black zone. The visions also instructed me on what was needed.

I was more than willing to provide a short distraction for Ver'Dak, but what the hell was he planning to do? Did he know Keela and the others were inside the black zone? I didn't finish that thought. *I'm on the way*, I shouted as I folded space.

A grand entrance was called for, and I went at it full-tilt, landing my larger Thifilatha between Ver'Dak and the black zone like a meteor striking the ground and shaking it with my impact. When the dust and debris settled, I roared and burst into flames, my wings fully extended and dripping fire.

"Come no farther," I shouted, coaxing my flames higher and hotter.

"Think you to stop me this time?" Ver'Dak challenged. "I have armored myself against you, Demon Witch." Raising his arms, his entire army, plus his wizards, appeared at his back.

He'd meant to distract me, and his ploy worked; once I'd focused on him and his brothers again, they were armored in shining, deepest black.

What the hell were they wearing?

"Go ahead, try to burn us now," Ver'Dak laughed. "I assure you, we will be protected."

Don't try, it's spell-glass, designed by Liron himself, a voice informed me. *It's what he used to form Avii Castle and it's indestructible.*

A man appeared at my left, far enough that my flames wouldn't affect him.

I recognized him now—and in the past.

Leare.

How and why? I began.

He's the Ear, another man landed beside Leare. *I am Cyrus, the Eye.*

"And I am the Voice," a woman now stood beside Cyrus. Something about both seemed familiar, but there wasn't time to dwell on those things.

"I thought you weren't allowed to directly interfere," Denevik appeared, with Zarigar beside him.

"When did that ever stop them before?"

My father, the god of war, had come.

"What the bloody hell is going on?" Zaria arrived, hauling Randl in with her.

"Enough!" Ver'Dak shouted. "This world is mine. I don't care who or what you are, get out of my way or die."

Thank you—that's all the time I needed to explain things to Jessil, a woman's voice informed me. *Although it wounds my heart to see Leare so close and never be able to touch him again. If you are true, you will be safe.*

And those who aren't?

They will die.

Then, everything went dark—and the storm came.

Keela

The storm is yours to control, Iris told me.

Now, with tears forming and drying in the space of a nanosecond, I roared my pain and anger against every living thing on Verillium, including the children of gods.

Only those who bore a certain light in their souls were allowed to live. I did it without thought, as centuries of powerful spirits flowed through me and poured from my fingertips, magnified by the ability ceded to me by my ancestors and their colleagues.

Screams of pain I ignored as I rolled with the force of the black zone all about me—this wasn't the time to cease my efforts. I wouldn't —couldn't—stop, until I'd covered the entire surface with the power and darkness built over centuries inside that murky barrier.

Only when I was done would I come back to survey the damage.

And the deaths.

Why hadn't I been more curious?

Why had I blithely gone about my recent days, thinking all was as it seemed on the surface, and that life would go on as I perceived it?

Why?

Somehow, the clairvoyance I'd been blessed with had been muted, and I hadn't guessed—likely by design.

No outside spells or power worked within the black zone, and I was intent on covering every inch of Verillium with that force. Abandoned babies cried; I could hear them. Children screamed as their parents disintegrated. Soldiers were reduced to nothing, along with the nanobots invading their blood.

Controllers?

I destroyed each one I encountered.

I *was* the black zone. No longer corporeal, I increased my might to engulf the planet. The power within the black zone was bequeathed to me, whether I wanted it or not.

Have no mercy, it whispered.

Take no prisoners.

Avenge the innocent.

I screamed in anger and compelled the black zone to rush over lands and waters alike; more swiftly than any machine could travel.

Destruction lay in my wake.

My name is Death, I whispered as villages fell.

~

Pauly

Nak's hands gripped my shoulders as we watched what Keela had become—a darkness enveloping the entire world of Verillium. Standing on the observation deck of BlackWing XII, our hearts beating painfully, we couldn't force ourselves to look away from the annihilation.

Nobody could have seen this—or predicted it—this black cloud that swept east to west, changing or destroying all in its path.

Nobody we knew could have seen this, anyway. Had my mind been working properly, I'd attempt to work out how it was even possible. This kind of power—I'd only heard tales of it in the hands of the most powerful. Seeing this went against anything I'd ever learned.

Even attempting to get messages through to Randl and Cassie failed; we'd already tried.

Several times.

Whatever the black zone was or had been, we had no explanation for it. Keela—our Keela—commanded it now, and our hearts would never be the same.

~

Leare

I never wanted to be here—not while this was happening.

Until I understood that it was inevitable.

I'd made an agreement in the past, and now the final payment had come due. Had I failed to read the fine print, as the saying went on old Earth?

Fury, like the winds of a hurricane, churned so swiftly about me that I couldn't see. The screams within that raging emotion forced me to shut my ears against it; it only spoke of anger, retaliation and death.

I cowered before the storm, making myself as small a target as possible. Without the ability to send mindspeech or reach out to the others, I had no idea whether I was alone in my distress, or if they were also locked in a battle for survival.

Ver'Dak wore impenetrable armor; he'd planned in advance for a war of some kind with the powerful among us. Was Liron's spell-glass protecting him in this assault? Would Ver'Dak and his brothers be among the few left standing at the end, to gloat over their victory?

I had no way to tell.

Cassie

I huddled into myself as the black zone's storm railed about me, whipping sand, dirt and debris against my Fire Demon's body. Zaria, in Larentii form, managed to grasp my hand; I knew it was her the moment our fingers linked. *She will listen to you,* Zaria told me, her mindspeech coming through her touch rather than her mind.

It was the only way to communicate during Keela's storm, I learned.

But I can't touch her, I pointed out, gripping Zaria's hand tighter.

You are *touching her. She has become the black zone,* my half-sister informed me. *She is the storm and howls about us, now. Only she will know Ver'Dak's status; we cannot see or feel him out.*

What can we do if his armor protects him, still?

I have a plan. We must see if Keela will listen.

Zaria sent words and images—of what would and wouldn't be should Ver'Dak survive. *We have to try,* she added at the end.

What she'd suggested could cost us everything, but then everything would be lost anyway if we failed.

We have to try, I echoed Zaria's sending. Gathering my courage, I relayed the message.

Keela? I sent, as her hurricane-force winds buffeted my body. *Tell me, do Ver'Dak and his brothers still live?*

Moments passed that felt like hours.

Would she answer?

They live, she replied, her sending filled with pain. *The armor,* she didn't finish.

Zaria and I, I began.

I know what you offer, she interrupted. *Are you sure? We could fail and die in the attempt.*

We know. We offer anyway. I sent her the images that Zaria had sent to me, so she'd understand the mission.

As do I, Randl joined our silent conversation.

I—see, she replied. *Prepare yourselves.*

Now!

Nil'Dek Third-born

The four of us—Second-born, Fourth-Born, Eighth-born and I, knelt together, our armored bodies dividing the winds of the storm as if it were nothing more than a breezy day. Liron-father's spell-glass armor was a creation of genius, and Second-born had worked many, many sun-turns to bend it to his will.

Liron-father had left the secret to shaping it with Ver'Dak, and that choice had been made with the utmost wisdom and care. Among us, Second-born was the crafty scientist, who learned far more quickly than Je'Dik ever did. What Ver'Dak had done to combat those we faced was nothing short of brilliant.

We need only wait for this one to expend all her energy, and then we will rise and strike her and the others down, Ver'Dak's comm, hidden within the spell-glass, informed us.

Was that a hesitation I felt in the storm? Yo'Dok Eighth-Born, asked.

She is tiring, Ver'Dak spoke with glee. *It will be soon, my brothers. Very soon.*

Keela

Exhaustion came. I'd used up everything I had—and that which had been given to me by all the others within the black zone.

Hold on, Cassie relayed to me.

I—can't, I struggled to return the message. *Ver'Dak and his brothers are still there, waiting.*

Gloating.

Admitting defeat wasn't something I intended to do, however; I would empty myself and die by my own choice, rather than allow these waiting filth to hand me my death.

We need more time, Zaria, Cassie's sister, begged.

You will have it.

I knew that voice.

I'd listened raptly through many of his lectures.

What was Master Leare doing inside my head?

I will explain later, he informed me. *My colleagues and I—we will keep your storm alive. Bear with us, I beg you, and treat the strength you receive as your own.*

Two things occurred then, simultaneously.

Ver'Daks' words, meant to be silently exchanged with his brothers, were transmitted clearly to my ears. *Time to rise and take them*, he ordered.

Through the blackness of my storm, even, I could see all four clearly as they rose from a kneeling position, their spell-glass armor untouched by everything I'd thrown at it. Not a single scratch marred those shining, perfect surfaces.

We only have a few moments, another voice, female and one I didn't recognize, observed.

Then we must put our talents together, Zaria noted. *If we are to survive this*, she added, as the four we faced pulled strange weapons from carriers at their backs and positioned them to kill us once my storm died.

Except…

Strength surged through me, the likes of which I'd never hoped to contain or control. I screamed from the pain of it, my shriek causing Ver'Dak and his brothers to cower.

Now, someone shouted.

And everything died.

CHAPTER NINETEEN

*C*assie
       Split-time created an eye within the storm. *I can only hold this for so long*, Randl said. *Hurry.*

I can only Change What Was *for the tiniest of spaces*, Zaria followed Randl's instruction with one of her own.

Keela, you must use your force to push me through that space, I took up the conversation.

And this must all happen in the blink of an eye, an unrecognized male voice advised. *Those weapons they hold are no ordinary weapons.*

What are they?

God-killers. Ver'Dak has been waiting for this moment for a very long time.

We had no time to carry on with this conversation. *Zaria*, I cried out.

I've got this, she said.

Somehow, Keela and I had been reduced to the size of the smallest filament, as Zaria employed her gift of *Changing What Was* to cut a hole through Randl's split-time stillness.

Until we reached Ver'Dak.

She was correct; we had to destroy him first, even if his brothers killed us afterward. He was the intelligence behind this operation, and terrifyingly adept at out-thinking us.

He'd done very well so far, it appeared.

There are nanobots inside that armor, Randl whispered to us. *Programmed to carry on, even if the armor's wearer dies.*

Ver'Dak.

He'd considered every fucking angle in this and screwed us all.

Let's do this, Zaria snapped.

We were committed, now, and there was no turning back.

Leare

I tuned my ears to hear Cassie, Zaria, Keela and Randl, while feeding my strength to Keela's storm, keeping it alive with help from Cyrus and Conner. Until Hank Bell, Cassie's father, joined his power to ours.

Smaller than that, Zaria instructed, as she and the others attempted to find a way past the spell-armor.

Find the time before it was what it is, Cyrus suggested. He, too, was watching—and listening—through me.

There was a moment's hesitation before Zaria replied. *On it*, she told us.

Keela

What's happening? I cried out when things went from lethal to worse than lethal. Caught as I was in Randl's split-time, I could only watch in horror as reality splintered and I saw two separate timelines butted against one another.

Who? Cassie asked as the tall man entered the timeline on the left. *Ah*, she said as he formed a dark glass ball in his hands and tossed the finished item onto a growing pile of other glass balls.

Except these glass balls didn't break.

Didn't splinter or scar, either, after hitting one another very hard indeed.

Spell-glass, Randl's voice breathed in my mind.

How can we sort the spell-glass given to Ver'Dak from all the rest? Cassie cried out. *We're doomed.*

Didn't you say there are nanobots in the spell-glass? I asked.

There are, Zaria replied absently.

What is she doing? I asked Cassie.

Sorting through the metal library, looking for the proper spell-glass, Cassie informed me.

This is taking too long, Zaria wept.

What if we can take control of the nanobots?

We can't—we already tried that with Nettle, Randl flung at me.

But what if there's a way?

You know a way? I'm listening, Zaria sobbed. *I can't find it—the information isn't here.*

I've already destroyed nanobots all across Verillium, I told her. *I finally figured out how they're different.*

Different how? Randl asked.

They all contain a tiny amount of copelis. It's how Ver'Dak can control them—he placed part of his power and information in them. That's why the spell-armor will carry on without him. Enough of him is in that armor to do it.

How do we control the copelis, then? Cassie demanded.

The same way the black zone is controlled, I sent a mental shrug with my words. *It's the reason I was born, oddly enough.*

The storm is dying, Leare shouted at us. *We've given you everything we have.*

No time, I breathed and reached out with everything I had left.

Leare

Like shutting a window against a hard rain, everything stopped suddenly. There we stood, on the Eastern Plains of Vorus, where every blade of grass, tree, shrub and weed had been scoured away by a storm so powerful few could stand against it.

Ver'Dak and three of his brothers slowly stood from their kneeling position and pulled weapons into their hands.

Those weapons—had he perfected something strong enough to take even the shining ones down?

We were about to find out.

I could only imagine that Keela and the others had perished in their attempt to get past the spell-armor; they were nowhere to be seen. I hadn't heard them cry out, either, so their deaths must have been instantaneous.

"Now, you die," Ver'Dak's voice taunted.

Get away, I warned the others. "Go ahead," I said aloud. "I have nothing left to live for."

We're staying, Hank Bell's gruff voice sounded in my brain. *That's my daughter he's murdered.*

My mother and my mate are in there, Zarigar echoed. *I stand here. If those two were dead, the Three would surely be here by now.*

A small amount of hope sparked in my soul at Zarigar's words. Ver'Dak and his brothers leveled their weapons at us, the guns thunking into glass-armored hands before the half-Krelk aimed. "Kill all but the Larentii," Ver'Dak growled.

At least he knew not to kill a Larentii—that truly would bring —*the One*.

"Fire," Ver'Dak shouted.

Triggers attuned to individual Krelk life signatures were pressed. I refused to close my eyes while waiting for my death.

And that's when it happened.

Nothing.

Nothing happened. Triggers were pressed again and again, with the same results. Ver'Dak cursed fluently in the Krelk language.

"Problem?" Zarigar crossed arms over his chest. I knew why he didn't turn each one of our assailants into sparks; ours were still in there somewhere, either trying to take them down or destroy their armor.

Or trying to get out.

That troubled me more than anything.

Shut your ears, Zarigar told the rest of us.

Obediently, I cut off all sound.

What's he doing? Cyrus asked as Zarigar continued to stand there. To us, nothing appeared to be happening.

He's trilling, Conner interjected. She'd know—she was mated to two Larentii and had given birth to two others.

Huh? Cyrus sounded confused, until one of Ver'Dak's brothers slumped to the ground, asleep.

One by one, the other three followed, with Ver'Dak going down last of all.

"We have to get them away from this filth, before they die or Ver'Dak wakes," Zarigar rushed forward. "He'll destroy the planet, next, if his weapons won't work."

Keela? I sent, striding quickly behind Zarigar.

Almost finished, she replied. *Give me one more moment.*

He's waking, Conner shouted as Ver'Dak stirred.

Eliagar

Zak pushed his breakfast sausages about his plate, refusing to eat.

"What troubles you, child?" I implored.

"I had another dream," he murmured.

"What dream was that?"

"Lironik," Zak shivered and hugged himself.

"Lironik?" I asked as gently as I could, although the word filled me with dread.

"The hiding place. They took me there, once. Ver'Dak said I wasn't smart enough to be placed in a wall." His breaths were ragged and filled with pain.

"What do you remember about Lironik? Is it a planet?"

"No. I think—now that I've read books and seen pictures, that it's a ship. In space. Ver'Dak said it was the final solution, if all else failed."

Zarigar, I sent terrified mindspeech. *Ver'Dak has a gunship!*

Queen's Palace, Le-Ath Veronis
Lissa

"A gunship? Where in the nine levels," Gavin shouted.

"No idea. Let's go." Drawing Gavin, Drake, Drew and Rigo into my wake, I folded space to BlackWing XII. If Ver'Dak had a gunship aimed at Verillium, then it had to be orbiting the planet, or close enough to destroy it.

Visions of ranos cannons or something worse raced through my mind as I found Pauly and Nak holding one another on BlackWing XII's bridge.

"Pauly," I snapped. "We need your talent. A gunship with power is out there somewhere, I just know it."

"What?"

I blinked—he and Nak were weeping, but Pauly answered anyway. "We need your help, honey," I said gently. "Now, before Ver'Dak's gunship destroys the entire planet."

"Can you detect the power? There has to be somebody on board who has it," Nak wiped wetness from his cheeks.

Pauly sat down hard on the navigator's chair. "Let me put out feelers," he said. "Nak, can you assist?"

"Here. Take what you need," Nak held out a hand. Pauly grasped Nak's fingers while his eyes lost focus.

Cassie

What's happening? Zaria demanded as the armor's pieces began to move apart on their own.

Burn it, burn it! Keela's shout filled my mind.

Without thinking, I released a conflagration.

Lissa

There! See it? Pauly sent a visual along with his shout.

The ship was there all right, cloaked in far too many shields and preparing to fire. The moment I gathered power to destroy it, the ranos cannon fired the blast to kill Verillium.

The scream of rage I heard turned out to be my own.

Zarigar

Fire bloomed about Ver'Dak, while his brothers pressed triggers on their weapons.

Incoming, Queen Lissa shouted in my head, while revealing the image of a ranos cannon's blast.

Mother, I found myself shouting mentally, attempting to warn her and the others.

Everything stopped.

Only one who stood with us held that ability.

The Eye.

I hear them; hold on, said the Ear.

I am holding their souls to their bodies, the Voice cried out.

What's happening? Lissa demanded.

Everything is frozen, I replied. *Except*, I sent her mental images.

Oh, dear heaven, Lissa whimpered.

You can let it go now, Keela's voice echoed in our minds.

Leare

Cyrus released everything.

Ver'Dak was immediately engulfed by fire. His brothers, still in the act of firing, were quite surprised when their weapons exploded in their hands.

Then they, too, began to burn while still trapped within their armor, their screams muted by the spell glass.

What about the ranos, Zarigar shouted to Lissa, who shrieked in all our minds.

She and those with her on BlackWing XII had been blown a lightyear away when the ranos cannon blast ricocheted off Verillium's atmosphere and hit the gunship that fired it to begin with.

Get ready; the armor will carry on with Ver'Dak's orders, Zarigar shouted.

No, Cyrus replied calmly. *Look. See for yourself.*

Zarigar

The armor was now a black pool of slag glass surrounding four grotesque skeletons. Where were they? Mother and those with her?

Mother? I sent.

There was no reply.

"Filth," Leare shouted as he strode forward, weeping. "Bloody, fucking filth," he added as he lifted a booted foot and crushed Ver'Dak's fire-bleached skull. The rest of Ver'Dak's bones were similarly crushed while I watched, until Lissa and four of her mates appeared beside me.

"Where are they?" Lissa's face was tear-streaked as she looked up at me.

"I don't know." I found that I, too, was weeping.

"Do you feel it?" The Voice approached, her arms open to embrace Lissa. "It's—impossible."

"What is impossible?" I wiped tears away.

"They're all entwined, now. I don't know if they'll ever separate."

"Entwined?" Lissa pulled away.

"They've become the black zone." The Ear, leaning on the Eye, approached. "I didn't know this could happen. I—don't know if it can be undone."

"Where are their bodies? It *can* be undone," my grandmother, the Mighty Heart, appeared. "It *must* be undone."

"Bodies were subsumed by the black zone," Leare said wearily. "It's all one, now."

Hank Bell, who had remained silent until now, turned full Thifilathi, threw back his head and roared in grief. Denevik arrived and did the same.

Next came Pauly and Nak, holding one another up, their grief evident in faces and posture.

"Where is Randl?" Dori arrived with several others, looking as if she were about to crumble. "He doesn't answer mindspeech."

"Oh, honey," Lissa stumbled toward her and wrapped her in a tight embrace.

"Gone?" Tamp now stood below me, searching my face for something I couldn't give him.

"We cannot reach them. The Ear believes they are transformed into the black zone. They are no longer reachable."

"Where is the black zone now? It was here," Travis arrived with Trent. "If they *are* the black zone, where is it?"

"Circling the planet," Nefrigar appeared. "Zarigar, come with me. The Larentii homeworld is in mourning. Afterward, we have many questions to ask."

"Of whom?"

The Ear, he sent. *Come now. Come with me.*

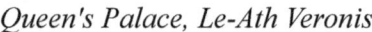

Queen's Palace, Le-Ath Veronis
Lissa

Once we left Verillium, nobody could get back on the planet. Every time an attempt was made, we were turned back. The black zone truly surrounded that entire world, and even the powerful couldn't get past that barrier. Six months had passed, and we were coming to grips with the idea that they wouldn't come walking through the door, or just show up because they felt like it or needed help.

We couldn't mourn properly since we had no idea how or what to mourn. I found tears on my face often, without realizing I'd been crying. Nefrigar sent a message, telling me we needed to speak with the Ear, but that he couldn't be reached as yet.

I had no idea what Nefrigar hoped to learn from that particular Shining One, but he believed there was something noteworthy in his knowledge of Verillium. I waited to hear what it was.

Yes, four of Liron's half-Krelk offspring were killed on Verillium, but the cost was too dear to the rest of us. Those we'd lost were the ones on the front lines of that battle, and there were still seven half-Krelk brothers out there, with nobody to carry on the fight.

As for what this whole battle for Verillium was over—the copelis quartzite—all traces of it were now missing from Verillium. That was verified by Nari and Tiri, whose talent for searching had yielded those results.

If the last act of Zaria, Cassie, Randl and Keela had been to remove what Liron's children wanted from that world, then it was probably for the best. That was one thing we'd learned from all the research on the nanobots; all of them carried copelis within them; it allowed them to store the memory and ability to move a constructed body on their own.

As for the trainees infected with nanobots on Sirena, they were still there—in stasis. Zaria had done that and for now, we were waiting for George and Barry to finish their counter-weapons—to free those souls from their overlords.

That was another thing we'd discussed since the loss on Verillium —whether Ver'Dak's living brothers now had control of those nanobots. It would be wise to assume that they did and could infect others if they held that same technology.

Every time I considered it, I was terrified. How many worlds could be infected already? When we wouldn't know unless we checked every individual residing on those worlds. The task was daunting and impossible, especially since the nanobots, if discovered, would instruct those they'd infected to commit suicide.

How long had Ver'Dak plotted this terrible move? How many had he infected? Once again, I wiped away tears and cursed him, his brothers and Liron.

"We'd come to depend on them too much, I think," Nefrigar arrived in my study, made himself smaller to fit the furniture and took a seat in front of my desk.

"I know." My voice trembled; my words followed by a half-sob.

"The Shining Ones are coming to speak with us," he went on, drying my tears with power. "The Mighty are also coming, as they need to hear these things, too."

I hadn't seen my sister Breanne since the mess on Verillium. She'd been in her own state of mourning, I knew, with Cassie and Zaria both taken.

Both daughters in one terrible event.

"Have you made any progress on those weapons Ver'Dak created?" I thought to ask Nefrigar.

"They would have been deadly, had the copelis chips not been redirected. A combination of upgraded and revised ranos technology, along with the copelis chips."

"They were redirected? The chips?"

"It is the only solution we could theorize," he shrugged—a very human gesture in a Larentii.

"Please tell me this technology will never leave the Larentii homeworld."

"It will never leave," he affirmed. "The weapons have been destroyed and there is only once source now of the blueprints to manufacture."

"Where nobody can reach them?"

"Exactly so."

"What if all his brothers have them, though?"

"Then we can only hope that those copelis chips will also be redirected."

"How soon do you think his brothers will act, now that Ver'Dak is dead?"

"I cannot say. Ver'Dak was cleverer by far than Je'Dik, his elder brother. We can only hope that the rest are of Je'Dik's caliber, rather than Ver'Dak's."

"We're here," Ashe announced as he, Breanne and Charles arrived for our meeting. The Shining Ones appeared only moments later. I sent a request to the kitchen for food and wine; I needed it, whether anyone else did or not.

～

Royal City, Sorvus
   Jek

"Brenna knows better than anyone what a family of six needs in the way of weekly food and supplies," I said. "That's why she's in charge of the former military storehouse."

"But the palace kitchen," the head chef complained.

"The palace kitchen is no more deserving than the least of any outside these walls," I snapped at him. "Make do with what you have or do without. The entire planet is under rationing orders."

"We have more coming from Vorus every day," he whined.

"We know how many are coming in," I said. "My people are at the gates, if you recall. Don't," I held up my hand. "If I hear Cjerl's name one more time, I will send you out to cook for the army—what little is left of it."

"Why are you in charge?" The chef wasn't done.

"I was asked to be. The one who asked, I don't turn down. Go back to your kitchen now. I have no idea why she let you live."

The chef's shoulders stiffened as he whirled and stalked out of the meeting hall. He damn well better get along and do his job; I really would send him to cook for the army.

"Commander," Chuk walked in, his long strides indicating urgency.

"What do you have, Lieutenant?"

"A woman in labor just arrived at the gate. Do we have anyone available who can help?"

"I'll come," I sighed. "Lead the way."

~

Karrideen
Ga'Dik Fifth-Born

"We must avenge our brothers," Si'Dak Sixth-born growled. "We have waited long enough. Let us begin with that wretched planet where they died."

"Do you think you can do better than the rest of us by getting onto it?"

"We do not need to get onto it. Send another gunship."

"So it will perish, like the last one?" Si'Dak was never the smartest of my brothers. Aside from Po'Dek Twelfth-born, he was likely the dullest.

"None of us were aboard that ship," he muttered.

"Do you think your presence would have made a difference?"

"I do."

"I don't, and I'm in charge, now. Shut up and let me think about this, all right? We still have the weapons Ver'Dak left for us. We merely have to find the time and place to lure the powerful in. Before they died, our brothers eliminated four of theirs, or do you not recall that rumor?"

"Ver'Dak should still be alive."

What he meant was that Ver'Dak should still be in charge. I growled, low in my throat. "He and the others died honorably. Leave, now, or place a challenge," I snarled. Wa'Dek Seventh-born and Lo'Dak Tenth-born stepped up to flank me, weapons drawn, as Si'Dak snorted and glared at me.

"We don't have the armor," he sniffed. "We should return for the armor." Lo'Dak took a single step forward, his weapon trained on Si'Dak's head. Si'Dak turned and fled before his brother fired at him.

"No sense," Wa'Dek grumbled, lowering his weapon.

"Less than no sense," Lo'Dak let his weapon drop. "If he were in charge, we'd all be dead by now."

~

Queen's Palace, Le-Ath Veronis
   Lissa

"Iris had the vision, not I," Leare defended himself. "She told me that all would be lost if we didn't," Charles cleared his throat, interrupting Leare's explanation.

"You planted a seed, then?" Charles crossed arms over his chest and stared—hard—at Leare.

"You told me to take care of it. This was the only way Iris and I could devise."

"And I lose my daughter to your machinations," Charles hissed.

"Fuck you." Cyrus, the Eye, rose from his seat and cursed Charles before disappearing. Conner, the Voice, appeared angry—at Charles and not Cyrus.

What just happened? I sent to Breanne.

I have to tell you later. It's something I've suspected for a while; I just couldn't bring myself to admit it.

Fine.

"Yes, Iris and I had a child, all right?" Leare snapped at Charles. "It broke our hearts to plant that child in the Queen's suite in Vorus after her baby died, but we did it. Jessil is our many-times great-granddaughter, and the one strong enough to carry the power necessary to wield the black zone."

"Heir to both kingdoms, then?" Nefrigar lifted a blond eyebrow at Leare.

"You knew?" Leare asked him.

"Suspected. Iris wasn't her grandmother's given name, was it?"

"No. She was a princess of Sorvus, rescued before her father could tap her with a controller."

"Those foul," Nefrigar's anger was deep—and unusual for a Larentii. But then Reah, his mate, had borne a controller at one time and he didn't relish the memory.

"Nevertheless, you interfered—far too much," Charles accused Leare.

"And what do you intend to do about it?" Ashe rose, eyes focused on Charles.

"He needs to be remade—as punishment," Charles huffed.

"I know whose he is, and I disagree," Ashe stiffened.

"Who told you," Charles' eyes narrowed at Ashe.

Frankly, the last thing I needed in my private study was Wisdom and Strength going after one another. Already, the walls were beginning to bow outward and I was helpless to stop impending destruction.

"*I* told him," Breanne entered the argument, rising to stand beside Ashe. "I know Conner is mine, although you thought to hedge your bets by fathering her physical body."

"She's right, you know," Conner agreed. "And I'm on Leare's side in this. You didn't give him specifics in the assignment. Do you recall that? He did the best he could with what he had to work with."

The walls bowed farther and began to crack. Hurriedly, I sent my paintings to Wyyld, for safekeeping. Charles and Ashe were about to destroy the entire palace. *Get everybody out*, I sent to Gavin and Tony.

"I have been the one," Charles hissed, "who has maintained communication with the Shining Ones. I have been the one," he went on vehemently, "who has given them their assignments. I am the one, therefore, who will hand out punishment."

"Do you think you're the only one who lost someone in this?" Breanne shouted at Charles. "That you're the only one suffering?"

"I demand punishment," Charles thundered, blowing out the wall behind my desk, sending stone, marble and other debris into the ballroom behind my study. "I will see to this myself," he roared.

CHAPTER TWENTY

*R*oyal City, Sorvus
  Commander Jek

The mother slept while the baby suckled. At least they were alive;
Hisan arrived to search out ruptured blood vessels, tying them off with
power so the mother wouldn't bleed out.

"Thank you," I dried my hands after a thorough washing. "I don't
think I could have done both things at once."

"Rade lent me power, it was the only way," Hisan shrugged.

"Then thank you both. They're alive because of you."

"And you, Commander," Skipp pointed out. "We don't have many
left on this world. We need every life we can save."

"How goes the emptying of Vorus?" I thought to ask Hisan.

"We're slowly getting it done," he sighed. "At least the bodies of
the dead weren't left behind. Burying them would have taken all our
strength."

"How much longer, then?" Skipp asked him.

"At least a month, even with the transports we've reclaimed. There
are far more men than women remaining in Vorus."

"And far more women than men remaining in Sorvus," I countered.
"Perhaps a balance can be achieved?"

"Perhaps," Hisan dipped his head to me. "Commander, I will get back to the business at hand unless there's something else."

"There's food at the palace, unless the chef walked out," I told him.

"I'll stay for a meal," he gave me a tired smile.

"Good. Come on."

Queen's Palace, Le-Ath Veronis

Lissa

"If you remake me, then you'll never know everything I do about Verillium and the black zone," Leare snapped at Charles.

"What do you mean?" Charles still sounded angry.

"You need to thank Leare, not punish him," Conner rounded on Charles with a hiss. "If you want to declare war on me and the others for searching and hoping these past six months, then do it now. We'll defend Leare until we die."

Leare's head jerked up at Conner's words, his eyes wide with surprise.

"And why would you do that?" Charles demanded.

"Without his power—and Iris' foresight—melded together within Keela, we'd never have gotten information about the weapons and nanobots Ver'Dak created with copelis. That stuff—at least we know what we're fighting now, even if our front line is missing."

Nefrigar's eyes bored into mine; we'd discussed weapons and nanobots earlier, although it felt like a lifetime ago after the anger of the Mighty destroyed my study.

"Could those weapons have destroyed us?" I blurted. "The ones that Ver'Dak created?"

"Yes," Leare sighed. "Until Keela asserted her will on the copelis chips they held. Same with the armor—it was set to carry on with Ver'Dak's mission, whether he lived or not. Copelis would have killed us all, before she took control of it."

"Where is that stuff now?" Charles demanded.

"Where you won't find it," Breanne snipped. "Besides, if anyone does find it, I think they may have a far more difficult time commanding it."

"What is so special about that stuff?" I breathed.

"You haven't figured it out, have you?" Leare turned toward me. "Iris and many, many others who were talented and held power, buried their minds and souls in that stuff. It can hold everything they are in the smallest piece. Ver'Dak figured it out and built his weapons with as much as he could find. He has a mountain of it, if my calculations are correct," he jerked around to face Charles.

"Do you mean that we can leave power in it, too?" Nefrigar sounded very interested.

"Yes," Breanne told him.

"You knew this?" Charles rounded on Leare. "And you didn't tell me?"

"Iris knew it," Leare said. "It was a secret known only to her—and her grandmother and mother. That's how she convinced me to have a child with her—to save Verillium. I extrapolated from her clairvoyance and determined it could save everything. And now, that secret is known to everyone here."

"Leare left his love there. She gave up her life in service to Verillium, locking her essence, her power and her memories inside her focus stone," Conner said. "Cyrus and I always knew he lost someone on Verillium, we merely didn't know who."

"Is that the focus stone that Keela had?" Bree asked.

"No. She wears Iris' grandmother's stone. Iris took her grandmother's name, once she got away from her father. I removed the focus stone from the original Iris' tomb to give to Jessil," Leare replied. "My Iris found her and trained her—through her own grandmother's stone."

"Does this mean the original Iris is also in that stone?"

"They have the choice of stepping out," Conner sighed. "She removed herself when she heard her granddaughter's call, didn't she?"

"Yes," Leare nodded. "How did you know?"

"Because I escorted an ancient soul to the gate. She told me many, many things before she crossed over."

"Still want to punish Leare?" One of Ashe's eyebrows lifted, while stars fell through the dark depths of his eyes as he glared at Charles.

"No. Wisdom lies in admitting mistakes. This was my mistake," Charles dipped his head to Leare. "You are also suffering, and I have overlooked that far too long. Strength, from now on, I will relay all my requests for help from the Ear through you."

"Thank you."

Charles folded away, leaving the rest of us blinking at one another.

"He could have fixed my study, first," I complained. "Since he's the one who broke it."

Royal City, Sorvus
    Hisan

"I miss her," Rade drew in a weighted breath.

"As do I. Are we always fated to lose the best of us?"

"Is she truly lost?"

"It has been six moon turns, Rade. What else could this be?" I hunched my shoulders—how heavy lay the guilt I bore. Guilt I would always bear, where Jessil was concerned.

Rade and I stood upon the topmost tower of the palace, looking out upon what was once Cjerl's Royal City. "Jessil—Keela—should have ruled here. Should have ruled both kingdoms," I amended.

A strong, fresh breeze chilled us as we stood upon the ramparts, considering our duties for the coming days. Jek was doing a good job, but he couldn't be everywhere, as he'd told us often enough. The rest of us were spread thin as we struggled to integrate the remnants of two kingdoms into one.

Additionally, there were many orphans to place with suitable foster parents, and that, in itself, was more than wearying. My eyes dropped to the palace courtyard, far below, where supplies were being carried inside by Brenna's troops.

"You think she's up there? In the black zone?" Rade asked. I lifted my head to look at him.

The black zone was now overhead, surrounding all of Verillium, although it didn't obscure sunlight. At night, a transparent veil would sometimes dim the moon, but that's the only time we were able to see that barrier, now.

"I suppose it's possible," I agreed.

"I prefer to think that's where she is, rather than the alternative."

"The one where she gave her life, alongside Cassie and two others, to rid Verillium of the enemy's scourge?"

"Yes." Rade shifted his shoulders uncomfortably. "I think," he had to clear his throat before continuing, "I think it should be called Princess Jessil's Veil, instead of the black zone from now on."

I blew out a deep sigh. "My friend, name it as it should be named."

Rade offered a quizzical look.

"Queen Keela's Veil," I breathed, lifting my head and my hands toward the sky. "We miss you," I shouted.

"We love you, too," Rade whispered beside me. "Now and always."

EPILOGUE

ELIAGAR

*Z*ak had already made breakfast when I returned from soaking in sunlight for two hours. He thumbed the screen of his comp-vid, reading while he ate.

"You appear happy this morning," I ventured. He looked up and smiled.

"I am," he replied. "I had a good dream—about four people. Their names were Zaria, Cassie, Randl and Keela."

I went still. "Child, can you describe the dream for me?"

"Yes," he grinned. "They live in the sky," he began. "They made me feel welcome and loved as I wandered through their home in my dream. They also told me not to be afraid; they have a plan. I still felt good when I woke this morning."

Nefrigar, Zarigar, I sent, *I believe I have important information.*

The End

This series will continue in *Wraith Zone, Future Wars, Book 3*